TAINTED DREAMS

S. C. Rafael

Copyright © 2025 S. C. Rafael

All rights reserved. It is illegal to copy this book, post or distribute it by any other means without permission.

This novel is entirely a work of fiction. Any names, characters or events portrayed are the product of the authors imagination, anything that gives any resemblance is coincidental.

Cover Work done by: AmbientPixel Designs

Beta/Proof Editing: Kenneth Rafael

ISBN: 9798314171301

To those who crave the danger in a smirk, the promise in a shadow, and the touch of a nightmare wrapped in silk. This is for the ones who love the hands that could ruin them, yet worship them all the same.

Scan the Spotify QR code to listen to the Tainted Dreams Inspired playlist!

Pronunciations

- Roenis— *Row-nis*
- Syra —*Sy-Rah*
- Sesha—*Sesh-ha*
- Avia— *Ah-Vee-ya*
- Sage—*Sayj*
- Callum—*Cal-lum*
- Ira— *I-rah*

- Dolion— *Dou-lee-on*
- Maya—*May-ya*
- Orson—*Or-Sun*
- Averill—*A-ver-ill*
- Datura—*Dah-ter-rah*
- Asani—*Ah-sa-nee*
- Kenji—*Ken-jee*
- Grifton—*Grif-ton*
- Mirein—*Meer-in*

Content Warning

This book may contain sensitive/triggering content. Reader discretion is advised. This book contains acts of Voyeurism, Slight Drugging, depictions of sexually explicit scenes, mature language/themes, and few acts of detailed violence. May not be suitable for all readers.

CHAPTER ONE

Syra

I feel it again.

The pull. The splitting of the images. The dark haze blurring my vision as I fight to focus.

My hand trembles as I dip it into the marbled basin's glistening water, the liquid cool against my skin. Purple wisps of my magic caress along my fingers, spiraling into the pool with precision. I strain pulling the vial from the top of the basin and tipping its essence into the water. A fragment of a human's dream, meant to be woven into something beautiful. Yet, no matter how carefully I weave, something always corrupts it.

Something dark.

The corruption seeps in more before I can stop it, black vapor swirling through the essence like smoke dancing on light. I jerk my hand away, heart pounding. "Fucking nightmares," I mutter, glaring at the spreading vapors as it mingles with my magic.

Failed. Again.

I keep watching the black swirl within. It's darkness calling to me with its whispering temptations, but I knew what it was craving. The pull is magnetic and seductive, wanting to consume and twist my magic. Their urge to steal the enchanting dreams I conjure, and kill it with poison. I finally break my stare from the basin.

Pacing to the diamond-shaped window, I lean into the frame, letting the cool stone bite against my skin. The shimmering glass hums softly with light from our realm, casting fractured rainbows along the walls. Below me, the five kingdoms stretch out like patchwork, their borders softened by distance. Some kingdoms radiate brightly, alive with magic. Others are shrouded, hidden by shadows too deep to pierce.

But one kingdom stands out to me.

It dominates the northern lands, its presence stark and unnatural, like a ragged line cutting across a perfect canvas. Even from here, its power casts shadows that ripple across our hidden realm. It's a constant reminder of the darkness my kingdom fights to contain.

Legends of the humans once said that dreams were a portal to a different plane of existence, if only the human soul knew how true that really was. They have long forgotten us. Our realm doesn't just shape dreams; it anchors time and space itself, keeping the human world stable. But balance comes at a cost. Our battles, the ones no human soul can see, combat in secret. The constant pull of peace and wrath, cycle after cycle. And every day, the darkness grows stronger. We only have ourselves here. Rinse and repeat sort of deal. My mother has told me the story multiple times, but the details tend to change every time she tells it. She would go on about how one day a black pit formed from a different element and complicated the way we work. This created the Dark Isle. The Kingdom of

Nightmares, and the god that ruled it.

Roenis.

His name alone sends shivers through me. From what my mother tells me, he's ruthless. Brutal and persistent. A demon cloaked in beauty and charm, hosting his extravagant balls every year to mask his schemes. My kingdom has no interest, and we never fall for his ruse. We've had centuries of bad blood with him. Our blood spilt by his hands.

Every daughter created to this kingdom has been trained to face him. Trained to kill him. Whether it be blades, magic, or mind work, our legacy is etched in combat and cunning skills. And yet, every single one of my predecessors has failed.

And died.

No pressure, right?

I flex my fingers, purple vines of magic weaving faintly in the dim light. My magic is unique; root-like, strong, and relentless. But even as I hone my skills, Roenis' influence seeps into everything, twisting my spells and unraveling my control. How am I supposed to stop him when every "daughter" my mother has conjured up for this exact mission, couldn't finish the job?

She never dives into how the others failed, just that Roenis killed them. And lately, she has been persistent on moving to the next phase.

My gaze drifts back to the basin, the black vapor still churning in its depths. This isn't just about magic or duty. It's about survival. To claim my throne and take my place as Goddess of the Dream Kingdom. I have to succeed where every woman before me has failed.

The mission is simple enough: seduce the God of Nightmares, and make him fall in love with me by the time of the Sundial Silitical. Then kill him.

Easy.

I let out a bitter laugh, my breath fogging a small patch of the glass on the window. "Fucking politics."

The sound of footsteps echoes down the hall, pulling me from my thoughts. The door creaks open, and right on time, my mother strides in.

"Syra, darling," she says, her voice like honeyed steel. "It's time for sparring with Orson."

My gaze shifts from her to the basin again.

Watching the vapors swirl like the chaos within me. I have to figure out how to prevent his power from corrupting my magic, but for now, maybe letting off some steam will help. Turning toward the door where my mother stands with her endless impatience, I finally huff out some words to her. "I could use a few sparring rounds. I feel like punching some throats anyway." I'm almost through the doorway when her hand grips around my arm. I don't even flinch. I'm use to it.

"I need you ready," she says, her tone sharp. "Everything has been set in motion, and this begins within the next couple of moons."

I whip my head around, shock splashing across my face. "A couple of moons? Excuse me? When was this decision made, and why wasn't I told?"

Her gaze flickers to the mess I made within the basin, lingering on the curling vapors as if she's only now noticing them. Without looking back at me, she speaks in her practiced, regal tone—piercing and calculated, each word sharpened to cut. "Because we're running out of time, and clearly, you're distracted from your main purpose."

Ah, there she is. The mother I know. The one who created my essence, as all gods and goddesses do. It's purely for their own gain and power. No love. No attachment. Just a tool. In her case, just another attempt. Daughter after daughter, all bred for one purpose.

I jerk my arm free of her grip, my voice dripping with venom. "I know my purpose. I just think you're impatient. Haven't your failures taught you anything?"

Her glare pierces me, her face twisting in a mix of anger and something that might have been fear, though it's hard to tell. "You know nothing but what I've taught you. Now, go see Orson. Afterward, we'll debrief on what's expected of you in the coming days."

I glance down the hallway, unwilling to meet her eyes as I ask the next question. "Did you ever love your other daughters?" The words barely leave my lips, a whisper drenched in bitterness.

She scoffs. "Love? How foolish."

The answer hits me like a slap, but I don't flinch enough for her to notice. Instead of responding, I start down the hallway. I feel stupid for even asking. She's a stone when it came to emotions. Her voice cuts through the air behind me, echoing with unrelenting authority. "You will not fail, Syra."

It's not encouragement. It's a demand.

My fists curl at my sides. I need to hit something—or someone.

Thank the gods Orson has such a punchable face.

CHAPTER TWO

Syra

I'm flat on my back.

I was completely laid out from the swipe kick Orson just landed on me. The impact still vibrates through my body, and dirt digs into my spine as I struggle to pull myself upright.

Fucking Orson and his tree-trunk calves. Seriously, who the hell is built like that? He's like a jagged boulder that came to life.

I plant my hands on the ground and force myself back up to my feet. My breathing is rough, each inhale sharp and painful thanks to the bruises forming on the right side of my ribs. The faint glow of my purple veins pulses beneath my skin, urging me to use my magic. I shut down that instinct. If I rely on it too much, Orson will say I'm weak without it.

He smirks down at me like the arrogant bastard he is. His face is all harsh angles. His bushy eyebrows that nearly swallow the tiny slivers of navy blue in his eyes, a nose that dominates his stupid face, and lips so thin they're basically nonexistent. And when he smirks like that? All teeth.

"What in the gods could you possibly be thinking about down there?" he taunts, his voice grating. "Did I finally knock that smart mouth out of you?" His chuckle is such a punchable sound, and he knows it.

Fuck him.

I raise my hands, covering half my face as I get my guard back up. "I was just thinking about the poor woman stuck with you one day. How's she supposed to get pleasure when your lips are thinner than my thong straps?"

His smirk drops, and the heat in his glare is immediate. A laugh bubbles up in my throat despite the warning bells screaming in my head.

Shit. That might've been stupid.

Before I can backpedal, he charges. Fast. Too fast. For a man his size, he moves like a damn machine, fast enough to kill. The ground shakes beneath his feet as he closes the distance. His bulk shouldn't allow him this much speed, but Orson defies every law of nature.

I hold my ground, bracing for the attack. He dips low, his stance wide, as if going for my legs. I've sparred with Orson too many times not to recognize a fake-out. He's baiting me into a defensive stumble, but I'm no novice.

As he lunges, I twist to his left side, hooking my arm beneath his and planting my foot behind his ankle. With a sharp sweep of my leg and a hard shove to his shoulder, I unbalance him completely. His massive frame crashes into the dirt with a thud that sends up a cloud of dust.

Gods the sound was so satisfying.

"Well," I huff, shaking out my limbs as I back away, "that makes us even, don't you think?"

He grunts, climbing to his feet like a bear roused

from hibernation. He shakes his head, sand flying out of his salt and pepper colored hair. His scowl could curdle milk, but there's something sharper in his eyes now. Annoyance, yes. But also... determination.

"Even?" he growls, brushing the dirt off his shoulders. "You wish."

Before I can give a clever comeback, he's advancing again. This time, there's no feint. He barrels straight at me, pivoting at the last second into a spinning elbow strike. I manage to duck in time, feeling the air whoosh above my head.

Damn, he's fighting seriously now.

I drop low, twisting into a low body kick aimed at his knees. He jumps, easily avoiding it, and counters with a heel aimed straight for my chest. I roll sideways, narrowly avoiding the strike, and spring back up just as he charges again.

"That's the best you've got?" I taunt, dodging his fluent combo of strikes. My movements are fluid, weaving between each one of his punches like a dance we've been practicing. "For a guy who brags about his training, you're looking pretty sluggish."

"Keep talking kid," he grits out. His strikes coming faster now, forcing me to stay on my toes. "You won't be able to when you're flat-out on the dirt again."

I grin, despite the sweat dripping down my brow. "Speaking from someone who just got thrown on his ass earlier."

His response is a snarl, and he changes tactics. Instead of brute strength, he shifts into a low, fluid stance unique to the Balance Kingdom's combat style. It was a type of dance-like rhythm that flows between offense and defense. The sudden change catches me off guard, and I'm forced to retreat. When he closes the distance, I'm able to block the precise kicks aimed at my weak points.

Damn it. Orson knows this style always trips me up. His knowledge on the other kingdoms tactics are incredible, and it's no wonder why he's the best sparring partner in the realm.

I grit my teeth and switch my approach, letting my movements mimic the sharp, unpredictable patterns of Wrath Kingdom's combat. It's a risk, but it might throw him off. My strikes become erratic, feints laced with subtle, twisting motions meant to disorient. I catch him off guard with a sudden upward kick that nearly clips his jaw. He stumbles, and I press the advantage, darting behind him to aim a jab at his ribs.

He spins, catching my wrist before I can land the blow. Our eyes lock, and I see the shit eating grin pulling at his lips. "Nice try." He says, yanking me off balance.

I twist, using the momentum to flip backward and land a solid kick to his chest. He staggers but doesn't fall.

"Nice try yourself." I fire back, breathing hard but refusing to give up.

For a moment, we circle each other, both of us battered, bruised, and too damn stubborn to back down. The pit feels alive around us, the air charged with the hum of magic we're both resisting the urge to use.

Finally, Orson lowers his stance, his breaths deep and measured. "We're done." he finally says, brushing past me with a bump to my shoulder that's less accidental and more petty.

"What? That was barely a session!" I argue, throwing my hands up. "We usually go for two hours. It's only been forty-five minutes."

Orson stops and glances back, his face red and wet from sweat. "Your mother has a meeting soon. I'm not wasting all my energy on you when your sparring is where it needs to be. You're good enough."

I blink. Did… did he just compliment me?

"…And before you get all mushy," he adds, rolling his shoulders, "I said 'good enough.' Not perfect. Not better than me. Now go clean up and make yourself presentable."

With that, he's gone, leaving me standing in the middle of the pit, speechless. Why does everyone want to rush all of a sudden?

I climb out of the dirt pit, dusting myself off with a groan. Orson's parting words linger in my mind. "Good enough." He's the only one who slightly praises me. I roll my eyes and mutter under my breath, "Not perfect."

The path back to the castle passes through the heart of the Dream Kingdom, a place that feels alive with soft magic. Patches of lavender mist hovers over the ground, parting as I walk. Towering weeping willows sway gently, their purple leaves trailing like whispers in the air.

As the castle comes into view, its ethereal beauty tugs at something deep inside me. The structure seems to rise from the clouds themselves, light filtering through the translucent walls and casting soft, shifting patterns of purple and silver on the ground. It's a sight that should feel like home, but today it feels more like a cage closing in around me.

Inside, the castle's halls are cool and quiet, the air tinged with the calming scent of purple poppy blossoms. I catch sight of myself in a nearby mirror and wince. My light blue skin is smudged with dirt, my white hair looks like a tangled mess, with the golden strands barely visible beneath the aftermath of sparring.

Perfect. Just the look I need for a formal meeting.

I enter my chambers and sigh a puff of defeat. I just need to soak and make myself presentable. I flick my wrist and the enchanted bath in the middle of my chambers begins to fill, the water rippling with soft shades of violet and pearl. As I strip out of my sparring clothes, I let out a long, steadying breath. The meeting isn't just another formality. It's the first step in a mission that could define my future, or end it.

The thought tightens something in my chest. Seducing Roenis isn't just dangerous, it's madness. But my choice has already been made for me. If I succeed, it won't just solidify my position, it'll change everything.

I sink into the warm scented water, letting it soothe my aching muscles as I scrub the dirt from my skin. My reflection in the water is blurry, but I can still make out my features. I was starting to see the faint glowing of my hair again. I wonder, briefly, if the God of Nightmares will find me beautiful, or if he'll see straight through the mask I'll have to wear.

Clean and refreshed, I step out and dry off. I slip into a simple gown spun from the softest threads, the pattern like woven starlight. It clings to me in all the right places. The sliver of gold strands in my hair is amplified now that it's properly brushed, and the fragrance of poppy flowers cling to my skin. I stand taller, pulling my shoulders back and willing my nerves to dissipate.

By the time I step into the grand hall, the council is already assembled. My mother stands at the head of the table, her Goddess figure framed by the room's soaring, cloud-like architecture. Her sharp gaze lands on me immediately, and I swear I catch a flash of approval before she speaks.

"Syra," she begins, her voice cutting through the air like a blade. "We have much to discuss. The time has come to fulfill your mission and your duty as the future Goddess."

I make my way to the seat next to her, nerves making my body tremble. My mother continues to speak to the other council members as if I'm not there. Her previous acknowledgment shadowed by the urgency of the mission. Averill sits on the opposite side of her, Orson across from me, and the other two members, who keep themselves hidden, occupy the far end of the table from Orson.

"We'll start with the journey," my mother begins. "She will travel alone, heading first toward the Kingdom of Balance. From there, Sage will take over. He has no idea of our plans, but he has allowed her to stay in his outside village while she makes her travel."

I whip my head toward her. "You brought the God of Balance into this? Wasn't this supposed to be a quiet mission?"

She dismisses my outburst as usual, but still gives me an answer. "Child, it is no secret we've been doing this for centuries. This time however, you'll glamour yourself and you'll attend his ball right before Sundial Silitical."

I'm raging inside. All of this kept from me, for what? This wasn't the plan.

"We've never attended the ball. Why now?" I spew.

Her gaze locks onto mine, and I cower under her cold glare. "Because it will be different this time. You'll catch him off guard with your glamour and make him trust you. We have all the plans and people laid out more thoroughly than the other times. Instead of the short-lived tactics we've used before, we are playing a longer game. Spend more time with him and make it seem like you're actually falling in love. The other attempts were too brief. Perhaps that's why he never cared for the others. It wasn't enough time for him to die when they tried."

"You are the closest thing to perfection Maya has created. We will use your beauty and your wits. He won't stand a chance." Averill states. He is my mother's right hand. Bald, but still possessing an old beauty to him. Orson shifts slightly in his seat, his eyes switching between my mother and I. "Besides, your fighting is packed with skill, and your blade training is exemplary."

I glare at him, but he merely shrugs his shoulders. The other members converse amongst themselves as I brew in my anger. I feel my magic heating at my fingertips, aching to destroy the very table we were sitting at. Unfortunately, that's not what the Goddess of Dreams would do.

I sometimes wonder if the others before me had this chaos brewing inside them, or if I'm the dud among all the perfections my mother has created.

Her voice breaks through my thoughts. "Then it's settled. We will pack tonight and send her off in two days time." Her smile sends chills down my spine, but I push my nerves down, and bring my confidence forward.

"I'll make this one hell of a show." I say, my words now growing with determination. I cannot deter from my path. If I have to adjust the plan, then so be it. Roenis will die. Whether by my blade or by love, I will come out alive and finally rid the realm of the poison he seeps. "Orson, help me pack and load up will you? Wouldn't want Mother waiting any longer now do we?"

My mother's eyes roll. "Not *tonight*, Syra. You still have prep and training. We will go over the exact plan a few times before leaving."

"Oh but why wait, Mother? We must make haste right? The sooner my charm sets in, the better, right? Come Orson, let's go." I flip my hair over my shoulder and gracefully storm out. Orson follows behind as we leave the grand hall filled with murmurs.

Orson chuckles, shaking his head. "You have a knack for pissing her off. It's oddly entertaining to watch."

I stop walking and turn to him. "Alright, what's

going on with you? You're usually all grunts and scowls, but you've been handing out compliments today like they don't pain you to do so. Should I be worried?"

He starts to rub the back of his neck. "Maybe I just figured it was about time I said something." His voice carried a sad weight. "Your mother was right. You're different from the others, always have been." He hesitated, "and depending on the circumstances, this might be the last time I see you."

That admission sent a strange pang through me, but before I could brush it off, he continued. "I guess I wanted you to know that you're one of the best fighters I've trained." He let out a low, embarrassed laugh. "Gonna miss you, kid. That's all. So do what you do best. Succeed. And kick his ass while you're at it."

I blinked, staring at him. It was strange seeing him like this. He was actually saying the things I had only ever felt in the way he pushed me, trained me. He had never been one for sentimental speeches, but somehow this felt more real than any praise I've ever received.

Warmth curls in my chest, but I waved a hand trying to play it off. "Um… yeah, no. This is weird. Let's just get to the room before you say anything else that might ruin your reputation."

Orson huffed out behind me. "Yeah, yeah, you're right. That was damn embarrassing."

I hesitate at the door, then glance over my shoulder back at him. To show him that despite my words, I heard him. And maybe it meant more than I'd let on. "Thanks, Orson. For everything. Also, I'm not a kid, I'm a century old, you know that."

He smiles. "Sure kid, let's just get you packed up."

I scuff, but a smile crept over my lips as we entered my room.

CHAPTER THREE

Syra

The next morning starts like it always does, with my arm stretched high above my head, rolling my shoulder as Orson circles me like a hawk.

"Precision first, then power. Aim correctly." He barked.

I exhaled sharply, rolling my dagger between my fingers before gripping it by the tip properly. Across the pit, a row of targets stood firm, with faintly painted markers where I'm suppose to strike. Orson stands beside me, arms crossed and his navy gaze tracking my movements.

I take aim and throw. The blade spins end over end before hitting the target—just shy of the red dot on the head.

Orson sighs. "Too much force. Go again."

Grimacing, I grab another dagger from my belt and adjust my stance. The weight of the handle feels balanced, but that isn't enough. I need control with the trajectory.

Breathe. Focus. Throw.

This time, the dagger hits closer to the center of the red dot. Still not perfect, but definitely close.

"Better." Orson said, nodding.

Frustration still gnaws at me. "What if I use my magic to guide it?"

"You could, if done correctly."

I flex my fingers, letting my vines unfurl and wrap around my wrist. I grab yet another dagger, and throw it the way I've done the past couple of times—but this time, I willed my vine to snake after it, nudging the blade slightly midair.

It strikes dead center.

Orson hums in approval. "Good. Just make sure you can do it without the magic assisting you. You don't want to always rely on it."

I nod. I go on for another hour. Sometimes using

my magic and other times without it. I throw until my arm aches, alternating between pure determination, and drowning frustration until Orson finally calls it.

"Your instinct and training must work together. You can't pick one over the other, but you are improving." He admitted.

My muscles feel tight. I squeeze my eyes shut, reveling in the feeling. Not knowing if I'll ever feel the sweet pain of good workouts after I leave for the mission. A small quiet nagging feeling nestled itself in the back of my mind. Was I truly prepared?

Orson slaps my back, whipping me out of my daze of self loathing.

"Stop doubting your skills."

I huff. "I'm not. I just don't want to fail."

"Whatever happens, your instincts won't fail." He says confidently. "Also, your mother is summoning you, she wants to see you in her chambers."

Great.

I climb out of the pit and collect my daggers. I don't bother cleaning up, I'm less worried about my appearance, and more anxious about the conversation we will have.

The corridor leading to my mother's private chambers is suffocatingly silent. The weight of expectations and centuries of her rule, presses hard on my shoulders the closer I get to her door.

I don't even get a chance to knock before I hear her voice call for me to enter. When I walk in, I see she is sat poised at her desk. Her back is impossibly straight, her hands folded atop an open book she had likely been reading before I entered.

She's poised like a statue carved to keep secrets, as if the realm itself dared not to ruffle her perfect composure. Her raven hair, cropped short just above the jawline, has streaks of gold that caught the light like threads of divine deceit—beautiful and all too easy to miss if you weren't looking close enough.

Her eyes, black as night, hold no softness. Just an endless pool of hardness, rimmed with a brilliant, unnatural pink that pulses around her pupils. They shine like a warning or a promise, depending on her mood. I used to stare into them as a child, wondering what she saw when she looked at me. Now I know clearly that I wasn't anything special, unless I succeed. Maybe then her expression will be different when she looked at me.

She bears the same blue skin I do, our shared inheritance from our Dream-blood. Hers is flawless, unmarred by the glowing veins that dances beneath my skin. It makes her look untouchable. Cold. Like she'd long since learned how to bury anything that ever threatened to make her lesser than the Goddess she had always been.

She doesn't look up immediately. She never does. A power move, one I had learned to get use to.

"You wished to speak with me?"

A beat of silence. Then, she lifts her gaze. "You leave for Balance at dawn."

"I know," I reply. "Orson and I did a little more dagger training and then we will finish packing up tonight."

"Then let's discuss how you will get into Nightmare Kingdom."

I stiffened. "What's the plan? I know you said glamour is involved."

"It is." She pauses while shutting her book. "New information about his Kingdom came to me."

I narrow my eyes. "From who?"

She waves her hand dismissing that question. "Roenis takes in strays, those without a home or who betray their kingdoms. He offers them shelter in exchange that they serve him. Some say it's loyalty. Others say it's debt."

The revelation sends an uncomfortable shiver down my spine. "And you learned this from where?"

A pause. Then, "It doesn't matter."

I clench my jaw. It was always like this. Information dangled just beyond my grasp, my mother deciding what I needed to know and when to tell me.

"It does matter," I push. "If we're using this to infiltrate—"

"It does not," she cut in. "You will enter as one of them. A refugee. A nameless, wandering stray seeking safety. The glamour will ensure you are unrecognizable. So you better not falter. If Roenis so much as suspects—"

"He won't."

Her fingers tapped against the top of the closed

book. "Confidence is good. Recklessness is not."

I ignore the barb. She's aware I have a bad temper, and that sometimes I can't control my reactions. Another flaw she loves to point out. "And what happens when I get close?"

"You seduce him. Start off small, nothing too forward that would draw attention. You observe. You learn. You wait for the right moment, and slowly make him fall in love with you."

The plan is solid enough, but I just feel like I'm missing information. This isn't a conversation between mother and daughter. It's an exchange between the player and her game piece.

"Got it." At this point I feel like if I press for more information, I'll just get shut down.

I turn to leave, expecting for her to stop me, but she doesn't. I look back before closing the door and she's back to reading.

◆

The light from my window is the only indication that it's time.

I tighten the straps on my satchel, fingers fumbling through the loops as if the act itself could erase my unease. The weight pressing heavily against my shoulder, though I had only packed a few essentials and some personal items. Behind me, Orson leans against the doorframe, his arms crossed, and his beady eyes tracking every move I made. He's been quiet since last night. Silence isn't unusual for him, and today his presence felt grounding, even if his expression betrays his concern.

"Are you sure you've got everything?" For a man who rarely shows he cares about anything, his worry is unmistakable now. It was there in the way his brow furrows, and in the way he hasn't left my side all morning.

"I'm sure," I reply, slipping a few vials into the hidden pocket of my satchel. Grabbing my blade next, it pulses faintly against my fingertips, its familiar power reassuring before I place it inside next to the vials. I tuck a map I'd found in my mother's office into the side compartment. The path to the outer villages of Balance were marked on the parchment perfectly, but my true destination lies further and deep into Nightmare territory.

Closing the satchel and tightening all the clips, I glance at Orson. "You don't have to hover, you know."

He snorts softly. "I'm not hovering. I'm making sure you don't forget something and end up in a shit situation. You're walking into the unknown, Syra."

"I know," I said, my voice twisting with uncertainty. I had never ventured beyond the Dream Kingdom's borders, never wandered through Balance, or any of the others. Now I'm setting off to enter the ominous lands of the Nightmare Kingdom, while beyond my home itself feels like uncharted territory. I had only the stories, books, secondhand tales and the view from my window to enlighten my curiosities of the others. A part of me craves the adventure, yet a quiet hesitation stirs beneath the surface. I smother it before Orson could notice, locking the doubt away where it can't betray me. He doesn't need to know about the battle raging in my head.

With my satchel secured, I swing it over and head out with Orson. I turn toward the spiraling steps leading out of the castle. He stands close behind as we descend. The soft, fragrant scent of poppies fill the air one last time, a comforting reminder of home. Outside, the weeping willows line the pathway. Their long, delicate branches brush against me like they are bidding me farewell. At the final arch of the trees, Orson stops and I turn to face him. His expression is serious as always, but his eyes are softer.

"You've got the training for this," he says, his voice low. "You've got the brains, the power, and the strength. Trust yourself out there, Syra. The villages are one thing, but Roenis..." He hesitates, his jaw tightening. "He's a different kind of obstacle."

I adjust the strap on my satchel. "I'm not to be fucked with, remember? I'll be fine."

He reaches out, his hand landing on my shoulder, giving me a firm but brief squeeze. "Keep your guard up. Don't smart-talk anyone in Balance, you tend to have a temper. Sage will meet you at the tavern, the one with the yellow curved roof."

He isn't wrong about my temper, but I nod anyway.

The weight of the mission settling heavily over me as I step through the weeping willows. The hazy purple dreamscape of my kingdom begins to fade behind me, replaced by the cool air of the borderlands. The path stretches wide ahead of me, and there is no turning back now.

As I walk on, I realize my mother hadn't bothered to see me off. A small part of me is glad. Her indifference stung less when I didn't have to see it.

CHAPTER FOUR

Syra

The new air is fresher beyond the Dream Kingdom, and I find myself inhaling deeply. I relax, basking in the fact that for a fleeting moment, I feel free. There were times when it was worth not using the portals —the shortcuts each kingdom uses to connect their lands for certain occasions. Sage had declined to open his, insisting I would raise questions appearing inside his castle. He suggested to my mother that arriving on foot and meeting in the village was a better idea. I didn't mind it. It meant more time to explore and think, or better yet to *overthink*.

The wind nips at my skin as I continue beyond

my borders of the Dream Kingdom. For as long as I can remember, I'd watched the world from my towers, the skies always tinted with our kingdom's lilac mist. But now, the world felt vast.

To my left, the hilltops of Time Kingdom rose, a stretch of rolling sandy landscapes that dance under the afternoon sun. Each hill bears patches of swirling sand dunes that traps anything too near. Even from a distance, I can feel the pull of something thrumming beneath the sands. Orson said the Goddess of Time, Sesha, created the dunes to store remnants of human's lifespans and their time left. They look harmless enough, but it still feels eerie.

To my right sprawls the Lake of Nimue, a massive mirror of water that catches the sky and holds it hostage. Its waters are so unmoving, so perfect, it was impossible to tell where the lake ends and land begins. I couldn't look away. The Kingdom of Balance lays somewhere ahead, to the left beyond that watery expanse.

My boots sink slightly into the mossy ground with each step. The ground shifting from the sandy road to now a more damp and cool surface. Golden leaves blankets the path, the air richer here, like honeyed earth and woodsmoke. The smell tickles my nose. The path isn't direct. It winds and twists like the stories I used to listen to at night from Orson. I already miss his presence, but if he were here, he'd tell me to focus and follow the road. The area feels a little narrow going over the small hills closer to Balance. The dirt trail is laced with tangled roots and the remains of fallen petals. Sometimes, the trail will disappear entirely, swallowed by thick meadows of white wheat that brushes my hips. I push through carefully, each step reminding me that I am outside the comforts of the Dream Kingdom. There are no lullabies sung to the trees here, no familiar stars humming above me. And yet, I feel no fear.

I pause to rest, sitting against a flat stone warmed by the afternoon sun and watching the clouds roll over the lake. I pull a small dream vial from my satchel and uncork it. A swirl of violet mist emerges, revealing the image of a laughing child chasing butterflies. It was meant to keep me calm, to focus weaving on daydreaming. But I let it fade after a moment, wanting to just bask in the reality of finally starting this mission. I lift myself up and continued on.

I spotted the first signs of civilization. There are stone posts with balanced scales carved into them, frost-covered and sturdy, shining from the suns reflection from a perfect sunset. My legs ache, my boots are stained, but my heart races with anticipation.

After the hours that felt like days, the world opens. Around the bend, the famous white trees of the Balance Kingdom come into view. Their glossy trunks glint in the sunlight like polished glass. The village nestled among them hum quietly with life.

Before reaching the villages, I ensure my glamour is intact. My once white hair is now dulled to a muted blonde, my light blue skin now appears pale and more humanlike. Even my lavender eyes darken to a nearly black hue. The effort leaves me feeling disconnected, as though I've cloaked my very identity. But anonymity is vital, and I can't risk anyone knowing the Goddess of Dreams isn't within her borders.

The village greets me with movement. Smooth stone streets spread outward like sun rays, curving around small buildings made of dark wood and the same glass from the trees earlier. Even the architecture obeys some invisible harmony, symmetrical and soothing. But it is the people that make it sing.

They wear sashes of warm amber and soft greens, their bodies relaxed yet filled with purpose. Laughter echoes from behind tiled rooftops. I wander past a circular square, where voices gather with excitement. It looks like a pit, and it feels extremely familiar. Almost the exact same structure as the one back home that I trained in.

Orson must *really* like Balance.

Drawn by instinct, I join the small crowd that encircle it. The pit is sunken, perhaps ten feet down, carved directly into the earth. At its center, two men face off, circling like predators. One is shirtless, skin glistening, while the other wears torn pants and a simple wrap around his knuckles and feet. Their styles are unmistakable: Orson's teachings.

I lean forward.

No wild swings. No reckless lunges. Every move is fluid, almost lazy circles of dance—until it isn't. One fighter strikes low with a feint, then twists his body into a high kick that snaps the other off his feet. I huff. *That* was definitely familiar. The crowd hisses and claps as the fallen man rolls, using the momentum to rebound and sweep his opponent's legs from beneath him.

I feel my fingers twitch in admiration. Orson would have barked at them for the oversight, but even he would've nodded at their control. The dance of strikes and dodges are beautiful, brutal, and well... balanced. Just like this kingdom.

After the match, I walk deeper into the village, drawn by the sizzle of oil and the sharp scent of spices.

Vendors line the paths, their carts filled with items I didn't recognize. One sells glass spheres that float above velvet pillows. Another offers tiny dragons, no larger than my thumb, that blink sleepily in glass jars. People squeal as they poke at the containers, and the dragons puff harmless smoke. Illusion magic at its finest.

I pause at a fabric stall, running my fingers along a bolt of cloth that gleam like dew. "Threaded with memory strands," the vendor states, eyes twinkling. "Wrap it around you before sleep, and you'll dream someone else's dream."

I smile politely and move on. I have enough dreams to deal with.

A savory perfume of spice, char, and sweetness curl through the air. My stomach growls in betrayal. I turn and find a small stand where skewers of meats roast over open coals, brushed with thick, golden sauce.

"Fresh wild meat," the vendor offers. "From the forests of Wrath. Fed on flame-berries. Want one?"

I hesitate only long enough to count the few silver shards I brought. Then I take a skewer.

The first bite nearly makes me weep.

Crisp edges give way to the juicy tenderness inside. The sauce is layered, sweet like dream-fruit, sharp with ginger, and just enough heat to leave a warm trail down my throat. I devour it embarrassingly fast, licking the sticky glaze from my fingers.

"Careful," the vendor laughs. "They say Balance food's cursed. One bite and you never want to leave."

I lick my lips. "Then curse me twice."

I continue wandering, tongue tingling, mind buzzing. Statues of figures holding scales stand watch between buildings, their expressions serene. They have one hand open, as if offering wisdom and warning. I stop before one without a free hand, a man with a scale in his left hand and a sword in the right. The tip of the blade is pointing to a different direction than the village. I follow to where it points and there, nestled away from the village, is the curved-roof tavern Orson had mentioned, standing apart with its golden doors. A breeze tugs at my hair, and the sun dips just enough to turn the sky amber. I finally make my way to meet with the bragged about God of Balance.

CHAPTER FIVE
Syra

Inside, the tavern is dim and it gives an unnatural feeling; a contrast from the outside. Only two figures occupy the space: a man half asleep at the far end and another sitting at a table near the entrance. My gaze lands on the latter, and I freeze.

Gods were always beautiful, but this man is radiant beyond reason. His sandy hair shines faintly, catching the only light in the room with every slight movement. His liquid orange eyes lock onto mine, a knowing smile spreading across his golden-tan face.

"Syra, I presume?" His voice smooth, almost like a musical tone. He stands, taking my hand with a deliberate, almost calculated touch and brushing a kiss against it. The gesture feels practiced, yet there is something unnervingly genuine beneath it. Charming but with a purpose.

"Yes," I reply, my voice steadier than I feel. "And you must be Sage."

"In the flesh." His smile widens as he pulls out a chair for me. "Though I pictured you differently."

I settle into the seat, forcing my posture to remain casual. "This isn't my natural look," I admit. "I prefer to keep a low profile."

His brows furrows, his golden gaze dissecting, like he's cataloging every detail. "Is there a reason to hide? I understand not wanting to raise questions, but when your mother spoke of you needing passage, she shared little else."

The piercing weight of his stare makes my stomach churn. He's testing me, and I can't afford to falter.

"I value my privacy," I say evenly. "Until I'm officially the new Goddess of Dreams, I'd rather remain unnoticed. It gives me the freedom to learn the lands without… distractions."

For a moment, a spark of amusement flickers in

his eyes, but it vanishes as quickly as it had appeared. "Freedom," he echoes. "An admirable pursuit. But in my lands, freedom is not without accountability. So, tell me, what truth lies beneath this freedom you want to learn?"

I swallow hard, carefully weighing my response. "I'm here to understand," I begin, "The Balance Kingdom has always intrigued me. Its equilibrium and its principles, there's much to be admired."

He counters, "Admiration is a curious thing," he states, his voice laced with skepticism. "Especially when cloaked in secrecy. You mention distractions. What distractions could you possibly face here?"

Irritation flares at his words, but I keep my composure. "The distractions I refer to are expectations," I say, my voice firmer now. "Being a goddess comes with its share of assumptions and scrutiny."

His smile thins, turning almost predatory. "Syra," his tone darker now, "Expectations are unavoidable. Even in the absence of titles, people will form their own. Are you aware that truth is paramount here? I don't like lies. That's not how I work."

His words hit me like a blow, but I keep my expression neutral. Clever. He's far more perceptive than I'd anticipated. I can see why Orson loved the Balance Kingdom.

When I didn't give him a response, he continued. "I've been the God of Balance for four centuries. Do you really think I'm unaware of the timing? I know your mother well, and I see she's doing things differently with you. But entering my lands comes with rules. We do not lie. To weave a lie is to unstring the core of truth. Balance crumbles when even one thread of deceit tips the scale. So again Syra, why are you *really* here?"

My mind races. Small truths. Nothing more. I can't afford to antagonize him.

"You're right," I meet his gaze head-on, summoning every ounce of resolve I had. "I'm being as truthful as I can be. You may not understand my reasons fully Sage, but they are mine to carry. I've learned to guard my trust carefully. I'm not like the others my mother has sent. They marched forward with reckless certainty, and look where it got them. I prefer a more measured approach. Lies, as you said, unravel balance, but so does acting without a plan. Perhaps balance isn't about answers, but the patience to let the scales settle on their own."

For a moment, the conversation lapses into silence, the weight of our unspoken thoughts hanging between us. Then, as if sensing the shift, Sage's expression brightens slightly, though the edge in his gaze remains.

All of a sudden, he chuckles. "Oh, I like you," he says. "Fine. I'm done pushing. But remember Syra, even the most pristine scales sometimes shift. The key is knowing *how* to let them settle."

"I'll remember that," I say with a faint smile. Despite the tension in our exchange, there is something magnetic about him, something that pulls me in even as I try to maintain my distance.

He leans in a little, "Enough of this serious talk for now. Im assuming you never tasted Balance's mead? It's said to be the finest in all of the realm."

I shake my head, allowing myself a small smile. "I can't say that I have."

"Then it's about time you do," he says as he

gestures at the sleeping attendant. His chair suddenly shaking him awake from Sage's magic. "Consider it a welcome gift. Just one sip and you'll see why this kingdom is actually worth exploring."

As the attendant approaches with two goblets of amber liquid, I relish in the temporary distraction. Perhaps this encounter won't be as daunting as I'd feared. Or perhaps Sage is simply better at disarming his guests than I'd given him credit for.

"Balance demands truth, Syra," he says, his voice almost a whisper now, "but it also demands courage. I'll be watching to see if you have both. In my lands civility reigns, so tread carefully."

As his words trail off, the door creaks open. A hooded figure strides in, his movements fluid and filled with purpose. He passes by us and settles at the bar with his back to me. Sage's smile fades as he excuses himself, moving to sit beside the stranger at the bar.

Curiosity prickles at me. I strain to listen, their voices low, but not completely muffled. It's just quiet enough to where I can't decipher the words. I tap a finger against my goblet, faking my disinterest as I lean back in my seat. A soft murmur from the attendant talking to Sage gives me the perfect excuse to shift. Casually, I stand quietly, as if adjusting my seat, but instead, I take a step toward an empty table just within earshot. I settle in, angling myself toward them.

My power plays at the edges in anticipation, sharpening my senses just enough to catch their words. Sage's charm alters, his tone firmer with the stranger.

"It'll be time soon," the hooded man states, his voice deep and smokey. "I need information, Sage. I'm not risking a repeat of before. My tactics need to change."

The hooded figure turns their head slightly towards Sage, the light giving me just a sliver of their jaw into view.

"I understand," Sage replies carefully, "but I won't interfere unless balance is threatened."

My magic stirs, starting to spill out. It's like an itch I can't suppress. It reaches toward the hooded man like a hidden thread being pulled taut. Panic flares within me and I swallowed hard. I try forcing the power down, but the connection won't break. The conversation halts for a moment. The hooded figure's head shifts slightly.

The realization hits me. My magic *never* reaches. The only time it did, was when my dreams were being tainted with that black vapor.

Fuck. It's Roenis.

The hooded man in front of me, has to be fucking Roenis.

My heart pounds as I fight to stay composed. If he senses me now, it will all be over. Still, I can't resist listening. A slow chill unfurls at the base of my spine. I press a knuckle beneath my chin, dismissing the hiccup of magic, as I lean a fraction closer. Whatever this is, it isn't a simple exchange of pleasantries.

Roenis is here for something important.

And I intend to find out exactly what.

"I need to question people. I need to know ahead of time. Any information will be useful." His head tilts again towards my direction. "Starting with the new girl." Roenis states, his voice sharp. "She's not from here."

Sage glances toward me briefly, his orange eyes betraying a slip of panic. "A visitor. She's familiarizing herself with my land."

"A visitor from where, Sage?" Roenis growls, his tone dangerous.

Annoyance surges within me, wiping away my fear. A visitor. As if I was some wandering human lost in the wrong realm. As if I wasn't sitting right here, well within earshot, fully capable of speaking for myself. My fingers tighten around the stem of my goblet, my irritation bubbling. Roenis isn't just questioning Sage, he is pressing him, demanding answers with a similar authority that grated against my skin when my mother used it. With Sage hesitating, the panic in his eyes tells me everything. He is trying to protect me, to defuse Roenis' situation. The very thought of being tiptoed around like some fragile secret, sets my blood on fire. I don't need protection. I don't need Sage scrambling for an excuse. And I certainly don't need Roenis speaking about me like I am a problem to be solved. My jaw tenses as Roenis turns slightly in my direction again. The way he does, it's like he already knows, like he's just waiting for Sage to fumble. The whole conversation sends something snapping inside me.

Before I can think better of it, my hand finds the cool weight of my dagger. Within those seconds, I hurl my dagger. Letting it fly straight for him. The blade slices through the air, grazing Roenis' hood, before embedding itself in the wall between him and Sage.

The room falls silent.

Now it's *my* turn to talk. Guess the plans have to shift. So much for keeping a low profile and taming my temper.

CHAPTER SIX

Roenis

The dagger thrums faintly, still lodged in the wall where it embedded itself. Its resonance is unmistakable. I know that blade. I know it well.

A smirk tugs at my lips. Well, this is new.

It nearly grazed me when it sliced through the air. Which is reckless, but precise enough to grab my attention. When I see the *type* of dagger, only then do I realize it has been thrown by someone from the Dream Kingdom. My curiosity flares as I shift my gaze over my shoulder, catching a better look at the woman.

She just stands there, and at first glance, she is nothing extraordinary. But then I notice magic. The faint glint of glamour clinging to her like an afterthought.

How interesting.

It's weak glamour, barely masking her true essence. Yet it is enough to intrigue me. My magic stirs, reaching out instinctively. Again, just like earlier. A surge of recognition hits me, sending a spark through my thoughts.

The woman standing there isn't *plain* at all. No, this is one of Maya's daughters.

One of her fucking daughters.

What in the shadowed hells is she doing in the Balance Kingdom? And more importantly, does she know who I am?

Her voice snaps through the air like a whip, drawing my attention back to her as she saunters closer to me and Sage. "Did anyone ever teach you that it's impolite to speak about a woman as if she's not standing right here?"

A brow arches of its own accord, and I turn my head just slightly, concealing a flicker of amusement.

Bold. I have to give her that much.

Still, I have no intention of revealing myself—not

fully. Not yet. I want to watch her, see how she moves, how her mind works when she thinks she's going unnoticed. So I cloak myself further, letting my magic dull the edges of my presence.

I grin at her, all teeth and mischief, and I'm rewarded with the sight of color draining from her face.

"Hard to be polite," I drawl, "when it's equally rude to eavesdrop on other people's conversations."

Her eyes light up like a fire sparking in the dark. Oh, this is going to be fun.

She steps closer, her lips shifting into a smirk that doesn't quite reach her eyes. "Eavesdrop? Hardly. Just constant buzzing in my ears from how loud you were talking. Figured I chuck a dagger to get you to shut up."

I chuckle, low and as a warning. "For someone who's new in the area, you have quite a temper that's too easy to ignite. You also missed, so should I be flattered or concerned?"

She doesn't flinch, but there's a subtle shift in her stance. Calculating. She's sizing me up, likely wondering if I'm worth the effort. It's almost charming.

Her eyes narrow, and for a brief moment, something dangerous flashes in them. "Concerned. Definitely concerned."

I let out a low sigh, keeping my gaze locked on her. "Oh, I'm trembling," I say, stepping slightly into her path. The faint shimmer of her glamour shifts under the dim light, just enough for me to notice again.

Sloppy.

Her illusion stutters when she's distracted, like she isn't used to the mask she's wearing. A novice's mistake. For someone trying to be subtle, she's doing a miserable job.

"Do you always carry a dagger for casual conversation?" I ask, pointing towards the still-humming blade in the wall. "Or am I just that special?"

She tilts her head, her lips curving into an almost smile—if not for the irritation beneath it. "Depends on who I'm talking to, but rest assure I won't miss next time."

I take a deliberate step forward, closing the

distance between us. "Oh, I'm counting on your aim being better next time. It's the only way this will stay interesting."

I lean in, just enough to unsettle her. "Let me guess, your temper is a bad habit and your dagger is a form of armor?"

Her expression doesn't falter, but her hand shifts ever so slightly to her hip. I know what that means—another weapon, ready and waiting. She's good, and very easy to push.

"I could say the same for you," she fires back, "men who wear shadows like armor tend to have both a temper *and* bad habits."

I bite back the laugh threatening to escape, letting a sly grin do the talking instead. "Checkmate. Though, you missed one thing." My voice drops, watching for any cracks in her composure. "Some of us don't just wear the shadows, we *are* the shadows."

For a moment, she doesn't respond.

I wait, wanting her to notice. She's clever enough, I can see it.

I expect silence, maybe even hesitation, but she

surprises me. She lifts her chin as she delivers her retort.

"I'd hate to see you in the light, then. Something tells me the shadows do you too many favors."

Her eyes were pure black, but for the briefest moment, the glamour falters again, and I see the liquid amethyst, swirling like a storm in her gaze.

Fucking beautiful.

The thought lingers longer than it should have. I didn't even realize I haven't responded until her voice breaks through my distraction.

"What's wrong, stranger? Gods got your tongue?" she says, finally letting a real sly smile curve her lips. She knows she caught me, and she isn't about to let it go.

Damn her.

Before I can reply, Sage decides it was time to intervene. Of course, he would. Perfect timing, as always.

"Listen," he begins, stepping between us like some self-appointed referee. "As entertaining as this is, this conversation has run its course."

I shift my gaze to him, narrowing my eyes. "She's

coming with me for questioning. I trust you see this is now a matter beyond your involvement." My voice is calm but edged with finality. I watch as Sage's gaze flickers briefly towards the woman, before returning to me.

"That's up to Syra," he states with maddening composure.

Syra. I haven't even thought to ask for her name.

She turns to Sage, swinging her head around with such force I almost expect her glamour to ripple again. "I just got here. What exactly do I have to be questioned for?"

I step in before Sage can indulge her with an answer. "No, not here. I mean you'll be escorted to the Kingdom of Nightmares for questioning by Roenis." I let the name roll off my tongue deliberately, testing her reaction, watching for even the smallest spark of recognition.

"You?" she asks, arching a brow. "You'll escort me there? And what exactly am I to be questioned about?"

"Since you hail from the Dream Kingdom, which is an educated guess confirmed by the craftsmanship of that dagger you threw, your presence has raised a few questions for me. Let's just call this due diligence." My gaze stays locked onto hers, searching for a crack, a tell, anything to reveal what she could already know.

But she doesn't flinch. Instead, she stares at me for a moment. As if gathering her thoughts before making her next move. Then she shrugs, as if I've just invited her to tea. "Fine. Sure. But only if you tell me your name, shadow stranger." Her eyebrows lift upwards, like she's testing me.

I pause, caught off guard again. She keeps doing that. One moment she's fiery, cutting with her words, and the next, she's nonchalant, as though this entire situation is some kind of game.

She doesn't have an ounce of timidity. No submissive deference, no doe-eyed fear. She definitely doesn't try to flatter or charm me.

She's a different type of daughter than the rest Maya has sent. Syra is an entirely new creature it seems, and it's already maddening.

What the hell are you up to, Maya?

I shift my gaze back to Sage, who merely shrugs,

clearly enjoying his role as a passive observer.

Typical.

"Noctis," I say, pulling the name from the depths of my memory. It once belonged to a former right-hand in my kingdom. A name that will suit my purposes now.

Syra tilts her head, studying me like I'm a puzzle she's half-interested in solving. "Didn't picture you with that name," she says lightly before turning her attention to the dagger still lingering in the wall. She strides over to it, gripping the hilt and yanks it out. "So, when do we leave? I just got here, and I'd prefer to at least rest and eat before we go."

I glance at Sage again. There's concern in his usually impassive eyes. It's a warning I don't need right now.

I take a breath, pushing down the irritation that her nonchalant attitude stirs in me. "We'll leave in the morning," I say, keeping my tone measured. "Until then, you'll be watched by my escorts. And no more throwing daggers." I add.

She huffs a laugh as her fingers trace the blade. "No promises."

Her defiance will be a problem, and yet, I can't help but admire the spark behind it. I whistle sharply, summoning my guards from the shadows outside the tavern. They enter, their frames casting long, imposing silhouettes against the warm light of the room.

Syra doesn't seem to care. Her gaze sweeps over them with casual disinterest, as if she's looking at toddlers, rather than two trained soldiers. No fear. No hesitation. It's a little unsettling.

"Escort Syra to the inn," I command, enough to leave no room for question. "Make sure she's settled. We leave at first light for her questioning with Roenis."

Grifton and Kenji exchange a brief, puzzled glance at each other. I catch the confusion in their eyes—referring to myself in the third person is going to be a trial.

Sage, never one to let a moment pass without a word, steps forward again. "I don't tolerate disruption in my kingdom... Noctis." He says the name slowly with unfamiliarity. "If there's so much as a whisper of commotion involving my people, you won't be welcomed back."

The warning is final, his tone as hard as stone.

I nod once, more to placate him than anything else. Then I cast my attention back to my guards. "You heard the God. Follow through."

Syra watches the exchange, her dark eyes darting between us. I can see the wheels turning in her head, can almost feel the energy of her calculations. She's trying to piece what *I* know, what *I'm* hiding, and what she can get away with.

She's fascinating to watch, a puzzle in her own right. My mind wanting to see her think, to see her plan. And I want to see what happens when she finally unravels.

She turns to Sage with a look of brief sincerity. "Sorry about the dagger."

Sage hides a smirk, shaking his head. "I said no lies, Syra."

For the first time, she smiles. A real, genuine smile that catches me off guard. It's gone just as quickly, fading as she turns her gaze back to me.

"Right," she says, voice softer now, yet still laced with her sharp edge. Without another word, she brushes past me, her shoulder barely missing mine.

That's when I finally catch her scent. Floral. A faint, intoxicating earthy flower that clings to her like a secret, it's delicate yet strangely potent. It lingers in the air between us as she strides ahead, leaving me momentarily rooted in place.

She's unlike anything I've encountered before. The others were all the same: strong perfumes that tried too hard or faint traces of nothingness, easily forgotten. But this? This is hers, undeniably.

Flowers suit her. Beautiful and laced with danger. A scent that draws you in even as it warns you to tread carefully.

Now I really want to see her without her glamour.

My guards fall into step behind her like shadows trailing the sun.

Outside, the crisp air greets us. The village gardens aroma mingles with the earthy undertone of the windmill just ahead. The inn then comes into view. It's a modest, two-story building tucked to the left of the massive structure. Its warm, glowing windows look welcoming, though Syra doesn't seem to notice.

She walks ahead without hesitation, her stride unhurried, confident, as if she owns the place. I follow at a short distance, letting my guards flank her. For now, I'll let her think she's in control.

But once we reach the Kingdom of Nightmares, all bets are off.

CHAPTER SEVEN
Syra

I can't walk fast enough. His two guards right on my tail, while Roenis keeps his distance in the far back. I'm feeling too worked up to enjoy the surroundings. My plan is shifting, and now I'm not sure exactly how to approach it. I'm suppose to meet him in Nightmare Kingdom and have the element of surprise, but now here he is. Literally escorting me to his castle himself. I'm not sure if he's aware I'm the Goddess, but I won't put it past him on already figuring it out. Something tells me he likes to play this game. He likes feeling in control and that I'm this dumb witted girl like the rest of them.

I like to believe I'm more cunning. That I'm more powerful. And damn it, I *will* be the one to succeed.

I make it to the Inn doors, grand and wooden, and so beautifully carved to perfection. I open the doors and inside is surprisingly warm, its cheerful contrast to the tension from the tavern. Sunlight spills through the tall, arched windows, bathing the space in a wave of gold. The walls are painted a soft cream, accented with decorative tapestries that depict scenes of harmony and balance. There is one with a river running between two equal banks, and another with the sun and moon locked in a half and half embrace. On the far end wall towards the back, two figures painted on the wall, balancing on opposite ends of a scale. A tree split perfectly down the middle with one side blooming with life and the other bare and steady.

Each table and chair surrounding the open space before the counter to check in, was crafted from a light color wood. Polished to a gleam and positioned evenly throughout.

I'll give it to Sage, everything so far is well thought out and…even.

In the center of the room was a circular hearth framed by stone. It's etching designs carved the same way as everything else in here. With patience and perfection. The fire crackles, filling the room with the scent of wood smoke and something sweet, similar to a human world smell.

Cinnamon and clove?

Conversations hum from nearby tables, a sense of companionship and respect. It really is a representation of the Kingdom of Balance, welcoming and warm, but reserved. Even with the inviting atmosphere, it doesn't hide the weight of the two shadows following me.

Roenis' guards, or rather, *Noctis'* escorts, since we are still playing that game, linger by the doorway.

Roenis is still keeping his full appearance hidden. I get a flash of his smile here and there and his eyes give off a glow, but every time I think I can make out all of his features with his hood up, the magic surrounding him blurs my view. It's so subtle, but affective as hell.

The guards hover, their constant presence feels suffocating. I can't decide which is worse: the shorter one, with his broad muscles, twitchy hands and a tendency to glare at me like I was the ugly one, or the taller one, who seems to think silence and lurking is the peak of intimidation.

Instead of heading straight to the woman behind the counter, whom I assume is the innkeeper, I go towards one of the carved tables. The men follow, and that's when *he* brushes past his guards and takes his seat.

Roenis gestures to the other chair across from him. I allow myself a slow stretch as I sit down. My movements minimal, as I ignore the stares. The guards stand at the edge of my awareness, quiet but ready to snap at the slightest provocation.

"Your guards seem tense," I remark, giving Roenis a raised brow.

"They're doing their job," he replies. His voice calm, but I didn't miss the edge in his tone.

I tilt my head back looking at the guards, almost facing upside down. "Afraid I'll escape? Or afraid I might put this dagger in Noctis' chest?"

The shorter guard stiffens, his jaw tightening even further. "We're here to ensure his safety, and to escort you to the Nightmare Kingdom," he states, his tone a littler quieter on that last line.

I feel like pushing. A little poke just to make things fun.

"Oh, his safety? What about mine?" I turn and rest my chin in my hand, giving the taller one an overly sweet smile. "I bet you can make me feel so safe."

The taller guard's mouth twitches, as if he's fighting the urge to smile. I guess intimidation isn't his strong suit. He quickly schools his expression into a neutral one. Roenis' gaze flies towards them briefly, his lips pressing into a thin line before giving me his attention again.

Leaning back on his chair, with a casual authority he states, "They take their loyalty to Roenis serious, you might want to try making their job a little easier."

I feign surprise, widening my eyes. "Easier? Where's the fun in that?"

He huffs.

I bend forward, lowering my voice to keep the men from overhearing. "So *Noctis*, do you always bring such...enthusiastic chaperones on your little adventures?"

He doesn't falter at the subtle emphasis on his fake name, but I catch the faintest sliver of curiosity in his eyes. Or what I can see anyway with his magic blurring everything.

"Only when the company requires it," he replies smoothly.

"I see." I let the silence stretch between us for a moment before leaning back in my chair, casting a sidelong glance at the guards. "Well, if they're going to be shadowing me all the way to the Nightmare Kingdom, I hope they at least give me good conversation. I get bored easily."

"And here I thought you preferred to keep people at arm's length." He assesses.

The comment is casual enough, but it's the way he says it, like a question.

Always searching for information. He's so nosy.

"Depends on the people," I say, propping my chin back on my hand. "Some are far more interesting than others."

He leans, his arm and hand inching closer.

"Interesting can be a dangerous thing."

I arch a brow, matching his tone with a hint of playfulness. "Only for the ones who don't know how to handle it."

For a moment, silence lingers about, thick with unspoken meanings. Is this really Roenis? Could I have assessed this wrong already?

The corner of his mouth tilting up, before swiping his hand to hit my arm slightly. The action causing me to lose balance since it's holding my chin, nearly smacking my face into the table.

Gods what an asshole.

He reclines back in his chair, his eyes never leaving mine. "This is going to be an amusing journey."

I sneer, the moment fades by his ridiculous prank. Keeping pace with his relentless comebacks is exhausting, but his playfulness doesn't deceive me. The real Roenis will emerge soon enough once we begin the journey. I can feel it.

My fingers toy with the hilt of the dagger at my side as I narrow my eyes in a silent glare. "Careful, Noctis. I told you I wouldn't miss next time. And you're definitely tempting me to throw this again." I motion my head to my thigh where the weapon is strapped.

The shorter guard scowls, but the taller one can't suppress a reluctant chuckle, quickly masking it with a cough.

"Enough," Roenis interjects, though his tone lacks any real bite. He gestures to the innkeeper, signaling for food. "The day ahead will be long. Save your stabbing tendencies for a more appropriate time."

I smirk as I put some distance between us. My eyes stay locked on him, watching. "Oh, I'm just getting started."

He tries getting close, resting his arms on the table, enough for me to catch his scent. Maybe his magic falters because I couldn't smell it before.

He smells like rain. Not just any rain, but that cleansing, earthy scent that lingers in dreams I often weave. There is also a hint of salt, and something similar to honey.

What a curious scent to have as a God of Nightmares.

As if sensing my distraction, he pushes even

closer, his voice dropping to a private murmur meant only for me. "You're cautious, aren't you? I wonder if you're always this calculated, or if it's just for me."

I keep still, not moving an inch, letting my voice drop to a similar pitch, "Maybe you're imagining it. Nightmares tend to do that, don't they? Inflict illusions?"

His expression don't stir, but there is a gleam in his eyes, a momentary spark of something dark and amused. He knows I'm playing a game, just as much as I know he is too, but neither of us want to lay our cards down. The question isn't who would win. It's who would make the first move.

The tension simmers in silence as the innkeeper approaches, setting down two bowls of what I assume is the daily special. The liquid is an ethereal blue, dotted with chunks of fish likely caught from the nearby river. The aroma is mouthwatering. The woman hesitates, clearly uneasy, before speaking. "Enjoy. I put my best effort into this meal for the God's guests." With that, she quickly retreats.

"Eat," Roenis instructed, his tone now firm. "Then

rest."

I glance at the dish, its appearance unlike anything I've eaten before. Scooping a spoonful, I taste it. The flavors are bold, a rich saltiness that dances on my tongue. I can't help but devour the entire bowl, noting Roenis does the same.

When we finish, he stands, gesturing to the guards and then to me. "Get some rest. We leave in the morning." Without another word, he ascends the stairs, the innkeeper trailing behind.

I watch him go, my mind buzzing with the situation I put myself in. Noctis, he claims to be. But the way he carries himself, the weight of command in his voice, feels too familiar as what Gods and Goddesses exude. Either he has been trained well, or he is exactly who I suspect him to be.

A sharp scrape of a chair against the floor pulls me back. One of the guards, the shorter one, has his dark eyes scanning me with caution. He jerks his chin toward the stairway. "Come on."

The other one simply exhales, stretching his arms upward before falling in step beside me.

For now, I comply. It isn't as if I have anywhere

else to go, and after tonight's little performance, slipping away unnoticed will be impossible. Better to bide my time, and get every ounce of rest I can.

The stairs creak beneath my steps, the inn is beautiful, but it holds a rustic feeling. I might've appreciated it under different circumstances. Shadows stretch long in the hallways, and I note how neither of the guards seem particularly concerned by them. It just feels out of place.

When we reach the upper floor, I catch a glimpse of Noctis—I still say Roenis—speaking in hushed tones with the innkeeper. He's negotiating. For what, I'm not sure, but his tone is obvious in the conversation.

The moment his head looks back, as if sensing me, I turn away before our eyes could meet.

The guard ahead of me stops before a door, pushing it open with the same ease one might swat a fly. "This one's yours," he mutters.

I step inside, and it's a modest space. A bed, a small writing desk, and a single window covered by dark curtains that barely sway despite the evening breeze sneaking through the cracks.

I exhale, feeling slightly defeated. "Try to get some sleep," he adds, tone gruff but oddly not unkind.

"Are you worried about me?" I muse, turning just enough to catch the annoyance in his features.

"Worried? No." He scoffs. "But if you try anything stupid, we'll have to deal with the mess."

"How considerate."

They leave, the tall one shaking his head as the other pulls the door shut.

Alone at last. Carefully, I peel back the curtains, peering outside. The streets below are nearly empty, save for a few stragglers. I'm still unsettled about seeing him. Noctis. Roenis. Whoever he is.

He's playing his role well tonight, but I've seen glimpses beneath the mask. Tomorrow, I'll be entering his territory. And I'll be watching.

◆

The light beams brightly in my face when approaching the open carriage in front of me. Its frame is dark, an onyx type metal etched with white engravings. In front are creatures made from shadow itself. Vaporous half-formed creatures resembling a type of mane. Their silver misty eyes cut through the stillness, as if trying to make me think twice before boarding. My lips tilt slightly in mild amusement.

What a dramatic God. His theatrics wasn't something I was told about.

I approach the creature slowly, their eyes growing darker.

The short guard speaks up, "They bite. Especially passengers like you. They have a taste for it."

"Good thing I'm not easy to devour then," I shoot back, climbing into the carriage. I settle into the plush seat, leaning against the black metal cooling my back.

The guards joining me in their places towards the rear. As for Roenis, he watches the exchange in silence. He's been playful so far, with his wit matching my own, but now as he climbs in and sits across from me, the mood feels shifted.

The air feels heavier, more suffocating.

His cloak sweeps over him like a dark shadow

and his posture is rigid. His fingers move to make a small knock on the side of the metal. Like an unspoken signal, the carriage jolts forward. The creatures surge on ahead, with movements so smooth and soundless, despite the uneven terrain.

The silence lingers even after riding for a few moments. All that is heard is a faint creak of the wheels and soft hisses from the creatures. I let my eyes drift to the landscape around us, though the weight of his presence is like a storm cloud, hard to ignore the feeling of electricity pressing into my skin.

The land changes from the beautiful views of Balance with its flowing river to the left, to a more darker view of land. A bleak, intense field of cracked earth with twisted dead trees that claw at the gray sky. White misty fog swirling in every corner of the rippling mountains near by. It also curls along the ground, moving naturally as if following the carriage.

I bring my attention back to Roenis, determined to pierce the wall he suddenly placed. "Well," I say, breaking the silence, "not much of a talker after all?

And here I thought I was in for an entertaining ride."

His silver eyes flicker to mine, but his voice lowers and is more restrained than before. "A journey requires more than idle chatter, your surroundings will leave you entertained enough."

I blink, caught off guard with the change of his tone.

It isn't what he said that upsets me, it's the sharp edge in his voice. I tilt my head studying him, but as usual, he's unreadable since he keeps his magic up, obscuring his true form. He turns his stare ahead, where the faint silhouette of the castle looms in between the mountains and mist.

The whole exchange leaves a sour taste in my mouth, and even the guards wear the wariness all over their face. Their earlier bravado now faded into the same silence that wraps around Roenis. What the fuck. Did yesterday even happen?

I shuffle in my seat, folding my arms across my chest.

Fine. If he wants to sulk, I'll let him.

I have no intention of showing how unnerved I

am, no matter how much the demeanor sets my teeth on edge. Yet, I can't shake the feeling that this is less of a journey and more of a warning.

It feels like hours, but finally the creatures slow.

The castle emerges in the distance like a phantom, its obsidian silhouette rising from the sharp tipped mountains. My breath catches, and I hate myself for it. The structure is unique, carvings that look like pure shadows. Its dark spires pierces the ashen sky, with white mist and black vapor curling around them like restless spirits. A faint hum of power vibrates in the air, making my skin prickle. As we draw closer, the land beneath us grows even more barren. The ground is blackened here, and even the air seems heavier.

The carriage comes to a stop before a bridge, expanding wide and stretching endlessly towards the castles monumental gate doors. The stones are uneven, etched with faded, cryptic markings. The sides of the bridge seems like a swirling abyss, too dark to discover anything alongside them. Towers linger beyond the main structure, their peaks barely visible through the vapor, making the castle seem alive, like it was expanding, and slightly moving—If you stare long enough.

Roenis disembarks first, breaking my trance. The guards move silently to flank me. I step down, forcing my expression into one of cool detachment, though my fingers tingle with nervous energy. Everything feels off.

"Welcome to the Nightmare Kingdom." He pauses. "Goddess." Roenis says, his voice a low purr that sends a bolt of irritation through me. His smile is unreadable, a look too sinister for my liking, as though he can already see the threads of my plan unraveling.

Wait…He called me Goddess.

The guards on either side of me both grip an arm and leave me feeling trapped. I snap my attention back to him. I go to speak but a phantom feeling slaps over my mouth, preventing me.

What the fuck is happening.

My gaze locks onto the massive gates ahead, the guards moving in sync as they carry me to follow after Roenis. "I hope it's to your liking," he murmurs, the amusement in his tone unmistakable.

I can't answer. My heart was beating a deafening blend of anticipation and unease.

He chuckles, "Not that it matters, you'll still be questioned, but until then, I can't have you creating a scene." He looks to his guards and nods his head. "Take the pathway for the dungeons. Keep watch until I send word for her to join the throne room."

They bow their heads in unison.

Fuck.

Another crack in the plan.

CHAPTER EIGHT

Roenis

I watch as they drag Syra off.

I wanted to approach things differently, but her being in Balance and at a time frame that's much sooner than the others, I have reason to be cautious.

I regret not talking more on the trip here, but my mindset needs to be clear. I can't have her in my head before this has even started. I turn, making my way through the doors and organizing the motive of this questioning.

The sound of my boots echo through the hall. I feel my vapors release, dancing along the smooth walls of my castle. They missed the presence of home. I ascend the steps towards my chambers, peaking out the small slanted windows, watching the white mist shift against the glass. Not even two minutes have passed and Dolion's lanky frame is trailing behind me. The newly appointed right hand, whose voice is a persistent buzz, starts ranting off the details of the evening to come. His slicked-back black hair gleams under the soft lights as we make our way up. It makes him appear more serpent like than a man. I barley even spare a glance as he speaks, my mind lingering on her. On Syra.

"The concoction worked as intended," Dolion states, his voice smug. "She's subdued, though resistant. Remarkable willpower for someone so small."

I stop mid-stride, my jaw clenching as I turn to face him finally. "You drugged her?"

Dolion's smirk drops. "A precaution, my God. You ordered her to be contained, and we couldn't risk her powers lashing out."

I step in closer, releasing some of my black vapors and shadows, flexing at the sides of him. His confidence wavers, his eyes darting around in a panic.

"I gave no such order," I growl, anger filling me. "She was to be contained in the dungeons unharmed. I don't need her drugged to keep control."

"Of course, my God," he stammers, bowing his head quickly. "It was a mistake—"

"Enough," I snap, silencing him. "If you've damaged her mind in any way, Dolion, you'll be suffering a far worse fate than her."

He swallows hard, nodding, and I call back my power. I turn and resume my pace, leaving him to scramble, but he follows me instead. My hands clench into fists at my sides.

"Leave." I state in a dark tone. I hear the sound of his steps hurrying away. The thought of Syra, her fiery attitude dulled by some stupid liquid, rubs me the wrong way. I'm trying to change the situation, not make it worse.

I wave my hand and the door to my chambers creak open. Blackened wood furniture fills the space, and a large mirror framed in twisted iron, stands against the wall facing the bed. I turn towards the basin of water sat waiting near the fireplace, steam curling lazily from its surface.

I shrug off my cloak, draping it over the back of my chair from my desk, and approach the awaiting water. The reflection in the mirror shows a man who is weary, though I'll never admit it. Dark shadows frame my silver eyes, and my red hair falls messily over my forehead. It looks tangled into my horns from wearing this ridiculous hood for the past two days. I drag myself into the water and splashed some over my face, letting the heat chase away some of the tension.

I take a moment to breathe. The scent of lavender hanging faintly in the air, an aroma meant to ground me. But today, it does little to settle the restless energy thrumming under my skin. Syra has ignited something within me. A sense of anticipation, curiosity, and a deep-seated unease I can't shake.

After awhile I get out, and dress swiftly, donning simple black clothing and a dark cloak that flows with each step. The weight of the fabric feels heavy tonight. My mind clouda with momentary hesitation. She's nothing like the others. I got too playful with her wits, which makes this all the more dangerous.

Is this an act? Her unpredictability, is it planned? Did Maya finally create a match to go against me?

My blood boils at the thought.

I make my way down, winding through the hallways and down the steps. When I enter the throne room, the vastness of the space greets me like an old friend. Tall, arched ceilings disappear into shadow, and a massive circular moat separates the room. Small bridges span the dark, rippling water, each one leading to a different direction in the castle. The one at the point, slightly longer and more defined, lead to my throne. The throne itself was carved from a black crystal-like stone. Its sharp edges glinting under the soft, eerie glow of the room. I climb up the dais and sit, leaning back against the coolness as I wait. The chamber is silent save for the faint lapping of water against the moat's edges.

It isn't long before the doors open, and my heart quickens with anticipation, despite the circumstances.

My two main guards enter first, their armor

clinking softly as they escort her in. Syra walks between them, though her steps are sluggish, and her movements unsteady. Whatever they gave her hadn't completely subdued her spirit, but it has dulled her sharp edges. Her glamour is gone now, her true form on full display, and for a moment, I am angry. This isn't how I wanted to see her unglamoured.

Her skin is a pale, luminous blue, as though kissed by moonlight. Her white hair falls in soft waves, streaked with strands of gold that shimmers with each step. She is taller than her previous glamour, her frame thin yet powerful, and her violet eyes hold a depth that draws me in.

The same liquid storm I've seen before in the tavern.

Beautiful doesn't seem adequate. She's otherworldly, a vision crafted from the dreams she weaves. And yet, there is a ferocity to her, even in her current state.

A Goddess for sure. Witty and deadly, standing before me with an unshakeable presence that defies the shackles of her condition.

The guards stop at the edge of the bridge, awaiting my command. I rise from the throne, descending the steps with intentional slowness. My steps echoing against the stone, the sound carrying through the room as I approach her. Her gaze lifts to meet mine, resistance bleeding in those violet orbs.

Or maybe it's recognition.

"Welcome, Syra," I say, my voice steady but is laced with a quiet intensity. "I trust your journey was... eventful."

Her lips part as though to respond, but no words come. The drug's influence still holds her tongue, though I can see the frustration stewing beneath the surface.

I gesture to the guards, and they release her arms. She stumbles slightly but catches herself, her chin lifting in a silent show of strength. I step in closer, keeping my movements slow, almost predatory, as I circle her.

"What's wrong?" I murmur, my eyes sweeping hungrily over her. "God's got your tongue?" I play with her comeback she had stated before.

Her sluggish movements betray her irritation, but

a spark of fire lights in her eyes. "I was right…" she begins, her voice hoarse but I hear the determination, "…The shadows *did* do too many favors."

A smirk peaks at the corner of my lips. "Still sharp, even when dulled. Impressive." I stop in front of her, meeting her brazen stare once more, neither of us speaking. The silence rolls on, heavy with crackling tension.

"Why Balance?" I ask finally, "Of all places to glamour yourself and play your little games, why there?"

Her gaze narrows slightly, a hint of calculation creeping into her expression. "The mead…" she states slowly, her voice still thick. "They don't water it down."

I raise an eyebrow, amused by her audacity. "Unlikely, and the timing?" I press. "Why now, Syra? What does mead have anything to do with the risk of wandering into Balance's kingdom, disguised as someone else?"

"Disguised…" she echoes, her lips quirking into a faint smirk. "That's a big word for someone who…

spends his time brooding in dark cloaks."

"Careful," I warn softly, though there's no real menace in my tone. "You're already on dangerous ground."

Her shoulders shift as she attempts to straighten, fighting the drug's effects. "Dangerous ground?" she mocks, her voice gaining strength. "You'd know all about that, wouldn't you? Tell me, how many of my people have walked these halls and lived to talk about it?"

I lean in closer, my voice dropping to a whisper. "That depends, Syra. How many of them had a plan made out to kill me?"

The splash of surprise crosses her face. "My plan…" she began, pausing as though weighing her words. "…was to see how much longer you'd hide behind theatrics."

"And?" I prompt, stepping back just enough to give her space, though my gaze never leaves hers. "Am I meeting your expectations?"

Her smirk returns, sluggish but undeniably present. "Falling just short."

I chuckle again, the sound genuinely filled with

amusement. "We'll see about that. What was your plan, really? Or shall I start guessing?"

She doesn't react, but her eyes follow me, aware despite the haze. She crooks her finger to summon me over. Of course my annoying curiosity beckons me forward. Then suddenly I see a purple glow radiating from her hand and a vine whipping out. It wraps tightly around my throat, restricting my airway.

Fucking bold ass woman.

I grip her magic in the air and break it. She blinks, completely shocked by the movement. "Your magic is worth shit here. I suggest you learn your place."

Her glare burns into my black soul. I applaud her effort. Even with the drug, she's relentless. As if the adrenaline wore off, I see her eyes falter and she falls backwards, my guards catching her. The magic must've drained her since she was already weakened.

"Bring her back to the dungeons, and send for Datura, I need to speak with her."

They bow and as they escort her, I return to the throne, my mind a tangled web of curiosity and conflict. This is only the beginning, and already, she is weaving herself into my thoughts, and being bold with moves to kill me.

Twice. Twice she has threatened me. The game has begun, and though I hold the advantage, I can't shake the feeling that Syra is far more unpredictable than I'd anticipated.

CHAPTER NINE

Syra

I pace around the cold, cramped, and pitiful excuse for a cell. If this is how my mission will play out, I'll lose my fucking mind. The smell is fucking unbearable, as if rotting flesh is embedded into the stone itself. It clings to the air, making it impossible to ignore. My head feels clouded, the lingering effects of the drug crawling under my skin, and my body tingling as though every nerve is screaming to be touched.

Damn it. That's the last thing I need.

But I feel him. No, my magic *reaches* for him. It draws out, stretching toward his presence.

I need him to want to get me out of this cell. If this

doesn't go the way I plan, this entire mission is a waste. Just the thought of Roenis sparks a traitorous sensation low in my belly.

Gods, this drug.

My skin feels like it's vibrating as my body reacts to his upcoming presence. I drop onto the pathetic cot to try to regain control of myself. It's barely large enough for a toddler, but I sit back anyway, letting the cold, damp wall cool the heat off my skin.

His face dances around in my mind. I finally saw him in the throne room, his beauty more devastating than I'd imagined even for a god. My legs spread of their own accord due to the drug I was given. It was a display of vulnerability and yet, I feel powerful. The memory of him draws out every impure thought I've repressed.

Roenis was an embodiment of temptation and power, his crimson hair falling into waves that seemed to defy the hardness he presented. His silver eyes were like liquid moonlight, piercing and endless, as if they could unravel the deepest spots in my soul with a single glance. His horns were magnificent. Black and elegant, curved around his head perfectly, their bases fading into a stark white that added a simple contrast to his otherwise dark aura. His features were sharp, sculpted with an almost unfair precision, every line and angle designed to captivate and unsettle.

And then when he spoke to me in the throne room, he sounded slightly different than at the tavern. His voice was smooth, laced with a sly humor that danced with the intensity of his words. I had expected cruelty, perhaps even indifference, but instead, he wielded his playful banter well, striking my composure with every teasing remark. There was an unexpected charm with him, and it was magnetic.

It caught me off guard, leaving me torn between irritation and intrigue. Roenis was not the one-dimensional Nightmare God I had prepared to face. I couldn't help but be drawn to the spark of challenge he ignited in me.

I tense. I sense him again, and my magic pulls me closer. It's strange, how his presence feels almost like an extension of my own, as though his essence threads through the air I breathe.

So fucking strange.

The room fills with a swirl of silver and black vapor, twisting and curling from the floor in a dark dance. The smoke forms a circle, and in its center, Roenis emerges. His grey eyes glow in the dim light, and his hair was now pulled into a loose bun, a few strands escaping to frame his face. Some twist wild near his horns.

My gaze lingers on those horns again, tracing the fading white at their base as they curl into dark spirals. He's almost too perfect. I snap my focus back to his eyes, catching the amusement that danced in them.

He takes me in with a slow, dragging look, his wolfish grin disturbing. "You've made yourself comfortable." His voice was like silk sliding over rough gravel, the sound curling around my body.

I spread my legs wider, making sure he sees every inch of me. "Actually, you're just in time for the show. My best one yet." The drug steals my control, my words dripping with challenge.

With a snap of thought, I conjure a chair behind him. It's jagged and crude, fitting for this cell. His gaze sweeps to it briefly, then returns to me, unfazed.

"Front row seating, just for you," I add with a lazy smirk. "Since you *love* theatrics." The drug comes in waves, leaving me coherent one moment and senseless the next.

I push my magic forward, forcing him into the chair. Purple chains erupt from the floor, wrapping around his wrists and ankles, anchoring him in place. If I'm trapped, then so is he.

His aura seemed calm, which was the complete opposite to the tension I was feeling in my body.

His eyes don't waver. There's no anger, no panic, only calculated indifference. "And why am I the one chained? As I recall, you're the prisoner." His tone is so infuriatingly flat it riles me up.

Infuriating God.

"Precautions," I reply coolly despite the heat boiling inside my skin. "I enjoy being watched, but I don't want any funny business. The chains are just insurance to keep your hands to yourself."

His brow arches slightly, but the flicker of amusement returns. He leans back, making himself comfortable as if we're back at the tavern. "You think if I wanted to touch you, these pathetic chains would stop me?"

His chuckle came out rich, almost sultry, and it wraps around me like a teasing caress, and my confidence wavers. He stretches, the motion causing strands of hair to fall into his face, the glow of his eyes cutting through the shadows.

"Let's get on with it," he says, voice hardening. "The sooner this pathetic performance is over, the sooner I can explain your future here."

This bastard thinks he's tough shit. Fine, I'll show him how its played.

His dismissiveness only fuels my stubbornness. I let the drug take over, my hands moving of their own accord. Slowly, deliberately, I trail my fingers down my neck, tracing the valley between my breasts. My shirt parts under my touch, the fabric slipping to reveal bare skin. I undo another button, letting the fabric fall open completely. His eyes follow every movement, his jaw tightening imperceptibly.

I don't stop. My fingers slip lower, tracing circles

over my stomach before dipping beneath my skirt. Inch by inch, I lift it, until I'm completely exposed. Vulnerable. And yet, the power of his attention fuels me more.

His gaze burns. For a moment, I see something primal flash in his eyes, a hunger he's too stubborn to show. But just as quickly, it's gone, replaced by that insufferable, coldness.

Gods, what am I doing?

This drug is troublesome. But isn't this my mission? Isn't seduction my weapon?

With that thought, I follow that initiative and let go. Let's make this interesting.

I take my first two fingers and push them into my mouth. Coating them with my saliva. I make sure I keep my eyes on his. My fingers then brush the top of my exposed mound. I dip lower, slipping through my folds teasing myself as I moan softly. The sound fills the cell. My body arches, chasing waves of pleasure I can't control. The tension coils tighter with every breath. I trail up and down in a slow rhythm, drawing soft gasps from my own lips. I peak another glance, and I notice his gaze has darkened, but his expression still remains controlled. Until it doesn't.

I smile as his eyes flicks to the glistening mess between my thighs. I see faint tiny black vapors emitting from him, and a glow in his eyes that were subtle, but still evident.

Thank gods this drug is clouding part of my judgment, otherwise I would feel a lot more embarrassed with my actions.

A sudden zap, a pulse of heat that was electric and sharp, hits me. My back arches, a loud moan tearing from my lips before I can stop it. My fingers felt hot, and my clit felt more sensitive.

This brute is using magic on me. His smirk confirms it, and another surge of heat rushes through me, simmering again, low in my belly.

Another zap.

I gasp, trembling as the pleasure builds, his power weaving through me like a lightning storm. He's playing with me, pushing me to the edge.

Bastard.

Like a switch, the drug fades abruptly, the heat of his magic receding. I'm left exposed, panting, and my body still buzzing with lingering desire. Not even finishing the ride. I got lost in the waves of pleasure, and now my awareness floods back. I peek at him. That smirk is still there, smug and insufferable. I'll wipe it off his face. I'll make him regret that.

An idea sparked within me.

Standing, I smooth my skirt down and fix my shirt. I stalk toward him, confidence burning in every step. I grip his chin, forcing his mouth open. "Have a taste," I purr, sliding my fingers past his lips. "Now suck…I'm delicious."

He doesn't fight me. Surprisingly his mouth closes over my fingers, his tongue swirling around them with aching slowness. The electricity is back, similar to earlier, and heat surges from his touch. I knew it was him. I suppress a shiver, clinging to my composure as it takes all my will not to tremble.

But I don't let him see it. Instead, I pull my fingers free and smirk. "Good boy."

I turn on my heel, sauntering back to the cot. Sitting down, I flash him a wicked grin. No one will make me feel weak. No one will break my determination.

"Now go on," I say, my voice filled with satisfaction. "Tell me my future."

CHAPTER TEN

Roenis

What. The fuck. Was that.

She hasn't tried to seduce me before. The others yes, but Syra was a little more defiant. So why now? Was it the drug? I can't figure out her plan, usually everything was laid bare and pretty fucking obvious before the others even arrived. The tales from her family are predictable in their intent. But as I stare at Syra now, that smug grin plastered across her face, my thoughts halter.

I can taste her on my lips. Instinctively, I run my tongue across them again.

Fuck. Why is that so arousing? That little display, her forcing herself into my mouth, it was reckless and infuriatingly bold. No one had dared to challenge me in that way before. I swallow down a growl, locking the memory deep within. I can't let her get to me. This was her aim, her ploy, her weapon, it has to be.

Fuck, now *I'm* the one getting sloppy. I need to focus. Then, like a shadow descending, clarity struck. I know what I need to do.

I focus on her, letting my earlier frustration drown the arousal out of my system. "About your future," I begin, my voice slicing through the tension. "I've decided you are now my guest, for a period of time. With conditions, of course."

Her grin drops, her arms crossing as she cocked her head to the side. "Like a fucking house pet?" she shot back, her voice singeing with disapproval.

That mouth of hers.

"Exactly," I say, "You can roam around, lick yourself clean, and follow my commands. Or," I add, letting the threat settle, "you can remain here in this cell until you smell like rotting flesh. Your choice."

I watch her carefully, knowing she will take the

deal.

"I can't bargain for anything?" she ask. "No say at all?"

I tilt my head, feigning consideration. "Like what?"

She rises gracefully from the cot, her movements suspicious. When she begins to step closer, I raise my hand, sending my vapors to coil around her ankles, rooting her to the ground. "Like. What?" I repeat.

She huffs, crossing her arms again. "Where would my bed be? With you, in a cage placed in your room? You said 'lick myself clean', does that mean I'll have access to bath necessities, or are we talking about pleasuring? Lastly, are your commands going to be enjoyable, or is this some kind of kink you've got?"

I pinch the bridge of my nose, shutting my eyes for a minute to think. Her boldness was vexing, yet its not unwanted. I take a breathe and I allow a smile to stretch across my face. "Your bed will be next door to my room. Bathroom included. My commands are mine to decide. And I don't care where or when you do your pleasuring, but it will not involve me."

She thinks for a moment. "And your kink issue?"

"It's none of your concern, as I said it will not involve me." I state, the image of her earlier flashing in my mind, causing desire to surge in my chest.

Her eyes burn with fury, her lips curling into a sneer as her power surged to life. I feel it instantly, whips of purple, vine-like magic snaked through the air, brushing against my chin, cold and crackling with hostility.

"You'll beg for it soon enough," she says, her voice venomous.

I wave a hand, dissolving her magic like smoke. "I've never begged for anyone," I reply. "What makes you think you'll be the first?" My tone is as polished as the bracelet I grip behind my back. I had it crafted by my finest brass maker Datura earlier. And thank the gods, cause I need it for this exact reason. I bend down until my face hovers mere inches from hers. Her breathe hitches, a telling tremor she can't hide. Her scent is intoxicating and maddening, basically sinking its claws into me. She doesn't recoil, instead, she breathes me in, showing her strength with those eyes.

She tilts her chin up, her eyes locking onto mine with a confident gleam. "Oh, by the gods. Trust me, you'll beg."

A growl rumbles in my chest, deep and dangerous. I seize her wrist in one swift motion, snapping the bracelet around it. Her magic flares briefly, but the bracelet glows, absorbing the energy until nothing remained. Her eyes widens, her lips parting as she examines the metallic band now fastened to her skin.

"What the fuck is this?" she demands.

I smirk, the predator in me flaring. "One of my conditions. Think of it as… your collar." I let the word hang between us, savoring the fury it sparks in her expression. "This little thing tamps down your magic. You can't use it against me with ill intent, nor can you remove it."

Before she can retort, I turn on my heel and stride toward the cell door. "Now, come along, little pet. We've got some things to discuss as you adjust." I release the vapors around her ankle, a sign for her to follow me.

The long trek out of the dungeon gives me time to steady my thoughts. Her presence is like a storm, chaotic, unpredictable, and striking. I hate how she had slipped under my skin already, but that's why I need eyes on her at all times. She is going to be trouble.

We exit the massive stone doors of the dungeon tower, stepping into a long arched hallway. The air shifts immediately, the damp chill of the dungeon replaced by the faint warmth of the castle above. My onyx stone doors, framed with silver linings, opens with a wave of my hand, revealing the grand stairway beyond.

I glance at her from the corner of my eye. She's stiff, her gaze darting around as though trying to commit every detail to memory. She barely had time to analyze the castle when she arrived, and now her curiosity was undeniable.

"Welcome to your new prison," I say sarcastically, my voice echoing off the high ceilings. "Though, I would like you to think otherwise."

Syra's lip twitches, as if she wants to retort, but thought better of it. Instead, she keeps her pace beside me, her eyes speculating the intricate designs that adorned the walls. The castle's architecture is my masterpiece, black stone veined with silver, every surface glowing faintly as though kissed by stars. Pillars rose like twisted obsidian trees, their bases wrapped in thorny silver vines.

"Impressive," she murmurs, her tone begrudging. "What is it with you and black stone?"

"It's durable," I reply, smirking. "Much like myself. But don't worry. You'll grow to appreciate its charm."

She rolls her eyes and says nothing.

Gods, it's like she's not even trying to reel me in. It must've just been the drug in the dungeon.

Yet, her stubbornness is refreshing.

I lead her through the main hall, its ceiling adorned with constellations that seem to shift and dance as we walk. She slows, her head tilting back to take it all in. Her lips part slightly, and for a moment, she looks enchanted.

"You like it," I say, unable to keep the satisfaction

out of my voice.

She snaps her head forward, her expression hardening like a mask. "It's fine."

Liar.

I guide her down another hallway, this one lined with windows that stretch from floor to ceiling, stained with colors. Beyond the glass, the landscape of the Nightmare Kingdom sprawls in eerie beauty. Dark peaks of the mountains rise against a swirling indigo sky, their shadows stretching like claws over the land below. Rivers of silver mist wind through the valleys, casting a simple glow.

Syra pauses by one of the windows, her hand brushing the glass. "It's not what I expected," she says softly.

"Disappointed?" I ask, stopping beside her.

She glances at me, her expression unreadable. "No. Just surprised."

I study her, noting the way her eyes linger on the view. There is no disgust, no fear, just curiosity. It's unsettling how easily she seems to slip past my expectations with a single glance.

Shaking off the thought, I continue the tour. We

pass the dining hall, its long table carved from a single piece of ebony wood, and the door to my library across the room is open. It is a vast chamber filled with towering shelves that stretched with magic. I decide to skip going near that area, avoiding the bridge that leads towards it. Syra slows again, her gaze darting to what plays across that bridge.

"Keep moving," I say, smirking as her lips press into a thin line. I use my magic secretly to close the library doors.

When we finally reach her quarters upstairs next to mine, I push the door open. The room is spacious, the walls lined with silver-veined black stone just like the hall, but the furnishings are luxurious in here. A plush bed draped in deep purple, a vanity of polished silver, and a private bathing chamber hidden behind an arched door, waits for her. I had the design made to make her feel somewhat at home. I needed her trust.

"This is where you'll stay," I say, stepping aside to let her enter.

She hesitates, her eyes squinting. "Why do I feel

like there's a catch?"

"No catch," I reply smoothly. "Consider it a gesture of goodwill. You're my guest, after all."

Her laugh is sharp and humorless. "Right. Your pet."

"Glad we're on the same page," I lean against the doorframe. "Now, settle in. We'll discuss your responsibilities later at dinner."

She didn't respond, her attention already on the room as she steps inside. I watch her closely, noting the way her fingers trail over the fabric of the bedspread, the slight furrow in her brow as she examines her surroundings. Every detail matters to her, every nuance cataloged and considered.

I should walk away now, but I linger, my thoughts churning. Syra is more than I'd anticipated. It feels like a broken record finally being replaced with a new one after being use to a murky sound. But one thing is certain: she is going to make my life very, *very* complicated.

CHAPTER ELEVEN
Roenis

The dining hall is a grand testament to the beauty and mystery of my kingdom. Long, dark tables made from ebony wood extend beneath chandeliers of intricate iron and brass, their candlelit flames flickering in crimson. Ornate tapestries adorn the walls, depicting scenes of nightmares that stuck with me. A stormy sea, a forest of endless paths, and a sky split by ragged light, but woven with threads of silver and blue that somehow transform terror into a kind of haunting beauty.

I sit at the head of the table, trying to focus on the task at hand. The candlelight catches on the edge of my goblet, and for a moment, I'm lost in the swirl of silver reflected there. My thoughts are broken when Datura leans back in her chair, the copper jewelry draped across her collarbone and wrists glinting. She's always been striking, her olive skin glowing against the dark tones of the room, her brown curls framing a face that's equal parts exotic and mischievous. Beside her, Asani sits comfortably. The man is a mountain, his massive hands resting lightly on the table, but his warm brown eyes soften the edges of his imposing frame. He's always been an anchor in this chaotic place.

"So," Datura begins, running her fingers along the rim of her brass goblet, her voice light and teasing. "The Goddess of Dreams dines with us tonight. Should I polish the good cutlery or prepare a net to catch her inevitable barbs?"

A low chuckle escapes me. "Both, perhaps. Syra isn't one for subtlety it seems."

"And you are?" Datura's brow arches, her smile taunting.

"I prefer to think of myself as... strategic," I say, "She's not here to enjoy herself. She's here to find fault. To prove to herself that everything about this kingdom is what she's been told. Whether she was taught or brainwashed, she thinks of this place as nothing but chaos and cruelty."

"And you think one meal will change that?" Asani's voice rumbles from across the table, his deep tone carrying weight, as always. His eyes meet mine, curious and calm.

"No," I admit, exhaling. "But, it's a beginning. People often see what they expect to see. My plan is to surprise her. Show her the parts of this kingdom that aren't so easily defined by fear. The beauty in the chaos. The life in the darkness."

Datura laughs lightly. "A noble cause, but do you think she'll even notice? Or will she be too busy glaring daggers at you?"

"Oh, she'll notice," I reply, letting a smirk tug at the corner of my mouth. "Syra would probably throw actual daggers instead of glaring them. She may be sharp-tongued and stubborn, but she's also curious. She can't help herself, I've noticed. That's why I need both of you at your best tonight. Datura, the brass centerpiece you promised me, does it reflect the glow of the dream vials I provided?"

"It does," she says, her smile widening. "The design is complete. When the light hits it just right, the shadows casted will look like flowers blooming across the table. Dramatic, yet delicate. Just the kind of contradiction you're aiming for."

"Perfect," I say with a nod before turning my attention to Asani. "And you? How's the menu coming along?"

"It'll be a feast, but not ostentatious. I'm balancing familiar flavors with elements unique to our kingdom. Dishes that remind you of peace, but have a twist: a hint of spice with a note of sweetness. Something that lingers." He boasts.

"Much like your charm," Datura teases, nudging his arm. Asani's ears turn slightly pink, but he doesn't lose his composure.

"I learned from the best," he replies, placing a gentle hand over hers.

Watching them, I can't help but smile. "You two make it difficult to believe this is the Kingdom of Nightmares."

"We're proof of what you're trying to show her, aren't we?" Datura says, her voice losing its edge for a moment. "That life here isn't what everyone imagines. That we can create something beautiful."

"Exactly," I say, my tone serious now. The weight of what's ahead settles on my shoulders. "If Syra sees even a glimpse of that, it's a victory. She doesn't need to love this place overnight, but she does need to see that coexistence isn't impossible."

"Well, then," Datura says, raising her goblet in a mock toast. "Here's to convincing a goddess over dinner."

"A bold endeavor," Asani adds, lifting his own drink. "But if anyone can do it, it's you."

I lift my goblet joining in. "Let's hope you're right. Otherwise, this might be the most eventful dinner we've had in centuries, and not in the way I'd prefer."

◆

I stop in front of Syra's room, pausing to smooth the fabric of my coat and steady my breath. For a moment, I consider walking away and going about this differently, but I push the thought aside.

Gathering myself, I knock firmly.

"Come in," her voice calls, hinted with suspicion.

I push the door open, stepping inside and immediately regret the decision of letting Datura pick her outfit. Syra stands near the window with her back to me, adjusting the delicate straps of her black gown. The fabric clings to her figure, accentuating every curve. The deep neckline exposes just enough to send my thoughts in impure directions. Her white hair, still damp from washing, tumbles down her back in loose waves, her few strands of gold catching in the soft light.

"Want to explain the dress that was placed on my bed?," she says without turning around, her tone laced with mock disapproval. "I'm still deciding if I want to join your little nightmare feast."

"If it helps, I'm still deciding if I want to escort you," I reply, earning a soft snort of amusement. "But seeing as I've already come this far, why not add a dress that matches the atmosphere and to offer my arm?"

She turns to face me, and for a moment, the Gods have stolen my will to breathe. The gown suits her too well. The elegance of the fabric, and the darkness it casts on her skin, is the perfect contradiction. Much like the woman herself.

She raises her brow, and crosses her arms. Her favorite pose. Her assessing violet eyes meet mine. "And what exactly am I supposed to take from this? That you're generous? Chivalrous?"

"You're new to this kingdom, Syra. You came here with preconceived notions and ideas about what we are and what we represent. I've arranged this evening to show you a different side of the Nightmare Kingdom, one that isn't what your people made it out to be. My only demand is that you remain civil and open-minded, and to avoid causing unnecessary problems for my people. That's your responsibility while you're here."

She studies me for a long moment, skepticism etched into every line of her expression. "Fine, but from now I will pick my clothing, black is not my first choice." She reaches for the dresser top, picking up her dagger and sliding it into her sheath on her outer thigh. The dress hides it well, even with the slit on the side.

Clever.

"You look appropriate," I say, deliberately understating. Her lips twitch into a smirk, seeing right through me.

"Appropriate?" she echoes, "Careful, Roenis. I might start thinking you're intimidated."

"If I were intimidated, I wouldn't admit it," I counter, offering my arm. "But we should go. It would be a shame to let all the effort put into this dinner go to waste."

"I wouldn't dream of it." She replies mockingly, but she hesitates at first before looping her arm through mine, her touch sending an unexpected jolt through me. "Lead the way, then. Let's see what this feast is all about."

The walk to the dining hall is silent, but charged. When I attempt to break the tension, asking what she thought of the castle so far, she comments on the dramatic shadows in the corridor.

"Your castle is like a stage in desperate need of better lighting." She states as we finally approach the dining hall. She'll change her mind about the lighting when she sees Datura's decorations.

The hall glows with warm light, the brass centerpiece on the table casting intricate shadows that resemble blooming flowers, just as Datura promised. The table is laden with dishes that held roast meats glazed with honey and spices, platters of colorful fruits and vegetables, and freshly baked bread. Goblets of wine and trays of desserts also spread out on the table, adding a playful push for the evening.

Datura and Asani are already seated, their smiles welcoming, but faintly amused as they take in the sight of us. Dolion sits farther down the table, his sharp eyes assessing Syra with interest. He's kept quiet ever since I snapped on him earlier. Good.

Datura is the first to rise, her jewelry flashy as she offers Syra a welcoming bow. "The Goddess of Dreams," she says, her tone teasing. "The guest of honor arriving with our God, and he's still intact I see. I'm impressed."

"Oh, he's intact for now. Though I can't promise he'll leave the same after dessert." Syra replies, her lips twitching into a faint smile. The exchange earns a laugh from Datura.

"We'll see if you say that after tasting Asani's spiced pudding," Datura quips, earning a laugh from everyone but Asani, who rolls his eyes.

Asani gestures to a chair, his broad smile softening towards her. "Please, sit. I hope you're hungry."

I can't help but watch the interactions. I observe her. I watch how she takes it all in, and a slight fraction of hope wants to form.

I turn my attention on Dolion, he remains seated, his dark eyes fixed on Syra. His silence is loud, and I know he believes this dinner is an unnecessary ordeal. I catch the faint tightening of Syra's shoulders as she takes her place in the chair next to Datura, which evidently is also across from me.

Conversation starts cautiously with Datura taking the lead. "So how did you end up meeting our God? I'm sure it wasn't just a nightly stroll encounter." Her eyes shined mischievously.

I shoot my glare at her. Insufferable woman, she just *loves* to start shit.

Syra's eyes flick to me, her gaze analyzing again, but then she smiles. "He was hiding in the shadows at a tavern. He clearly needed a lesson on manners, and what better way to teach respect than a well-aimed dagger to keep him in line."

Datura's mouth drops. She slowly turns her head to me. "Well damn, I would've paid to see that."

The banter draws a small laugh from Syra, but her wariness remains. When she does speak, it's with precision, carefully choosing her next words. "And what exactly do you do here Datura, besides humor Roenis?"

"I'm a brass maker," she replies, "I create beauty from metal and fire. And sometimes, I offer advice to stubborn gods who think they know everything."

Syra looks down to her bracelet and then to me. "Sounds like a full-time job."

"Exhausting," Datura agrees, her grin widening. "But worth it."

The humor between them is light, and I catch myself watching Syra more than I should. Half-expecting her to bring up the bracelet, but she doesn't.

"You're quiet Roenis. Would you like to add to the conversation?" Syra says, he eyes glinting with mischief.

Dolion breaks the levity with his gravelly voice. "Our God speaks when he wants to."

Syra's attention shifts to him, her expression sharpening. "Oh he finally speaks, nice to meet you as well. But I'm afraid my question was directed to *him* not you."

I decide to break the agitation before it got worse. "That's enough Dolion. I'm capable of speaking for myself." I brace the back of my hand under my chin. I hone my stare on Syra.

"I was just holding my tongue and letting my council get acquainted with you. If you wanted to hear my voice so bad, you could've just said so."

Her eyes narrow, that same tension from earlier threatens to overtake the room. Asani intervenes this time, his deep voice calm. "The food's growing cold. Let's enjoy the meal."

Datura smirks up at me. Questions swirling in her eyes.

Shit, I'll hear about that later.

Gradually, the conversation resumes with Syra now ignoring me. Asani speaks of his time in the

Peace Kingdom, his tone warm and nostalgic. Datura teases him about his "obsession" with perfectly plated dishes, and Syra listens, her responses sparse but increasingly engaging. By the end of the meal, Syra's wariness hasn't entirely disappeared, but she's no longer reserved.

When dinner is over and our conversations turn silent, Asani offers to escort Syra back to her chambers, in which she obliges. She says her goodnights and only drifts her eyes to me, without a word. The silence between us feels less hostile, but it's not warm either.

Tomorrow may bring its own challenges, but tonight, I allow myself the smallest ray of hope.

Dolion gets up and bows, taking his leave. I'll have to consult with him later. His attitude needs to be fixed. I can't have him sabotaging our chances of civility.

Datura on the other hand, is a whole other issue.

"She's damn delightful," she purrs. "Nothing like the others."

"I know." I state whole heartily. "I knew that from the tavern."

Shit.

"Yes, about that." Her tone shifting. "So she threw a dagger at you? You left that little detail out. You said she was fiery, not that she already tried to kill you once."

"Twice." I correct her. "Well…if you count choking me as a move to kill me."

She stares at me stunned. "Yet, she lives? Damn Roenis." She shakes her head, smile getting bigger by the minute. "Oh I'm going to love this Goddess."

She stands, making her way past me. She places a hand on my shoulder, and speaks in now a softer voice.

"Just keep your feelings in check. I can see that this one can be dangerous." Her presence drifts away and I'm now alone in the hall.

I wipe my hand down my face and groan. "I'm already aware of that." I say to myself.

Fuck, this is going to be a long two months.

CHAPTER TWELVE
Syra

I sprawl out on my bed, utterly confused.

Still in my gown, I stare at the ceiling, wondering what the purpose of the dinner was really for. Datura and Asani had been a surprise. Their conversations were pleasant and easy to enjoy, but I can't shake the feeling that their presence serve some hidden agenda. Datura had proudly claimed her role as the brass maker, which all but confirms she's the one that forged the wretched piece of metal that now adorns my wrist. Perhaps I can convince her to take it off. The thought offers a tinge of hope, quickly dimmed by the realization that nothing in this castle will come easily.

Roenis had barely spoken the entire night, his demeanor a silent storm looming at the edge of the table. He was fully committed to observing, his gaze had weighed on me, as if expecting and hoping everything went well. When he showed up at my room before dinner, I had caught him by surprise. My lips curved into a small smile as I recalled the way his silver eyes had lingered, the feigned indifference that didn't quite hide his thoughts. He even tried to lie, of course, but his eyes had betrayed him. Maybe my charm was already working. Maybe the others had gone about this all wrong. Roenis seems the type who enjoys the hunt, who thrives on arguments and games of wit. Someone not easily pleased and poses a challenge.

I can do that. Though, I can't promise that my temper won't flare out a few times.

I pull myself off the bed and begin to undress, the silk fabric sliding from my shoulders. An abrupt knock startles me, and I scramble to cover myself.

"It's me. I wanted to check in before you went to bed."

The infuriating God of Nightmares. Of course, it's

him. I swear to myself that if he makes a habit of knocking at the most inappropriate times, I might actually stab him.

Wait. A slow smile spreads across my lips.

"One moment," I call out sweetly, tying a silk robe from the wardrobe loosely around me. *Very* loosely.

When I open the door, I nearly laugh at the sight before me. He too, is wearing a robe, black with red trimmings. It hangs open just enough to display his chest, it's chiseled and ashen gray, streaking with jagged silver veins. My eyes flick upward quickly, hoping he didn't catch me staring.

He smirks. Of course, he noticed.

"What do I owe the pleasure?"

His gaze sweeps over me, sparking tension between us. How does he always do that. "I wanted to properly thank you for attending dinner," he says smoothly, "and to ensure you get some rest. I also wanted to ask what type of clothing you'd like stored in your room so I can make the arrangements."

I tilt my head, surprised. "I like comfortable clothes. Nothing too loose. Nicely fitted, and no dull or dark colors."

"Not a single dark article?" he asks, almost pleading.

I relent, just a little. "Fine. A few, I don't want my whole wardrobe lacking light like this castle. I do have a request, though."

"Of course you do."

"I want bath oils, specifically purple poppies. The smell… comforts me."

He nods without hesitation. "Done, I'll try."

Well, that was easy. "Not going to fight me on it?"

He smiles. It was striking, and I notice his canines. They never showed before.

As he turns to leave, he waves a hand dismissively. "The smell suits you. Now sleep."

◆

When I wake the next morning, it feels like I slept without interruption for the first time in ages. The unfamiliar sensation is a little jarring. I turn to the side and notice a folded note resting on the other pillow.

***

Put something nice on. Your closet has been filled. Meet me in the back of the castle. The guards will escort you there.

Don't be late, pet.

I scoff aloud. What would happen if I was late? And how had he managed to fill my closet overnight? My curiosity propels me out of bed, and I practically run to the wardrobe. Sure enough, it's brimming with an array of gowns, tunics, and other garments. The colors vary beautifully—blues, violets, pinks, whites—with a few tasteful dashes of black and gray. Shoes line the bottom in every style imaginable, and a drawer that holds an assortment of accessories.

This God could tailor a curse in golden thread and call it divine fashion

I choose a simple purple sundress, light and flowy, and slip on a pair of comfortable white flats. As I pass the dresser, I notice a silver tray holding several bottles of oil. Another note resting beside it.

***

I couldn't get my hands on the poppy oils you wanted, as they are rare and mostly found in the Dream Kingdom. Obviously, I'm not a wanted guest there, so I had oils made of a similar, if not more suitable, scent. If you care to use them.

Curious, I uncork one of the bottles and dab a little on my wrists and neck. The scent is subtle, a blend of vanilla and pepper with an underlying sweetness. Odd, yet unexpectedly comforting.

I feel ready, I open my door to find two familiar guards waiting. Dressed in tight black leathers with minimal armor and long spears strapped to their backs, they look as formidable as ever.

"Well, hello, men. I've missed you," I tease. "Are you here to escort me?"

They remain silent, their expressions plain. Roenis had clearly given them strict orders.

"I can deal with your silence," I say with a shrug. "But I actually want to roam around before meeting up with him."

Their eyes meet briefly, as if silently debating how to proceed, but I didn't give them a chance to argue.

I step between them and start my own tour, their shadowy footsteps trailing close behind.

The castle seems different in the light of day, though "light" was a relative term here. A mute grayness filters through narrow windows of stained glass, casting fragmented hues of crimson, deep violet, and cold blue onto the polished black stone floors. The shadows have a life of their own, curling and stretching in the periphery, never fully retreating even when illuminated. The air carries a faint chill, as though the walls themselves breath an ancient, icy sigh.

The ceilings rise so high they appear to scrape the never-ending sky, supported by immense pillars carved with intricate patterns, appearing like black tree trunks. The trunks are wrapped with silver vines on the base, catching the light and creating a haunting glow. I notice the tapestries again, hanging between the columns, massive and dramatic, each one depicting a surreal landscape that felt plucked from a nightmare, or even a dream. The ones lining the hall are more terrifying, a forest of skeletal trees stretching endlessly under a blood-red sky. In another, shadow figures dance on the edge of a dark ocean, their faces indistinct but their movements drawn hauntingly graceful. The sheer artistry of the castle's decor are both mesmerizing and unsettling, a constant reminder of where I am and who rules here.

I make my way to the throne room, the echo of my footsteps being swallowed by the oppressive silence. The grand archway looms before me, and I hesitate just inside its frame, taking in the sight. It's unrecognizable from the hazy, drugged state in which I'd first seen it. The room lengthens out in all its dark glory, vast and impressive. The obsidian throne sits proudly atop a dais at the far end, its jagged crystal edges gleaming like onyx under the fractured light streaming from the stained-glass windows. The moat that sits in the middle is unique on its own, setting a barrier not to be crossed, yet inviting enough to want to explore. Each bridge leading a way to a different part of the castle. At the North point of it, the throne itself seems alive, almost pulsating with an aura of authority and danger. Its design a statement of power. Behind it, a massive tapestry hung, depicting a swirling storm of shadows and stars, as if the essence of nightmares had been captured in cloth.

Stunning.

I continue my tour, making my way around the moat and taking the bridge that's to the right of the throne. The floor beneath my feet shift to a mosaic of black and silver tiles, forming an intricate pattern that seem to move as I move. It's hypnotic, drawing my gaze downward as if it might reveal some hidden secret if I stare long enough. The windows here line the walls, but is not of glass. They are frames over carved stone images with fragments of light seeping through somehow. Scenes of chaos and beauty: a water type dragon winding through constellations, a crumbling tower engulfed by a storm, and a solitary figure standing against an endless tide of darkness. The artistry was unparalleled, each image imbued with a story I was not yet familiar with.

Such sadness flow in these images. I swipe my fingers along the cold stones of the figure in the last one.

A faint breeze stirs through the hall, though there are no visible openings. It carries a faint metallic scent, as if the air itself remembered the past. I shiver and pull my gaze away, feeling the weight of unseen eyes on me. This area is both a sanctuary and a trap, a place of authority that demands respect and submission. I hear the two guards shift uncomfortably.

After a long moment, I force myself to move on, my footsteps quicker as I exit the throne room and wander deeper into the castle. The hallways feel endless, their dark stone walls illuminated by dim orbs that gleamed with soft light. Each corridor has its own character, some narrow and winding, others vast and lined with tall windows that offer glimpses of the barren landscape outside. Doors dot the halls, some simple and unassuming, others grand and ornate, their surfaces carved with elaborate designs. I ascend back up the steps leading to all of the other rooms. I pass my room, noting the two sets of stairs on either end of the hall, making it two separate routes to get here. So I decide to keep going in this opposite direction. Sure enough, after a few feet, one set of double doors that bear the image of a serpent coiled around a crescent moon, its eyes glowing as if in warning. I hesitate, temptation to explore, but I move my glance to the guards. Their eyes tell me everything, this is Roenis' room.

The guards fidget nervously, their unease practically radiating from their stiff postures. My fingers hover over the handle, but before I can grasp it, the taller one finally speaks up.

"I'd advise against that, Goddess." His voice quivers ever so slightly, betraying his shaken confidence.

I arch an eyebrow, curiosity sparking even higher. "Is that so? Tell me, what exactly is behind this door that warrants all this… caution?" Even though I'm fully aware of the answer.

Neither responds immediately, so I shift tactics. "You know," I tilt my head with feigned nonchalance, "I don't believe I ever asked for your names." My voice dips just enough to sound casual yet still convincing.

The taller one hesitates, glancing nervously between me and the door, clearly weighing his options. The shorter one stays silent, his sharp eyes locked on me as if expecting some sudden move.

"It's only fair we get better acquainted," I press, letting a faint smile curve my lips, a mix of charm and persuasiveness. I let a little of my power, or what is allowed with this bracelet, to conjure a small vine that caresses the cheek of the tall guard. My magic is definitely weaker, but still affective.

Finally, he relents, exhaling in defeat. "Kenji, Goddess," he says with a quick nod, motioning toward his companion. "And this is Grifton."

Grifton's scowl deepens. Clearly, he's not pleased with Kenji's compliance. Interesting.

"Well, Kenji," I begin, letting my voice soften and pulling my power back, "I can assure you I only want a peek. I'll keep my hands to myself, promise. Surely, as a guest here, I'm meant to be familiar with the castle?"

I step closer, just enough for me to whisper like a secret, "Unless, of course, you'd like me to mention to Roenis that his guards were uncaring and denied a chance to explore his fine domain. I'm sure he'd love to hear about this… oversight."

Kenji swallows hard, looking towards Grifton. He still hasn't said a word, but I can see his jaw tighten.

"I only need a moment," I add with a casual wave of my hand, as though the matter has already been decided.

Kenji's resolve crumbles, and I see it in the slight sag of his shoulders. "Fine," he mutters, stepping aside. Grifton lets out a barely audible growl of frustration but doesn't protest.

I smile, satisfied. "Wonderful. Your cooperation is duly noted."

I crank down the handle and push the doors open cautiously, stepping inside. My gaze sweeps over the room. It was surprisingly simple, almost stark compared to the rest of the castle. The bed is large and unadorned, covered in dark sheets that look impossibly soft. The headboard is chiseled from black wood, its surface polished to a mirror-like sheen. Speaking of mirrors, he has a large one framed with twisted iron that stands against the wall facing the bed. Shelves line one wall where the fireplace is, filled with books whose spines bear no titles, their covers a uniform black. Interspersed among them are odd trinkets, a crystal orb that seems to swirl with shadowy smoke, a silver dagger with a detailed hilt, and a collection of small glass vials filled with liquid in varying shades of red and violet.

A heavy desk sits in the corner, its surface strewn with papers and what appears to be maps. Some are marked with sharp, precise notations, while others have smudges and hastily scribbled notes. A single candle burns on the desk, its flame steady despite the faint draft that seems to permeate the room. The air here feels heavier, tinged with a faint scent of ink and something darker, almost like burnt wood. I didn't linger long, the intimacy of the space starts making me feel like an intruder. I did however notice twin glass doors across the room. It didn't look like a closet entry or any type of wardrobe. It has to lead somewhere. As I head towards it, Grifton finally speaks.

"That's enough for now." He states coldly. Seems I was pushing the boundary, so I will definitely have to come back and look on my own.

Exiting the room with a coy smile on my face, I

make my way down the opposite stairs. It leads me back towards the dining hall I am already familiar with. Circling back around I approach the moat again and decide to take the left bridge. It's the area Roenis refused to take me earlier yesterday.

This hallway seems never ending, its cold, empty opening was somberly lit with torchlight. Each step I take reverberates back at me, the endless expanse of shadow and stone swallowing me. The walls pulses with an undercurrent of magic, their veins of silver thicker in this area of the castle. But no matter how imposing the corridor is, it's nothing compared to what awaits at its end.

The doors.

They stand like a monument to power, taller and more resplendent than anything I'd encountered in this castle. Forged of radiant gold, they pulse faintly, as though they have a heartbeat of their own. Entangled patterns weave across their surface, depicting gods and mortals, dreams and nightmares, all locked in some eternal battle. The golden sheen reflects unnaturally, shifting with hues of deep amethyst and midnight black, as though the doors can't decide if they want to beckon me closer or warn me away.

A faint hum beams from them, and my own magic stirs in response, unbidden. The familiar sensation of my vines rippling beneath my skin sends a shiver through me, but this time they move differently. Like they are hesitant, almost reluctant. Then come the whispers. Soft at first, like the rustling of wind, but as I draw closer, they grow clearer, more distinct.

They call to me.

Not by name, but the pull was unmistakable. A low, melodic hum weaving promises and warnings all at once. I clench my fists, feeling the pulse of my magic pushing toward the doors, yearning to touch them, to yield to whatever power lay beyond.

Behind me, the guards are silent, but I can feel their presence like knives pressing against my back. They didn't have to say a word. I know they are watching, waiting.

I swallow hard and force my gaze upward. The faint glow of the torches on either side of the doors flicker violently, as though the flames themselves fear to burn too close.

My steps slow as I approach, the weight of those golden doors pressing down on me like a physical force. This is no ordinary threshold, no simple entry into another room of the castle. This is a test. And whatever lays beyond isn't waiting for me to open the doors. It's waiting for me to challenge it. This magic has to be woven by Roenis as a precaution. Something useful has to be inside.

The whispers grow louder, their words gliding through my thoughts like a phantom, and despite myself, I reach out. My hand hovers just above the intricate carvings, my magic surging forward in quiet defiance, seeking answers to a question I didn't dare ask.

When I try the handles and give a tentative push, the doors don't budge. Frustrated, I lean against them, pressing my ear to the gold. Silence greets me, the door thick and impenetrable. The voices go quiet, and a shield whips in place. Whatever secrets lie within, they are not meant for me, at least not yet.

Sighing, I move on. I go past his throne towards

the back, and come across an office space right before the arched ending of the back entrance. Unlike Roenis' bedroom, this room is meticulously organized, every item in its place. The desk here is massive, crafted from the same dark wood in the other rooms with silver accents. Documents are spread across its surface, along with a few scattered quills and ink bottles. One paper in particular catches my eye, its surface covered in strange, looping symbols that seem to writhe if I look at them for too long. A large window dominates one wall, offering a sweeping view of the landscape behind the castle. The desolation outside contrasts sharply with the richness of the room, a reminder of the isolation that comes with power. But I notice something. My eyes had to have been wrong, I swear I see a garden.

Shaking my head, I trace my fingers along the edge of the desk, my thoughts swirling with questions. What plans were hatched here? What decisions made? The room feels so alive with purpose, the air thrumming with an energy I can't quite place. It's both fascinating and unnerving.

I feel like I have my fill of wandering, the rooms making me feel quite small, so I make the decision to leave. The guards, who have followed me silently through my explorations, exchange a look of what can only be relief as I finally make my way through the arch, reaching the back of the castle.

CHAPTER THIRTEEN
Syra

Overcast clouds and crisp cool air greet me when I walk out the castle doors. My footsteps make no sound on the smooth marble steps, a refreshing change from the clacking sounds inside. Kenji and Grifton stop at the entrance and take post. It leaves me to walk alone. A nice silence to bask in. As I walk on the simple path, an aroma tickles my senses. It's the same scent from the oils I used in my room.

    Of course, that smell leads me to Roenis. He's at the edge of… is that a garden? Surprise hits me. I *knew* I saw flowers from the window. And there he is, standing amidst a sea of white spiked flowers. As I get closer I notice they are Queen of the Night flowers, which shouldn't be correct. These flowers only bloom at night and are quite rare. I believe they bloom once a year and for only a few hours, but here he is, standing in a whole bushel of them.

Roenis is crouched low as he cuts the stems of a few. His red hair gleaming under the sun, it's almost unnatural to see him in such a way.

Behind him, Dolion lingers like a specter, his ever present scowl deepening as he catches sight of me.

"Finally," Roenis says, not looking up. His voice carrying slight amusement. "I was beginning to think you got lost."

"Your castle is rather labyrinthine," I rely smoothly, stepping closer. "I had to ensure I knew my way around if I were to be spending my time here."

Dolion lets out an irritated huff, but still says nothing. Roenis stands, holding a fresh cut flower. "Or perhaps," he starts, "you just enjoy making an entrance. Though I am surprised, no dagger this time."

I tap my hand on my outer thigh. "I do come prepared of course, and anticipation is half the pleasure." I shoot back.

He holds out the flower, the gesture oddly out of character.

I take it, fingers brushing his for the briefest moment. "How are these in bloom?"

He looks back at his small field of them. "Magic. I had a friend entrap time, or in a manner, the space around them, to keep them like this."

Roenis eyes shift over to the emptiness behind the garden. He turns back to me, his expression questioning again. "There is something I want to show you. It's why I asked you out here today."

"Oh? Is this like your little dinner you planned?"

"In a sense yes, its' to help you understand my kingdom better. But this, it's not to be spoken of outside of here."

I narrow my eyes. "Am I that untrustworthy?"

"I think you're dangerous," he replies matter of factly. "And sometimes, dangerous things must be tested with certain truths."

The weight of his words settle roughly in my chest. After a moment, I oblige. "Very well."

He steps past the edge of the garden, gesturing for

me to follow. I trail behind him, my hand brushing the hilt of my dagger. Dolion's muttered complaints are little more than background noise as we venture through dense hedges . The air splinters with magic, brushing against my skin like a soft caress. It isn't until we pass through an arch of twisting vines that the scenery shifts entirely.

A village expands out before us, hiding within a valley cloaked in a glamour enchantment. The homes are simple but beautiful, their walls built from dark stone and their roofs adorned with glowing white flowers. Lanterns hang from trees, casting warm light that dances across cobblestone paths. People move about, their faces serene, their laughter soft and genuine. It's breathtaking.

I stop in my tracks, the sight rendering me speechless for a moment. "This place... it's not on any map. You don't have a village noted in any document."

I take in the information. This is where the refugees are. I was beginning to wonder if Datura and Asani were the only ones.

"It's not meant to be, and clearly I do." Roenis

states, his tone uncharacteristically solemn. He stands beside me, his gaze fixed on the village below. "I've kept it hidden, glamoured, for centuries."

I turn to him, curiosity now blazing. "Why?"

"To protect them," he says, his expression unreadable. "The people here are vulnerable. Some were from other kingdoms, others born with magic too fragile to help. And a few humans."

Humans.

My head felt dizzy. Impossible. Having humans here is dangerous. My mother didn't mention that. Is she aware of it?

Roenis continues. "The island past the Dream Kingdom and Wrath Kingdom has a portal—an unstable one. Sometimes, humans fall through." He runs a hand through his hair, his horns slighted coated with pollen from the flowers. "Most don't survive. But those who do, arrive with nothing but fear and desperation. They speak of lives they were willing to leave behind."

My pulse quickens. I have never heard of such a thing. Humans slipping between realms? It's forbidden. Unnatural.

"I know what you're thinking," He states, his voice quiet. "It shouldn't happen. It's against the laws of our world. But when I saw them, lost and broken, I couldn't bring myself to turn them away. I don't know why. Maybe because I understand what it means to be stranded in a place that isn't meant for you."

I want to argue, to tell him he was reckless for sheltering humans, but something in the way he he speaks, like he too, was searching for belonging. I drift my eyes back to the village. "So you took them in."

"If they wanted to stay," he admits. "Some longed for a new life, one not bound by the rules of their world. Others were simply too afraid to return. I gave them the choice."

A choice that shouldn't have been his to give.

He continues. "They've made this place their home, and I..." He hesitates, the words catching in his throat. "I couldn't let them be destroyed by the politics and judgement of *any* realm."

I study him, the rawness in his voice striking me

in a way I didn't expect. "So you became their God?"

"If you want to call it that," he shrugs. "They made a choice. They have nothing to do with the nightmares I embody. They don't deserve to suffer for it, so I keep them safe."

His words hang heavy in the air. "Why tell me?"

He finally looks at me, his silver eyes piercing. "I trust you to make your own choices as well, Syra. What you do with this knowledge is up to you. But understand this—if this village is ever harmed because of your actions, there will be no forgiveness."

My gaze returns to the village one last time, watching as a child darts across the square, their laughter ringing like bells in the early morning.

It's so contradicting to what he represents.

This feels like life, like a dream. Then the moment was over, he whips his hand back and the village is glamoured again.

Roenis' eyes observe me. As if waiting for a piece to fall. Something he can use, or dissect. It's a little unnerving, and I didn't want to buckle my resolve.

"So, was that all I was needed for? May I be dismissed now." I say with little to no emotion. Even though inside I am burning with this information. I need answers of my own, but I can't ask him yet. How come my mother knew about the refugees, but nothing about the humans? How come he hasn't shown this to the others.

Unless he has.

Probably dead before any word got out.

Roenis moves his head down, softly closing his eyes and letting out a blown out sigh. "Yes my pet, you may leave."

With that, I make my way back inside his castle. The nerves crawling up my body with all the information that was shoved down my throat. It burns. This feeling of the unknown, it just feels like its only the beginning.

The days start to take on a strange rhythm after that, each one blurring into the next. Every morning, Roenis waits for me, punctual as ever, with something new to show or teach me. He seems to enjoy surprising me, not that I'll ever let him know. The gardens where he lets me sit and observe the village are also active. I watch in silent fascination as his people live happily in his village. Though in secret, I am awestruck.

Dinner with Datura and Asani has become a nightly ritual, one I've grown to enjoy more than I expected. At first, I kept answering their questions with clipped words. But now, Datura's wild laughter and Asani's sly jabs feel like a challenge I'm all too eager to meet. I even manage to outwit Asani a few times, earning a look of grudging respect from him and outright glee from Datura. Somehow, these meals have become a comfort. Dinner was never like this in my kingdom. My mother was cold, never welcoming or loving. It was a reminder that even in a kingdom built on Dreams, it lacks the hope and wonder it's suppose to bring. Roenis lives that dream everyday here. So why is nightmares his source of power?

The library though, that's another story. Its doors stand tall and quiet now, the golden surface pulsing with magic, but still silent since I tried the previous time. I've tried everything. I used brute force, subtle enchantments, even a bit of charm directed at the guards to open it for me.

Nothing works.

Roenis caught me once, watching from the shadows with an infuriating smirk as I muttered curses under my breath. "No use, Syra," he'd said, his tone far too smug for my liking. "It'll never open for you."

I'll get in eventually. I have to.

Kenji and Grifton have become my reluctant entertainment. Kenji's fragile demeanor cracks when I prod just enough, and Grifton's exasperated sighs are almost musical at this point. One afternoon, I convinced them to spar with me, just to see how they handled a blade. They surprisingly let me, and a small part makes me think Roenis allowed it since I've been asking them for a week. All of a sudden, they finally said yes. Grifton grumbled the entire time, but Kenji's sharp movements caught me off guard. "Not bad," I'd said, circling him with a grin. He didn't respond, but the faintest twitch of his lips told me he appreciated the compliment.

With Roenis, he's always there, watching me,

challenging me, pushing me to see things his way. Sometimes it feels more like tests designed to frustrate me into revealing something, or to fumble. I've learned to hold my ground, to meet his gaze without flinching. He's infuriating, yes, but I'd be lying if I said I wasn't learning from him.

At this point a month has passed and I feel like I've gotten nowhere with seducing him. It's hard. I can't fake my tone. I feign interest, gather information, but now I'm starting to question who's in the wrong. The days slip by so quickly here, and I stopped trying to count. I tell myself it's just part of the game, part of the plan, but deep down, I know the truth. I'm starting to understand this kingdom, its people, and its God. And that realization is more dangerous than anything I've encountered so far.

I need to start *really* seducing.

CHAPTER FOURTEEN
Roenis

It's been a month.

Thirty days of quiet restraint, thirty days of watching Syra adapt. Her natural chaos has started to dim. The tension once etched into her shoulders has melted, the sharp edges of her laughter softened into something warmer, less guarded. But I see everything.

She thinks I don't notice the glances she steals at me, the way her fingers brush against the castle walls like she's trying to read the history chiseled into the stone. She masks her curiosity beneath an indifferent tilt of her chin, cloaking it with edged words and glares. But it's there—tucked between stolen gasps, her frustrated attempts to solve the puzzle of the library doors, and the fleeting curve of her smile when leaving dinner every night.

I watch her, because it's easier than admitting how much I want to step into those stolen moments. To pull apart the layers and find what she's hiding in that stubborn, clever mind of hers. Her reactions have slowly chipped away at my walls I've fortified over centuries.

She's been training with Kenji and Grifton. Sparring, weapon drills, thinking I'm unaware. As if the castle walls don't murmur to me, as if my vapors don't curl through every hall, carrying whispers of conversations like faithful messengers. I know every movement, every spar session, every dinner, and every breathless laugh. She moves like she belongs, even if she doesn't admit it.

I pretend ignorance, because acknowledging it means facing the itch beneath my skin, the one that wants to be more than an observer.

Today, is different.

I'm in my office instead of the library, the place that feels like an extension of myself, because I still can't trust Syra there. Instead I'm in here with Datura flipping through notes, because a nightmare that I weaved is getting out of control. The room is heavy with the scent of dusty papers and ash, the firelight casting distorted shadows that mimics the nightmare that sprawls across my desk. It twists and coils, a mass of darkness that breathes. This isn't an ordinary nightmare. It pulses with a hunger, its form shifting between clawed hands, fractured faces, and the hollow echo of screams. Syra sits across the room, slouching lazily in a chair, a calculated distance from the chaos. She looks almost unbothered, her expression a mask I know too well.

This human's nightmare is spiraling. Its darkness is different, volatile. I can't twist it with desire because the only things this one craves, is death, revenge, and pain. It's been a long time since I've encountered one this strong.

"It doesn't respond to the usual methods," Datura mutters, flipping through my older notes, frustration etching deep into the lines of her face. "It's like its adapting."

Syra leans back in her chair, crossing her arms, the

cursed bracelet flaring under the dim lighting. She taps it against the armrest, the metallic sound sharp in the tense silence. She looks like a ball of light in the darkness.

"Speaking of usual methods and adapting," she drawls, voice light but eyes pointed like glass, "I could help in a way since I weave dreams. Plus, don't you feel guilty about this lovely accessory?" She dangles her arm, letting the bracelet slide down to her wrist.

Datura doesn't even look up. "If by guilty you mean proud, then yes. Also, not sure your magic would work with this."

Syra huffs a laugh. "Charming as always. I'm sure it's a masterpiece of magical suppression. But surely, with all your brilliance, you should know I could help if you removed it."

Datura finally glances up, one brow arching. "I could. But where's the fun in that?"

"The fun would be me not struggling to weave when I try to summon an ounce of magic."

"It fits you. A little humility looks good on you, Syra."

Syra rolls her eyes. "Humility? This thing is less about humility and more about shackles. You made it. He clamped it on. And here I am, a walking, talking magical paperweight."

"A very stabby paperweight," I murmur without thinking.

Her glare pierces me. "Glad to know I'm leaving an impression."

I ignore the witty comebacks that trickle into my mind, and put my focus back to the nightmare. It ripples against the constraints of my magic, tendrils of shadow lashing out, leaving scorch marks on the desk. Its whispers crawl under my skin, a scraping worse than nails, promising things it has no right to promise.

"This isn't like the others," I say, my voice edging with something I rarely let slip. Uncertainty.

Syra leans forward, curiosity behind her wary gaze. "What's different about it?"

"It's shifting without me."

She stiffens. Good. Fear is rational here.

"Why does it look like that?" she asks, her voice quieter now, stripped of its usual bravado.

"Because it wants you to be afraid," I reply. "And it's very good at getting what it wants. When I weave, I have to tear it apart and rebuild. This one is refusing, actually fighting back, and getting stronger."

She doesn't flinch, but her fingers curl tighter around the armrest.

Datura leaves to fetch more notes in the library, we share that secret nod so we won't tip off Syra. The door clicks shut, leaving just Syra and me with the nightmare filling the space between us.

"You shouldn't have to deal with this alone," she says eventually, though there's no softness in her voice. Just confusion and wariness.

I don't look at her. "I was cursed with this power. I never asked for any of it, so I won't burden others with it."

I place my hands on the vapors. Concentrating, I close my eyes, trying to unhinge the screeching madness.

She gets up and steps closer, her voice softer now. "Maybe not. But you're still here, handling it. And it seems you have Datura's help."

Her words sink deeper than I expect, lodging in places I thought I'd sealed shut.

"This power isn't something I handle," I admit. "It wields me. It was probably meant to be a punishment, a curse. But I… I've made it a part of me because what choice do I have?"

She doesn't respond, and the silence feels heavier than the nightmare itself. I sneak a glance and her expression looks like sympathy.

Before I could stop her, she lifts her hands to the vapors. Her magic flickers weakly because of the restraint, but she still tries. Her brows furrow and a bead of sweat already forms in between the crease on her forehead. The nightmare reacts violently, lashing out. Syra's eyes widen.

"It's just a child." She whispers.

I nod, already knowing. The unfortunate life this child had, was nothing shy of cruel. Sometimes I can't fix the nightmare, sometimes I can't stop the chaos, no matter how bad I want to, I'm cursed to give anyone their worst fears and desires. Nightmares are made, given and forced.

Syra screams, yanking her hand back. The vapors

cling on her magic, tangling with mine, forming a sludgy angry vine. It snaps across the room, missing her by inches before coiling around my throat.

I roar, the sound shaking the walls. "GET OUT! NOW!"

Syra hesitates, eyes wild with disbelief. Datura bursts in, her face draining of color.

"Shit, Roenis!" she shouts. "You need to get it under control!"

"I'm trying," I choke out. "Get Syra out of here! N—." My words are cut off as the vine constricts, darkness bleeding into the edges of my vision.

Fuck.

I never wanted her to see me like this. But there's only one way to stop this nightmare.

I have to become one.

CHAPTER FIFTEEN

Syra

The realm fractures with a thunderous sound.

A deafening roar erupts, not from Roenis' throat but from the very air itself. It cracks like a storm splitting the sky, reverberating through my chest, rattling my ribs, and leaving a hum in my ears. His vapors thicken, pulsing outward from him like a heart beating violently. The ground trembles beneath my feet, dust cascading from the high columns spreading out in the office. The flickering firelights lining the walls blow wildly and then die out, swallowing the darkness whole because of him.

Datura's arms lock around me like iron bands, her grip bruising, anchoring me as if my very soul might rip from my body. "Stay back," she hisses into my ear, though her voice is a distant echo against the cacophony of the nightmare unraveling before us.

Roenis is gone.

Where he had stood, a creature writhes, a shifting mass of shadow and smoke, merging into something with shape but no true form. Waves of darkness lashes out like whips, slamming into stone with the force of waves crashing against walls. Silver light flickers within the void, like stars swallowed by a black hole. And his eyes—gods, his eyes—blazing silver orbs flashing through the darkness, piercing, hollow, and ancient.

His beastly form is a grotesque masterpiece. Towering and twisting, magic clinging to him like living armor, pulsing with an unnatural rhythm. His horns, black with streaks of bone-white at their base, curl around his head like a crown forking out even more than usual. His once fiery red hair transforms into cascading strands of pure silver, devoid of even the faintest trace of color. His limbs are elongated, too long, too thin, ending in claw-like talons that seem to tear through reality itself. He is dripping with darkness like ink bleeding into water, and his chest rises and falls with ragged breaths.

Terror claws at me, my instincts screaming to run, to flee from the monstrous thing before me. My heart hammers, each beat a frantic drum against my ribs. But beneath the fear, is something else.

Awe.

He's beautiful.

Not in the way a sunrise is beautiful or the delicate bloom of a rare flower. No, Roenis is the beauty of a dying star collapsing into itself, of the ocean in the heart of the darkest night, untamed. His power is absolute, unfiltered, and terrifyingly magnificent.

The echoes of the child screams, a high, keening wail that splinters the air, and Roenis answers. His shadow form surging forward with impossible speed. Darkness meets darkness, and the clash of their magic erupts in a shockwave that sends cracks spider-webbing across the floor. Datura stumbles, dragging me back, but I can't tear my eyes away.

Roenis' power wraps around the child's

nightmare form, not with cruelty but with precision, restraining rather than destroying. His monstrous shape changes, the darkness folding in on itself until it is no longer terror but a cage. An inescapable prison crafted from the very essence of fear.

The child's screams faded to whimpers, then to silence. Roenis remained still, his form rippling. His head snaps towards us, and he lets out another roar.

The rumble of it still hasn't faded, even when Dolion appears, sprinting down the corridor like a man fleeing death itself. Only, he was running towards it. His eyes, wide with terror and disbelief, snaps to the cracks snaking across the floor then to the monstrous figure within, recognition slamming into him with brutal clarity. Without hesitation, he shoves past us, a sharp command dying on his lips as he crosses the threshold. The door groans under the weight of the magic seeping from the room, but Dolion didn't falter. He spins, his face a mask of grim determination, and slams the doors shut with a resounding thud. Magic flares over the door, sealing us out, and himself in.

My breath hitches. Is he still Roenis? The man

with sharp wit and softer edges buried beneath—trapped within that nightmare shell?

I didn't realize I took a step forward until Datura's grip tightens again. "Don't," she whispers. But the warning is lost to me, drowned by the thundering of my heart and the pull to reach for him. Datura leads me away, walking me back to my room, to be consumed by my own thoughts until the new morning. I see him in a different light. His once perfect manner, fracturing into a godly beast with power.

Because no matter the terror clawing at my chest, I saw him.

And he was breathtaking.

CHAPTER SIXTEEN

Syra

The God is… brooding.

Ever since last night, he's been silent and distracted, a heaviness weighing him down. He moves like a man lost in his own existence, making him something unreadable, something that makes even Dolion worry. I expect him to be volatile or cruel, but instead, he just craves my presence.

It's fascinating to observe. Even with a single word not spoken, his thoughts seem loud. I can't get the image of him last night out of my head. He also hasn't mentioned anything about his shifting.

I don't know if I should be satisfied that it's me he wants beside him, or frustrated that I don't know what to do with it.

We pace the halls, his steps erratic and jumbled, like he's lost in his own mind, running circles he can't escape. His shoulders are tense, his body rigid with an unspoken burden. It's unlike him. He's usually composed and unfazed. That nightmare he worked on last night really messed with his head.

His brows furrow, deep enough to carve a permanent crease between them, an expression so human it almost unsettles me. Small beads of sweat form at his hairline, making his skin appear like wet stone. His eyes dulled to a stormy gray, stripped of their usual glow.

What I would do to get a vial of his soul. To weave it into a dream, to pull apart the shadows of his mind and see what truly haunts him.

Wicked dreams. The thought slithers through me before I can catch it.

Why do I want that?

I shake my head, trying to dispel the intrusive urge, but before I can gather myself, Roenis stops so abruptly I collide into his back. The impact is firm enough to knock the breath from my lungs. He tenses further, his entire form rigid like he's bracing for impact. He looks slightly over his shoulder, like he's listening for something.

"Fuck." The curse is a quiet snarl. Then he moves. Fast.

Before I can react, his hand clamps around my wrist, dragging me toward the nearest door. I barely register the small space before we're swallowed by darkness. My back hits a solid surface, a shelf I realize, the sound of glass vials rattling in protest. The only light illuminating the room is from the bottom of the door and a few fae light bugs in jars on the counters. The air is thick, and it has nothing to do with the dust, and everything to do with Roenis' scent.

The pantry is small—too small. Our bodies are flush against each other, my chest pressing against his as he looms over me. Heat coils between us, a slow-burning ember waiting to be stoked. I part my lips to make a remark, but his hand is suddenly there, covering my mouth in a swift motion.

The shelves tremble again at the force of it.

"Keep quiet," he murmurs, his breath brushing

against my skin like a hot whisper of fire. He is so close. He smells so good. And I'm aware of every area his body is pressing against.

I hear it then, footsteps outside the door. Dolion's voice slips through the cracks, his tone edged with irritation. He's looking for Roenis.

Somehow, Roenis knew he would be. He's been on his ass since closing us out of the office and sealing it shut.

We stay frozen, the only sound is us, the slow inhales of our breathing.

I can feel the silent tension humming in the space we occupy. When the hall beyond the door finally falls silent, Roenis exhales sharply, his hand dropping from my lips. His forehead rests against the wood behind me, his body still too close, too warm, too much.

He's unraveling before me. And I don't know why, but I want to touch him.

Without thinking, I reach up, my fingertips grazing along the sharp cut of his jaw. The contact sends an electric pulse through me. His skin is fever-warm beneath my touch, and his breath hitches just slightly. He leans into it, eyes slipping shut for a fraction of a second, as if savoring the sensation.

"You're acting different," I whisper, the words falling out before I can consider their weight.

His eyes open, seeking mine. They're still that dull, troubled gray, but something else lingers now.

"Can I ask for you to distract my mind?" His voice is breathless.

A crack in his armor.

I jump at the opportunity. "In a small space like this, my body alone pressed against you should be distraction enough."

His gaze drops. Awareness dawns on him, slowly, as if truly registering the way we're tangled together. His fingers flex toward the door handle, but then shifts to gripping my waist instead.

I freeze.

His touch is careful, but searing. His thumb brushes lazy circles at the dip of my waist, an absent, soothing motion that only tightens the coil winding inside me. His head dips lower, his breath ghosting along my jaw, then near my ear.

"You are always a distraction," he murmurs. "Whether it's your sharp tongue, your defiance, or your soft body pressed against mine."

My breath stutters. His lips are so close. He moves his face back to mine. His stare dropping to my mouth, lingering, waiting.

I think he's asking for permission.

Then—

"Kiss me," he demands.

Okay, not asking. Demanding.

I narrow my eyes, searching for the reasoning behind this game. "Are you pressuring me? Why would you want me to kiss you?"

His smirk is devastating, that gods damned cocky curve of his mouth that I want to wipe off his face. "Honestly? It's an excuse. But fuck, have I wanted to kiss you since you threw that dagger at me in the tavern. And then you made it worse when you choked me in my own throne room."

My heart stumbles.

"So please, just fucking kiss me."

Demanding, infuriating, masochistic little God. But even without the demand, I would've tried kissing him.

My fingers slide up his neck, twisting into the fiery strands of his hair. His horns not far from my reach, but the temptation will be damning. His own grip tightens, his free hand sliding behind my neck, fingers threading through the base of my hair and tugging just enough to tip my chin up.

A perfect angle.

"Say it," he pleads.

The tension between us crackles, a pull neither of us can ignore.

"I'll kiss you."

Then his lips crash into mine.

It isn't gentle. It isn't careful. It's hunger and frustration, fire and ice colliding, a battle of willpower slipping through fingers that can't grip tight enough. His mouth is hot, urgent, parting mine with a passion that demands I surrender. And damn me, I do. I match his intensity, pressing closer, drinking in the sensation of his body against mine. His hand on my waist tightens, fingers digging in as if I'm the only thing tethering him to this realm. To this moment.

I should stop this. But I don't. I prefer this wilder side. Something snapped last night and I'm not sure if it was his power, or his bravery.

Then suddenly, his hands slide lower, gripping my thighs and with startling ease, he lifts me, pressing me against the shelves. The vials rattle around us, but I barely register the sound, too caught in the way his body aligns with mine in the deepening pressure of his kiss.

Fuck he's a good kisser.

Heat pools low in my stomach with the way his grip tightens, his fingers digging into my flesh just enough to send a sharp, pleasurable ache through me.

His lips move with a constant hunger, claiming every gasp, every shuddering breath I give him. His tongue brushes against mine, coaxing, summoning, until my body melts further into his hold. Every touch sends sparks across my skin, his hands roaming, tracing paths of fire along my thighs, pressing me closer as if he can't get enough.

I break the kiss to breathe, my head falling back against the wooden shelves and he chuckles, the sound dark and alluring. His eyes show untamed hunger as he takes me in—swollen lips, heaving chest, my sundress hiked up and legs wrapping around him like I belong there.

"Fuck, Syra," he rasps, voice thick with desire. "You have no idea what you're doing to me."

I feel it. Gods, I *feel* it. The press of his arousal against me, the way his fingers twitch against my thighs as if restraining himself and he's quickly losing. Then his grip shifts, his hand grazing over my exposed undergarments, and I realize he notices just how wet I am. A shudder runs through me at the way his breath hitches, his nostrils flaring as if the very scent of me is driving him insane.

A low growl rumbles in his chest, and his lips crash back against mine with renewed fervor, as if a primal beast gave permission to take more. His fingers dig into my hips, rolling me against him in a way that makes my breath catch, my nails biting into his shoulders.

And just when I think he might completely lose himself, he stills. I feel the exact moment he hesitates, the tight coil of restraint pulling him back just before he can cross the threshold of no return. His breath is ragged as he presses his forehead to mine. His hands loosen their grip, his lips leave mine, and then slowly, almost reluctantly, he lowers me back to the ground. A charged silence creeps in. My body now missing the warmth it had.

Breathing hard, he takes a step back, his eyes now a luminous silver. But in his face I can tell he's conflicted. "I can't," he mutters, more to himself than me, before he turns and leaves without another word.

I stay frozen in place, my breathing still uneven, my heart still pounding.

What the fuck just happened?

I press my fingers to my lips, trying to understand the heat still lingering there. I was supposed to be seducing him, gaining control, but for the first time, I feel like I was the one unraveling.

Gods help me, I think I wanted it.

CHAPTER SEVENTEEN
Roenis

My lips still tingle with the remnants of her taste, the memory etches into every nerve ending like a cruel brand I can't scrub clean.

It replays in my mind relentlessly.

The press of her body against mine, the arch of her spine as if daring me to lose control. The soft, involuntary noises she made when my mouth claimed hers, the shudder in her breath when I lifted her like she weighed nothing at all.

For one reckless moment, I was consumed by her, drowning in the intoxication of her being. It wasn't just distraction from the horrors of the night before. It was something far more dangerous. It was surrender.

She saw me.

Not the polished mask I wear for the world, not the carefully calculated God of Nightmares. No, she saw the monster beneath, the fractured pieces stitched together by rage and regret. And she didn't flinch. She didn't fear me. There was something else in her eyes when the beast came out. Her expression was one of fascination, of admiration and wicked desire. When the dust settled and I wrestled the nightmare back into its place, all I could think was, why wasn't she afraid? While Dolion lectured me, and help stabilize the situation, I found myself walking to her room. I stood outside her door, a coward disguised as a God. I didn't knock. I told myself it was the adrenaline, that she'd wake from the spell of the moment and remember to be terrified.

But then there was that damn pantry.

The walls were too close, the air thick with the scent of her. I felt it, undeniably. Desire. It radiated from her, eclipsing her previous intent to kill me. For one small moment, I believed it. I let myself drown in it. I wasn't Roenis, the God of Nightmares. I was just a man desperate to feel wanted, to escape the thoughts clawing at my mind. I wanted to know what it was like to be touched without fear, to be kissed like I was something worth craving, I wanted to feel her want me.

I shake my head, trying to exorcise her from my thoughts as I stalk down the hall. My body betrays me, heat lingering where her hands had been, where her mouth had claimed. I adjust myself with a sharp breath, irritation bubbling beneath the surface. I almost crossed a line—almost lost myself to the very thing I swore I'd never indulge in again.

I need answers. I need control. And for that, I need my library.

The doors swing open effortlessly, the magic woven into the frame recognizing its master. Syra would have some snarky comment about how easy it is for me to bypass the wards, her face twisted in that perfect blend of annoyance and begrudging amusement. The thought tugs a reluctant smile from me before I can stop it.

The shelves shift as I walk, responding to my

intent without hesitation. The endless rows and shelves realign, guiding me to the book I'm looking for. Syra's book.

It hums with a pulse that matches my own, a violet cover marbled with black veins, like our magics have already started to entwine despite my best efforts. It radiates danger, a soft, ominous glow of purple aura that feels like a challenge—a dare wrapped in temptation.

Every kingdom has a unique way to store or use their power, while I keep mine tucked away in secrecy. Every human, every God or Goddess, every living thing that can dream or have nightmares, is stored in this library as a book. It makes it easy to form, to plan, and each one holds their desires and fears.

I've told myself a hundred times not to look. That her unpredictability is what keeps me sharp, but she's a reckoning I can't chart, a Goddess who refuses to be contained. And Gods help me, that excites me more than it should.

Still, I can't afford it. Not with her. She knows too much already, sees too deeply. I've worked too hard, sacrificed too much. I need to know what lies beneath her surface, what threads I can pull, and if her motive is still the same.

I tell myself this is right. That opening this book is about strategy, not obsession. That it's about control.

But as my fingers brush the cover, I know I'm lying.

I open her book, and magic washes over me. It pulls at my very being, wanting to combine with my own magic. I part the pages, and the room flips.

Desire comes first. It always does. I felt hers before, or so I thought, but seeing them is a different matter. The vision flutters, then rearranges and I'm thrown into her book.

At first, the images are vague, but as they sharpen, I feel the undeniable weight of *me* within them.

Her phantom hand traces the ridge of my jaw. Her lips wet with desire, burning with intent, brush against my throat. Heat ripples along my spine as I try not to react, nervous I will alter the vision. I see flashes of fingers threading through my hair, nails dragging down my back, her wicked want tangling in the thrill of control, of testing boundaries she swore to despise.

But the vision shifts again. My vapors whispering in the moment.

Kill. Him.

In the same breath, the vision darkens. The silver strands of desire twists, morphing into something colder. A dagger gleams in the air before pressing against my throat. Her breath is close, her expression hard, but her intent burns clear.

Her face keeps changing, filling with uncertainty, as if her very soul has not yet chosen which reality to embrace.

The contradiction within her is stitched into every fiber of her magic. She wants to kill me. She wants to keep me. She wants to ruin me. She wants to be ruined. The Gods have a cruel sense of humor.

This time, the violet haze twists into the shape of a woman. Maya. Syra's mother stands within my reach, a spectral figure draped in authority, her eyes as biting as frost. The image wavers between two realities.

In one, Maya reaches for Syra, a hand extending,

not warm, but not rejecting either. The longing in Syra's gaze bleeds through the magic, her mother offering something, almost like approval? Love? Acceptance? In the other reality, Maya turns away, her expression lined with cruelty. No words. No acknowledgment. Just distance. Shadows gathering at her feet, swallowing the space until Syra is left standing alone.

The pages are trying to kick me out. Torn between the two possibilities, unable to settle. The fear of failure wove through her book, bleeding into every edge. Not just failure in killing me. Failure in proving herself. Failure in earning her mother's acceptance. Failure in being enough.

The magic starts to fracture, the spell within it unstable, as if it too was trapped in her uncertainty, struggling to decide which path to follow.

I exhale slowly, willing myself out of the trance and back into my reality. For once I didn't force for more information. I close her book gently, the aura fading between my fingers. I let it be carried back to its spot on the shelves, the bookcase already reforming.

Her desires are constantly changing. She *did* want me, but that urge to kill me is still there. Somewhere in the tangled mess of uncertainty, I became a crossroad for her.

I run a hand through my hair, exhaling slowly, because I know one truth she has yet to admit to herself.

The moment she decides which path to take, whether wanting me or killing me, there will be no turning back.

CHAPTER EIGHTEEN

Syra

As I stand outside Roenis' chamber doors, I hesitate.

I haven't seen him since our kiss in the small pantry two nights ago. He's been avoiding me. Purposefully. The only trace of him was the note left on my pillow, his elegant script summoning me here when night fell. No explanation. No reassurance.

A shiver snakes down my spine.

Did he expect something to happen between us? Did I?

My fingers brush my lips, as if the memory of his touch still lingers there, as if it hasn't haunted me since. The scent of him clung to me that night, seeping into my skin, and my *almost* surrender, taints my mind. I barely slept. My body burns with a need I didn't understand, and worse—I resent the part of me that wants more. The war between desire and duty twists deep within me. I shake my head, banishing the thought, and push open the heavy door.

The chamber is draped in shadows, the only light filtering in is from the tall twin glass doors on the opposite side of the room. I'm still unaware on where they lead to, but the air is thick with silence.

And then I see him.

Roenis sits at the edge of his bed, facing the door as though he's been waiting. His robe hangs carelessly from his body, the black silk slipping off one shoulder, baring the smooth plane of his chest, aside from the raised veins. His head is bowed, red hair spilling forward, which was a striking contrast against his pale grey skin. His hands resting loosely on his thighs. He doesn't look up or acknowledge me. A small tinge of familiarity hits me. When my mother would summon me and not even give me a glance. But, this doesn't feel like dismissal, more like caution on his part.

Something about him is different. His presence, normally charged with power, feels... fractured. The weight of it wraps around me, pressing against my chest. Then his voice cuts through.

"You are the most confusing creature I have ever encountered."

There is no teasing in his tone, no wicked amusement. Just frustration. I endure it, caught between caution and curiosity. His head sways slightly, as if fighting the weight of his own thoughts, before his gaze finally lifts to mine. His beautiful silver eyes, they burn. I haven't seen this expression on him before.

"Come here," he commands.

I stiffen, remembering the last time he ordered me like this. My pulse jumps in warning, and I try to ignore the way my body betrays me at the sound of his voice. "I don't see the nee—"

"I advise you not to question me," he interrupts, his voice dipping lower, the authority rumbling through me. "Come. Here."

A slow heat unfurls in my stomach again at the sharpness in his tone, a thrill filled with something dangerous. Every warning bell in my head rings at once. But there's something in his voice—something I can't resist. I step forward cautiously, and within seconds, his hand snaps out, gripping my arm. A startling breath escapes me as he yanks me forward, lifting me with ease, forcing me to straddle him.

My hands collide with his chest in reflex. It's warm and solid beneath my touch. I fight the blush clawing up my face, but my body is already betraying me. He's unpredictable. I don't know how many sides he has to him, but this one—this controlled chaos—is the most dangerous.

Yet, it's the most exciting.

"Now you stay quiet?" he taunts, his voice a low rasp. "Was it the stolen moment we had in that pantry? Or was it sitting on my lap that finally made you listen?"

Asshole.

My palm meets his cheek before I can stop myself. The crack echoing in the room.

Shit I *really* need to learn to control my temper.

His head turns slightly from the impact, and a wicked grin slowly stretches across his face. He looks at me like I am the most fascinating thing he's ever seen, like this man is enjoying every second of this.

"You really are unpredictable," he murmurs, amusement now curling at the edges of his words. His tone switching yet again.

I grit my teeth. "You can't just kiss me like the world revolves around us, disappear and ignore me for days, then summon me here only to throw me onto your lap and mock me."

He studies me. "Do you know why?"

"Why what?" I snap. "Why you kissed me? Why you ignored me? Or why you made me straddle you? Please, do enlighten me."

His lip quirks, but there's no humor, I see the change in his eyes, a wall, a guard. "No. Do you know why your family has always failed to kill me?"

The abrupt question slams into me. He watches me, reading every conclusion that passes through my mind. I frown, the answer automatic, though it is tainted with uncertainty now. "Because you didn't love or care for them."

"Wrong." His fingers tighten slightly on my waist, grounding me. "You have only one side of the story. You have lies."

My stomach knots. "You think you have me all figured out?" I bite back, trying to regain control of this moment, this conversation. "You think I don't know why I was sent here?"

"I think you don't know the full truth," he counters smoothly. "I think you're starting to realize that yourself."

I hate how he gets under my skin, how he picks apart my defenses like they're nothing but broken glass. I hate that he might be right.

"The thing is, you aren't like the others she has sent. You have curiosity. You have fire. And you don't hate this kingdom or its people. Yet, you still desire to kill me." His statement makes this all too real. This mission is meaningless if he just knows everything.

I clench my jaw. Mind games. He's playing mind games. "You don't know me. I'm not some piece to figure out in your puzzle." I grind out.

"I know you more than your kingdom does," he

counters again. "I bet I've seen sides of you your own mother chooses to ignore. You have a little darkness in you. I haven't killed you because I don't want to. Your magic fucking *calls* to me. And I kissed you because I fucking wanted to." His frustration is palpable, his confession like a spark of electricity in the space around us.

"Love is dangerous," he continues, his voice quieter now, like a confession meant only for me. "It makes magic call to magic. It leaves you vulnerable. Anyone can kill a God or Goddess of this realm. Because love shouldn't exist here. That is why it is the easiest way to kill one."

I inhale sharply, his words scraping against the carefully constructed lies I have clung to my entire life. He's giving me information my own mother wouldn't tell me.

"So I'll ask again. Do you know why the previous women your mother created have always failed?" He pauses, giving me time to think, but when I don't respond, he gives me the answer I've been deprived of. "Because in order for it to work, they have to love me back. To kill me is to kill yourself.

To love me is to be loved back. That's why they failed. I would fall, but they never would."

Wait.

More time. She said I needed more time.

The plan had changed because my mother was doing something different this time. She told me I needed to make him care for me, to lure him in deeper. But why? The answer is glaringly obvious now. If I needed time to make him fall… that meant there was also time for me to fall.

The thought slams into me like a physical force.

Did she know? Did my mother foresee that I would begin to care for him? That I would start to doubt, to hesitate?

And if Roenis is right—if killing him would also mean my own demise—then I was never meant to survive this mission.

A pawn. A sacrificial piece on a board I never controlled.

A slow, festering rage unfurls inside me, winding around my ribs, coiling tight in my gut.

This can't be real. This has to be some kind of manipulation. A trick.

My head pounds. The air constricting, stealing the air I breathe as my own thoughts turn against me. My mind racing through every conversation, every calculated decision made on my behalf. The lies, the omissions, the way my mother never once entertained my questions, only demanded obedience.

I dig my fingers into my scalp, squeezing my eyes shut as if I can block out the truth clawing its way into my mind.

Then—warmth.

A firm squeeze against my thighs, anchoring me. Roenis.

His voice cuts through the noise. "Do you think it's fair?"

Something inside me snaps.

I see red.

My mother. Orson. The council. Roenis. Everyone.

They knew. They had to know. And I—I was left in the dark, expected to walk blindly into whatever fate they had decided for me. I can't tell what's real anymore. What's true, what's deception, what's just another piece in someone else's game.

A deep, seething anger erupts from within, and my magic rises in tandem, curling at the edges of my vision like… smoke? The pressure inside me builds, black and unrelenting, swelling, consuming.

I open my eyes—

And everything feels like darkness.

"You still want to kill me," he says, voice low, confident.

His body shifts beneath mine, and before I can fully process the motion, I see my dagger, twirling between his fingers. The blade hums, the magic caressing against my skin, thrumming in recognition.

Roenis meets my gaze with a cold indifference. The dim light casting sharp shadows over his features as he lifts the dagger between us. His silver eyes gloomy as he says, "Kill me then. Stab me right now."

This God is stupid.

I scoff, my lip curling in disgust. "That's not how it works."

He shrugs, unbothered. "How would you know?"

He's right. I don't know. I never figure things out

for myself. I was taught, molded, manipulated. And now, with everything unraveling, how can I even be certain of the truth?

My fingers wrap around the hilt. The blade poised just above his heart, and still, he watches me, waiting. His chest rises and falls in steady breaths, but his eyes burn with confidence. He wants this. He's daring me.

What if I'm wrong? What if he can die without love?

"Do it," he coaxes.

"Why?" My grip tightens. "You could die."

He studies me for a long moment, then, with the same maddening calm, he delivers the words he knows will ignite my fury, like dry tinder to a flame.

"Your mother doesn't love you."

A snarl rips from my throat as I drive the dagger forward. Magic bursting from me in a violent blast, the air shaking with energy as my rage consumes every rational thought. The bracelet on my wrist holds back the worst of it, but it can't contain the wildfire burning inside me.

The impact is visceral—I feel the blade sink into

flesh, the vibration of the force traveling up my arm. My breath comes in short, rapid gasps as I grip the hilt, my knuckles white. And then—reality slams back into me.

My fingers loosen. My heartbeat stutters.

I push myself off his lap and step back, horror clawing up my throat as Roenis looks down at the dagger embedded in his chest. He blinks once, slowly, before lifting his head to meet my gaze.

"Roenis…" My voice barely makes it past my lips. "I—I didn't—"

But then, he laughs. This. Asshole. laughs.

"Damn," he muses, running a finger along the hilt as if I'd merely pinned a brooch to his robe. "That was a powerful thrust."

My entire body bristles. "What the hell is wrong with you?" I snap. "Why would you provoke me?"

He moves—fast. I barely have time to register the shift before he's on his feet, gripping me roughly and throwing me over his shoulder like a child.

"To prove a point, see? I'm not dead." he says, striding toward the door with effortless strength.

I pound my fists against his back. "Put me down!"

"Not yet." His grip tightens. "I told you the truth, Syra. I know you better than you realize. And you need to start questioning *everything*."

Something in his voice, something desperate, something I don't want to acknowledge, makes me stop struggling.

"...Why?" The word falls from my lips in a quiet plea. It was all I can muster up.

He doesn't hesitate. "Because you're powerful and smart. And you deserve to know everything."

The door to my room flies open with a single kick, and he strides inside, placing me onto the edge of my bed. He lingers, his fingers brushing my cheek, then trailing up to tuck a loose strand of hair behind my ear. The weight of his touch makes my breath stutter.

That sensation, the one he always draws out of me, deepens and spirals tighter in my stomach.

Roenis pulls back, his hand slipping away. My eyes stop at his chest, where my dagger still juts from the middle where his heart is. Before I can say anything, he grips the hilt and wrenches it free with a quick, nasty pull. The blade clatters to the floor, gleaming with the evidence of my wrath.

He steps in closer. His fingers tilting my chin up, his touch uncharacteristically gentle.

I don't think. I just *breathe*. "Can I ask you to distract my mind this time?" My voice is barely more than a whisper.

A smirk ghosts across his face. He leans in, lowering himself until our mouths are mere centimeters apart. His breath fans over my lips, warm and teasing. Then, he darts his tongue out, dragging it slowly along my bottom lip. A traitorous tremble runs over me.

And then—he pulls away.

"Not this time, pet," he murmurs, his smirk deepening as he straightens.

The loss of contact is instant, frustrating. Desire and rage burn inside me in equal measure. I clench my fists, ready to throw a punch, but the bastard is already walking toward the door.

"Goodnight, Syra," he calls over his shoulder.

The door clicks shut.

I let out a breath, staring at the empty space where he stood. A growl of frustration rumbles in my throat, and before I can stop myself, I hurl a pillow at the door with all my strength.

Infuriating. Insufferable.

The taste of him still lingers on my lip, a tease of what could have been. My body is still humming, aching from the fire he stoked and refused to put out.

To hells with him. I've been worked up for days now. My breath is unsteady as I let my hand drift down, my fingers tracing the heat pooling between my thighs.

If he won't give me what I want, I'll take my pleasure into my own hands. I *will* have my fun.

CHAPTER NINETEEN
Roenis

I lean my head against the door of her room, my breath coming in rough exhales. The restraint I had to show, to not take her right there, to not claim her in the way every part of me demanded, was excruciating. Her scent, her desire, the way her pulse pounded beneath her skin, I could drown in it. The beast inside me snarls, my self control a flimsy cage barely holding it back.

I push off the door and lean my back against the cold stone wall, fingers curling at my sides. The second I put space between us, I feel it again—stronger, richer, pulling at me like an unseen thread. I inhale sharply, and my cock twitches in response.

Fuck. What is she doing to me? Her desire is *flaring*.

I close my eyes, shifting a secondary vapor. My form twists and shapes, shadows whispering as I let myself drift, let myself seep back into her room unseen. I don't have to be there physically to experience it. My vapor-self moves like a second skin, an extension of my being. I can see. I can feel. I can taste.

And gods, what a sight she is.

She's sprawled on the bed where I left her, but now her hand is between her thighs, fingers buried in her wet cunt. Her back arches, her lips part in a silent moan, and the expression on her face is pure sin, pure ecstasy, it makes my blood burn.

What a deviant little pet.

She doesn't care about rules. She doesn't care that she's unleashing all of her desire knowing I can feel it, knowing I am somewhere near. If she truly wanted me to resist, she wouldn't be doing this.

She wants me to break. I remember her saying she enjoyed being watched. And damn myself, I am definitely watching.

My cock aches, heavy and thick as I palm myself through my robe. The friction is nowhere near enough, but I savor the pulse of pleasure anyway. Every stroke is in sync with her moans, every movement of her fingers matched by mine. The thrill of watching her, of knowing she's thinking of me while she writhes in pleasure, is almost too much.

Does it count if I touch her like this? In this form? Does it count if my hands are made of vapor, my tongue of shadows?

My power reaches out, unnoticeable but felt. A cool stroke along her leg. A teasing brush against her inner thigh. She gasps, her body stilling for a moment as her eyes snap open. The confusion that crosses her face is quickly followed by realization. She tilts her head back, a delicious, wicked smirk forming on her lips.

She likes it.

A dark chuckle rumbles in my chest, even as I clench my jaw to keep from groaning too loudly in the hallway. My fingers tighten around my shaft, stroking myself harder. The heat is unbearable, pleasure pulling tight in my stomach, but I don't stop. I press my vapors against her, gliding up the smooth skin of her thighs, curling around her hips like a lover's hands. And when she spreads her legs wider in silent invitation, I give in to the temptation.

My vapor grips her thighs and pulls them apart farther, forcing her open for me. Her breath catches, and she lifts her head slightly, searching for the presence she can't see. The disappointment flickering in her eyes makes my cock throb painfully.

You want me that badly, don't you?

I lean in closer, my whispers curling around her ear. "Your release is mine to consume."

A violent shudder runs through her, her body arching into the force around her. I don't give her a moment to react before I slide my shadow tongue along her clit.

She chokes on a moan, her fingers flying to grip the sheets as I lick her again, achingly slow and purposefully. Her head thrashes against the pillow, thighs trembling. Her moans grow desperate, panting, and I match her rhythm with my strokes.

Each roll of my hips into my hand syncs with the flick of my tongue against her.

"This is what you wanted, isn't it?" I taunt, my voice a soft echo against her skin, everywhere and nowhere at once.

A giggle spills from her lips, breathless and teasing, and fuck, I'm going to ruin her.

I swirl my tongue over her sensitive bundle of nerves before slipping a vapor inside her.

"Gods, Roenis!" She cries out, her hips bucking, her hands flying to clutch her thighs.

The way she moans my name, the way she writhes beneath my touch, is almost enough to push me over the edge. My hand tightens around my cock again, squeezing at the base to hold back. The pleasure is unbearable, my tip leaking, aching. I stroke myself harder, faster, each jerk of my wrist mirroring the thrusts of my vapor inside her.

Her magic flares, her vines reaching out, searching for something to hold onto. Searching for me. My darkness curls around her light, entwining, pulling her deeper into the pleasure. She's darkness coated in stars and glamour. I itch to see the wickedness come out, to show she has that darkness too.

"Look at you," I whisper, my voice dripping with satisfaction. "Falling apart for me."

She moans in response, her legs twitching, her breath coming in frantic pants. She throws her arm over her face. She's close—I can feel it, the way her muscles clench, the way her body bows. I refuse to let her hide from me.

I snap another vapor around her wrists, yanking them above her head. She gasps, her chest rising and falling rapidly. My grip is firm. I want to see her. I want to watch her come undone with nothing to shield her from me.

"Let go," I whisper darkly. "Let me see you fall."

And she does.

She cries out my name as she shatters, her body convulsing, her magic lashing wildly as her pleasure peaks.

It's my undoing.

I groan, biting my lip hard enough to draw blood as I spill over my hand, my release hot and thick. My body shutters as I turn to face the wall. I grip the stone for support as I ride it out. My forehead hits against the cold surface, my breath ragged.

I glance down at the mess I've made, a laugh escaping me.

Never in my immortal life have I felt like such an adolescent, jerking off in a hallway covered in my own cum.

Dolion would fucking die if he saw me like this.

But gods, it's exhilarating.

I close my eyes, a wide smile stretching across my face. This is only the beginning. I can't wait to see how she reacts when I pretend none of this happened. When I let her believe she conjured up the whole thing in the haze of her own pleasure.

Oh pet, you have no idea the games we're about to play.

CHAPTER TWENTY
Roenis

The morning light barely filters through the dining hall windows, casting soft shadows over the long ebony wood table. The air bubbles with anticipation and satisfaction from the night spent unraveling Syra.

I sit at the head of the table, lazily swirling a spoon through the dark liquid in my cup. Across from me, Syra is still quiet as ever, though her shoulders are just a little too stiff, her fingers curling just a little too tightly around the silverware. And most notably, she is absolutely refusing to meet my gaze.

Which, of course, makes this all the more

entertaining.

I lean, resting my chin on my hand, watching her as she cuts into a piece of fruit she has yet to actually eat. "You're quiet this morning. Trouble sleeping?"

Her grip on the knife tightens.

"No," she says, far too quickly. Then, as if catching herself, she lifts her chin, eyes burning with questions. "Why do you ask?"

Gods, she is making this too easy.

"Just curious. You look... well, a little restless. Perhaps overstimulated?"

Her knife scrapes against the plate.

She takes a steady breath, unimpressed. "I slept great. Fully energized."

I offer a knowing smile. "Are you now?"

The way she stiffens was delicious.

A war rages behind those violet eyes, one I imagine involves every moment of last night flooding back to her. Her mind is likely battling itself. Confusion and lingering want flashes through those eyes, I had done my job correctly. Her mind must be clashing around.

She thinks it was me. Perhaps *knows* it was me. But I had left her just enough room to doubt herself.

She huffs and finally, *finally*, turns to look at me fully, and Gods, she is astonishing when she is pissed. "You know, I had the strangest dream last night."

I raise a brow. "Oh? Do tell."

She leans in slightly, her voice seductive. "It felt real. Unbelievably real. And you were there." She continues cutting her fruit.

I hum as I tear off a piece of bread. "Mmm, fascinating. Dreams can be quite vivid, but you should know that better than anyone."

Her jaw clenches.

I take a slow bite, watching the frustration dig into her every muscle. "But, please, continue. I'm intrigued."

Her eyes turn into slits. "You—"

"—must have made quite the impression for you to summon me so vividly in your sleep?" I finish for her, letting the words burn.

Syra rolls her shoulders, trying to brush off the comment. "I didn't summon you."

"Didn't you?" I watch her squirm. "Your dreams are powerful, Syra. Perhaps your desires were simply strong enough to manifest me on their own."

For a moment, she just stares at me, her lips parting slightly before pressing into a tight line. I can practically see the uproar behind her eyes, the doubt, the struggle to hold onto her certainty.

Then, ever so quietly, she mumbles under her breath, "Bastard."

I grin.

Her fingers curl into fists before she forces them to relax, her spine straightening. "Fine. Let's say, for a moment, I did conjure you in my sleep. Then tell me this, Roenis—" she inclines her body, her voice booming with confidence, "—why did it feel like you? The cunning words, the vapors, even the touch on my thighs. Quite familiar to the time in the pantry."

Oh, she's good.

I bite back a laugh, dragging my thumb along the rim of my cup. "Why, indeed?"

Her nostrils flares, her frustration reaching its peak. "You're insufferable."

"And yet," I muse, "you keep dreaming about me."

Her fork clatters onto her plate and with a dramatic sigh, she pushes back her chair and stands. "I think I've had enough breakfast."

"Shame." I stretch my arms behind my head. "You'll need your strength, for later."

She freezes mid-step.

Oh, this is torture. Cruel and entirely worth it.

Slowly, she turns to glare at me, cheeks just a shade darker than before. "For what, exactly?"

I let my gaze drag over her in a way that is far from proper before meeting her eyes once more. "Whatever your dreams conjure up next, of course."

She scoffs, rolling her eyes again, but I don't miss the way her breath catches. Without another word, she spins on her heel and strides toward the exit, her steps just a little quicker than necessary.

I watch her go, waiting until she disappears beyond the threshold before exhaling a satisfied sigh.

Gods, that was fun.

I reach for my drink and take a leisurely sip, savoring the taste. Yes, I will definitely need to do that again.

"And what was that about?"

I nearly choke on my drink.

Datura leans against the doorway, arms crossed, expression nothing but amusement. I grimace, setting my cup down. "How long have you been there?"

"Long enough to see you act like a smug bastard and enjoy every second of it." She saunters over, plucking a grape from a bowl and popping it into her mouth. "So? Are you going to admit you're obsessed with her, or shall I state the obvious?"

"She's the one obsessed with me."

Datura snorts. "Right. That's why you were the one watching her walk away like she hung the damn stars."

Now *I* roll my eyes. "Do you have a point?"

"I do, actually." She sits across from me, resting her chin on her palm. "We should take Syra to the village."

I frown. "Why?"

She shrugs. "Because if you want her to understand your world, she needs to see it. The real parts, not just the castle. Let her see what your people think of you."

I study her for a long moment, then sigh. "Fine. But if she causes trouble—"

"Oh, please." Datura grins. "That would be the fun part."

◆

As I approach Syra's door with Datura, nerves churn in my gut. It's an unfamiliar feeling, one I don't appreciate. I tell myself it's because I want her to understand my people, to see them and not judge. But, if I'm honest, there's another layer to my unease. She has kept the village's existence a secret, unexpected, but somehow I knew she would. It's a small but significant display of trust. A part of me is grateful.

I knock, and it takes her longer than usual to answer. When she finally opens the door, I'm momentarily speechless.

Her white hair is damp and braided, framing her face in a way that sharpens the angles of her jawline. The strands shine, a few golden ones catching my attention. She hasn't worn her glamour since the throne room incident.

My chest tightens.

There's something captivating about seeing her this way, especially after seeing her last night in a different light. It makes it impossible to look away. When it's just us, with no pretense, no kingdom's gaze on her, when I have her all to myself, her beauty radiates into something I can't get enough of. Like its all mine to take.

Datura's elbow slams into my ribs.

I cough to cover up my pause, scowling at her as she bites back a laugh.

"Datura and I are heading into the village to start gathering prep for the ball," I say, pushing past my momentary lapse. "We want you to tag along."

Syra's brows lift. She looks genuinely shocked. "I've been before, but never ventured into town. Is it really okay for me to walk around there? They know I'm from Dream Kingdom, right?"

I nod. "Yes, which is why I'm sorry to ask if you could possibly glamour yourself again? It's just to avoid unnecessary questions, and to keep the villagers from being nervous."

Something flashes in her expression. In that brief second, I think it's disappointment. But, just as quickly, she slips back into her usual composed state.

"Right," she says. "That's best. Just give me a moment to change."

The door shuts, and I exhale roughly.

Datura is too quiet. When I glance over, she's watching me like a cat waiting to pounce.

"What?" I finally ask, already regretting it.

"Nothing. It just looked like you were stunned for a moment. She on the other hand, looked nervous to see you."

I frown. "That's not what I saw. She looked more disappointed that I asked her to glamour herself."

"Ah, so you are observing her, you are so interesting to watch lately." She teases.

I cross my arms. "Why are you pestering me?"

"Because it's fun. And because I haven't seen you this worked up about one of Maya's daughters before."

I say nothing. She's right, Syra is definitely under my skin. But after last night, something changed.

Datura tsks. "I think she's different. I don't have the same worries about her that I did before. It's okay for you to open up, you know. No judgment from me. Dolion on the other hand, is a different matter though."

"I don't give a fuck about what he thinks." I scoff.

Before she can respond, the door opens again. Syra steps out, her glamour fully in place.

It shouldn't make a difference. I've seen her in both forms. And yet, it brings me back to the tavern. The memory makes me smirk a little.

Suddenly, I'm hit with an unexpected wave of feelings, a little bit of desire. It isn't *full* desire. Not the kind I usually recognize, this kind is simmering deeper. I felt it when I saw her mother in her book.

Approval. She wants *my* approval.

The realization is startling. I don't know what to do with it.

I scratch my head to cover my reaction. "Well?" she asks, arms crossed, watching me expectantly.

I let my gaze linger for a beat too long, as if testing

a boundary. There's no immediate spark of irritation from her, no usual sharp retort. Just a hint of vulnerability beneath her guarded stare.

"You look…good," I say. My voice rougher than intended.

Datura squints her eyes at me, muttering something under her breath as she starts toward the hall. "Come on, we don't have all night."

We fall into step beside each other, making our way toward the back of the castle where the hidden village sits. The corridor is quiet, save for the occasional echo of footsteps. The castle is emptier this morning. Dolion, Kenji, Grifton and Asani already went ahead of us into the village.

Syra remains quiet though. She isn't sulking, but there's a weight to her silence.

I should ignore it. I should let it go.

Instead, I say, "You didn't have to look so put off about the glamour."

Damn, that came out accusingly.

Her head snaps toward me. "I wasn't—" She exhales sharply, shaking her head. "Forget it."

I arch a brow. "No, please, tell me. I love when

you keep things bottled up."

She glares. "It's nothing. Just… it's strange to feel unwelcome in a place you're meant to understand."

Something twists in my chest. I don't like the way she says it. And worse, I don't like that I might have made her feel that way. "You aren't unwelcome, the villagers are just wary. Dream Kingdom hasn't exactly been kind to us."

"And what about you?"

I frown. "What about me?"

"You act like you want me here," she says carefully. "But then you ask me to hide who I am."

I don't have an answer for that.

Or maybe I do, and I don't want to admit it.

Because the truth is—I don't want her to hide. Not really. But, the part of me that's always thinking five steps ahead, the part that understands how fragile the balance of power is, knows that keeping her disguised is necessary.

And yet…

Yet, I find myself regretting it.

The rest of the walk is quiet, but the silence between us feels tight now. Charged. Weighted with unspoken things. She doesn't wait for an answer, like she already convinced herself with one.

As the castle's back gardens come into view, the distant glow of lanterns from the hidden village casts light onto the opening path. I should be focusing on the day ahead, on the villagers, and on the preparations. But, all I can think about is her, and how every thought I have, weaves her into my mind every time.

And how I no longer hate it.

CHAPTER TWENTY-ONE
Syra

I hate this.

I know I used my glamour before, and I was prepared to use it most of the time, but after everything that happened, I didn't expect to have to use it again. Yet here I am, following Roenis as we enter the village, my true form concealed beneath a veil of magic.

I have never truly gone past the small entrance before. The last time I lingered at the edges, the weight of curious stares made me feel as if I didn't belong. But this time, I force myself forward. As I try to distract myself, the memory of last night replays itself in my thoughts.

It *had* to be Roenis.

I knew his magic like my own, familiar. I had felt it in my room, curling around me in the dark. I had heard his voice, felt his presence. And I was certain he had lingered outside my door after. But, in the morning, he played his little game, never answering my questions fully, never admitting it. I was ready for an apology, ready for an admission when he came up to my room, but instead I was simply told to hide myself.

A bitter part of me wonders, is it because he doesn't like how I look? Am I a reminder he wishes to forget?

For once, I say nothing. I just swallow my pride and follow him. The village unfolds before me, breathtaking and bigger than I expected.

Lanterns hang from iron posts, their glass panes giving off an unnatural light that isn't hindered by the daylight. The sky above is concealed in thick, storm-gray clouds, instead of casting the village in gloom, the overcast sky only allows the lanterns to illuminate the streets in an otherworldly glow. It's as if the town exists in a twilight all on its own.

The streets are far larger than I imagined, stretching outward with pathways made of dark cobblestone. People of all shapes and sizes move through the roads, their appearances as diverse as their origins. Some have obsidian skin with cracks similar to dried out lava, etch across their arms. Others bear horns or iridescent scales trailing down their necks. There are those who look human, draped in robes or well-worn casual gear, while others have wings the color of fire embers, tucked against their backs.

The scent of food thickens the air, roasted meats, honey, and spiced pastries carry scents both floral and smoky, that makes my stomach ache with longing. Steam curls from small cauldrons where vendors stir bright-colored liquids, their hands moving with practiced ease as they pour into tankards and bowls.

Shops buzz with activity, some open to the streets with cloth awnings flowing to catch attention, while others are nestled behind dark wooden doors with signs and colorful decorations. Conversations fill the air, a symphony of voices I didn't recognize, mingling with the distant echo of music that drifts from a part of the town I can't yet see.

I must've been smiling, because when I turn, I catch Roenis staring at me, his silver eyes filled with excitement.

I don't hide it this time. Instead, I let the wonder settle into my bones, allowing myself to drink it all in without resistance.

Roenis reaches for my hand, the gesture so natural and unexpected that it sends a jolt through me. His fingers are warm against mine, calloused yet tender. The feeling foreign.

"Come," he states, voice gentler than before. "Datura is heading to her shop, but you can come with me to the Cloth Designer."

I nod, letting him guide me through the winding streets.

The cloth store is burrowed between two tall buildings, its arched doorway framed by sheer veils of silk that respond to the magic in the air. The sign above the entrance is elegantly etched with delicate golden script, Mirein's Woven Wears.

As soon as we step inside, the scent of something

rich and musky—perhaps aged fabric, or the remnants of incense, tickle my nose. The store was a dream of color. Bolts of silk and velvet line the walls, cascading like waterfalls of shifting hues. There are fabrics that resemble a star-dusted night sky, others that hold the soft iridescence of dawn. Some cloths appear woven with liquid metals, while others bear intricate embroidery stitched with actual glowing thread.

One fabric catches my attention immediately, a sheer material that seems to trap moonlight within its threads, shifting between shades of blue and violet as I reach out to touch it. It's unlike anything I had ever seen, yet familiar in a way that sends a chill down my spine.

This is from the Dream Kingdom.

My fingers trail over the fabric, tracing the patterns of swirling clouds woven into it, memories tugging at the edges of my mind.

"You recognize it," a voice says behind me.

I turn to find a woman standing there, her dark eyes studying me with quiet intensity. She is older than me but not by much, her long, raven-black hair twisted into elaborate braids adorned with tiny silver charms. Her skin has the same faint luminescence as those from my homeland.

She's Dreamborn. A runaway.

My lips part, but before I can speak, Roenis steps forward, his voice calm. "Syra, this is Mirein. She owns this shop."

Mirein folds her arms, gaze flicking between us. "Syra. Well, I assume you're glamoured since I don't see the resemblance of the Syra I *do* know."

The weight of her stare burns a hole in my chest. "You—"

"I left the Dream Kingdom a long time ago." Mirein's voice is steady, but I still hear her pain beneath it. "I was not welcome there, so I made my own home. Here."

I look to Roenis, searching for an explanation, and he exhales softly.

"This village is a sanctuary," he states. "For those who seek safety, no matter where they're from. No matter what they've done." His gaze holds mine. "Not everyone is given a choice in where they belong. Sometimes, they have to carve it out for themselves. Which is what I've explained the day I first showed you the village."

I swallow, glancing at Mirein again. She doesn't look angry. Just… resolute. Strong in a way that makes me question everything I had been told about those who left my kingdom.

I had always been taught that those who fled were betrayers. But maybe, they were just survivors. And maybe, Roenis wasn't the monster I had been told he was, if she's still alive here.

I reach for the fabric again, running my fingers over the soft material. For once, I don't feel so alone with something from home to make me feel slightly at ease.

Mirein studies Roenis with an assessing gaze, her arms still folded like she's deciding whether this is just another transaction, or something else.

"So," she says, "I assume this isn't just a casual visit."

Roenis' eyes glaze over the vast array of fabrics before settling on her. "I need something for the ball. The usual standard of elegance, but with something unexpected."

Mirein taps a finger against the wooden counter, considering. "Your last gala ensemble was a simple black robe with red cuffs and golden buttons." she concentrates, then turns towards a shelf, fingers grazing over the fabric bolts like she's listening to them. "I assume you don't want to repeat yourself?"

He tilts his head slightly. "You assume correctly."

A knowing smirk crosses her mouth. With a twist of her hand, bolts of cloth drifts off the shelves, unfurling mid-air before us.

I suck in a quiet breath.

The first is a black silk so deep it drinks in the surrounding light, like the void between the stars. But as it shifts, thin veins of silver flick in and out of sight, like the cloth itself is threaded with captured lightning.

"This, is woven with nightshade fibers. The silver will only be visible under certain lights, just enough to make you look untouchable, but still a presence no one will ignore."

Roenis runs a hand over the material, his expression impressed. "Not bad."

Mirein gloats. "You'll love it, but let's not pretend

you don't want options."

With another motion of her fingers, the black fabric rolls itself back into place, replaced by another. This one is a dark navy, almost midnight blue, with a faint opalescent sheen that catches the light hostage, forming a mirage. Subtle swirls of deep purple are etched into the silk, so faint they only appear when the fabric turns at certain angles.

"This one," Mirein continues, "is imbued with shadow wisp magic. It moves like a dream, clinging only where it needs to. Regal, but not predictable."

Roenis studies the options, but I'm not expecting him to turn to me. "What do you think?"

I blink, caught off guard. He wants my opinion?

I hesitate for only a moment before stepping closer. The navy silk was cool beneath my fingertips, impossibly smooth, shifting under my touch like settled water.

"The first one makes a statement," I admit, my voice quieter now. "It's power. The kind that demands attention the moment you enter the room. The silver threading will catch just enough light to keep people on edge, like they're waiting for something to happen." I glance at the second bolt, lifting it slightly. "But this one, it's something else. It's mystery. It's something you think you understand, only to realize you never did."

Suddenly, I'm aware of the silence. Roenis is watching me. The intensity in his gaze makes my stomach flip, but I refuse to look away.

Mirein lets out a quiet chuckle, as if she's enjoying the moment far more than I am. "She has an eye for this."

Roenis considers my words, then murmurs with his approval of my opinion, "The second one, then."

Mirein hums, rolling the fabric back with her magic. "And what about your guest?" she asks, her eyes sliding to me. "Does she need something as well?"

I tense, shaking my head. "I—No. I wasn't planning on—"

"She'll need something," Roenis interrupts my spiral.

I shoot him a look, but he doesn't return it. He motions to Mirein. "Show me what you have in royal purples."

Mirein doesn't even blink. Without hesitation, she reaches for another section of the shop, pulling forth a bolt of deep violet silk so rich it almost looks black in the dim lighting. Gold undertones run beneath the surface, and instead of a uniform shine, they curl and move like clouds of a dream, floating and twisting about with every movement.

"This is—" Mirein starts, but my attention already drifts. My gaze sweeping over another fabric, the one I had touched earlier. The one from the Dream Kingdom.

A piece of home.

Mirein notices immediately. There's a recognition in her eyes, but she doesn't acknowledge it outright. She focuses on Roenis. "I assume you want to purchase these, then?"

Roenis sees it too. His silver eyes assessing me, catching the way my gaze switches between the pieces of fabrics.

And without hesitation, he beckons to Mirein. "And add that one."

I inhale. "Roenis, I—"

"You kept looking at it," he states, his tone soft

but absolute.

I stare at him, unsure what to say.

Mirein, to her credit, leaves no comment. She simply smiles and binds the fabrics in protective enchantments, wrapping them in golden thread before placing them on the counter.

"That'll be—"

Roenis doesn't even let her finish. "Send the bill to me."

Mirein lets out a soft laugh. "Of course, my God."

I expect Roenis to bristle at the title, but when he doesn't, I sneak a peak at him. There's something almost amused in his expression, like the name didn't hold the same weight in this place as it did everywhere else.

He gathers the bundle of fabrics, holding them effortlessly under one arm before turning to me. "Let's go."

I wait for only a moment before following, my fingers brushing one last time over the dream fabric. It has been so long since I had touched something from home.

And now, it's mine.

CHAPTER TWENTY-TWO

Syra

When we exit the shop, Roenis seems like a different person. The shadows that usually cling to him have thinned, revealing a sense of contentment. A soft smile tugs at his lips, and it's so unfamiliar on him that I find myself staring.

"A few more shops and we can head back," he says, his voice lighter.

I nod, unable to form words. As we walk through the streets, his people greet him with warm smiles and casual waves, their admiration evident. They love him. It's not forced, and it's not out of fear. It's genuine. There is no way he can be a monster. If someone was truly cruel, they wouldn't be celebrated like this.

I follow him mindlessly, taking in every piece of his world. We pass a shop filled with a warm golden glow, it's definitely Datura's brass shop. She stands inside, surrounded by bursts of magic, molten metal reshaping beneath her precise hands. This must be where she spends her days before dinner. A few doors down, the rich aroma of spices return in the air. Asani's Cooking Delights. The scent is the same intoxicating one from all the dinners I've tasted. I should've known it was him crafting those flavors.

As we weave through the streets, I spot Dolion outside a tavern, deep in conversation with a hooded figure. The way they stand, tense and uncomfortable, makes it clear this isn't a casual chat. I can't make out the face, but my gaze catches other familiar ones. A few feet away, Kenji and Grifton sit at an outside table, drinking and playing a card game with some other men. Kenji grins widely and waves when he sees us. Grifton, surprisingly, looks relaxed. He lifts his mug in acknowledgment before whipping his head back and yelling about someone cheating while he was distracted.

We stop at a local perfume place, then the next, shopping for decorations and accessories. When he whisks me away from the shopping, the atmosphere switches the moment Roenis pulls me into a quieter part of the village. The warmth of the buzzing streets fade as we turn a corner, and an unnatural stillness settles around us. We stop in front of a small building. No lanterns hanging outside, no welcoming signs. The wooden door is aged but functional, its frame slightly warped with time. When we go inside, my nose is hit with dust. I swipe my hand in front of my face to rid of the particles, suppressing a cough.

"What shop is this?" I ask, covering my mouth.

"It's not a shop." His voice is strained now. "This was supposed to be the home of the first daughter your mother sent here."

I freeze. What? My words stuck in my throat.

So he *had* shown the others before me.

"I thought I was the only one you've shown the village to," I state, my voice filled with disappointment. I'm not sure why, but foolishly, I had felt special.

His gaze softens. He reaches forward, fingers tilting my chin up so I'm forced to meet his eyes. "She was here, yes. But under very different circumstances. You are the only one here with this much freedom. I brought you here to share a truth." His voice carries a rough edge, like guilt is choking him.

"What happened?" I whisper.

Instead of answering, he moves past me and pulls a heavy, stained curtain that covered a doorway. When he steps aside, my stomach lurches.

A bed sit in the center of the room, draped in wilted flowers. The air feels stale, but my eyes lock onto the body wrapped in aged linens, mummified by time. Chains lay slack against the corpse, a silent testament to what happened here.

Roenis grips the doorway. "When Maya sent the first daughter, her plan almost worked. I fell for her. I fell fast and hard. The night after the ball, on Sundial Solitical, I brought her here, told her she could stay in the village if she wanted. I believed we could create something new—meld our powers, find a way forward." He pauses, the memory thick in his throat. "But when the moment came, her demeanor changed. She lunged at me with the same dagger you carry. Stabbed me in the heart. Right here in this room."

His hand skates across his chest, rubbing absentmindedly at the spot. I feel sick.

"She was supposed to love me back for it to work," he continues. "But she never did. I realized in that moment, that I had been nothing but a pawn in her game. And when the blade didn't kill me, something inside her cracked. Her eyes glazed over, like she wasn't in control of her body anymore. Then she turned the dagger on herself." His voice is barely a whisper now. "She died in my arms. The dagger faded away after that, almost like transport magic."

The room presses in around me. I can't breathe.

"It was always a lose-lose situation," I mutter. "I was meant to die either way."

Roenis grips my arms, holding me in place as his silver eyes burn into mine. "No. I'm tired of her controlling the narrative. I wanted you to know the truth. You *are* different."

I shake my head, my vision blurring. "Stop. You knew the whole time, didn't you?" My voice cracks. "Why didn't you stop me when you saw the dagger in the tavern?"

His lips forms into a broken smile, but there was no amusement in it. "Because you were bold. Fiery. Different. I felt your magic, Syra. I never felt that with the others. I wanted to give you a chance, but I had to have a few precautions in place first."

The air. It was constricting. I'm trying to remain calm but I feel like I'm drowning.

As the tears stream down my face, the reality of how little I actually know slams into my gut. Every carefully laid belief, every lesson drilled into me by my mother, crumbles into dust beneath the weight of this truth.

If I fall for him and kill him, I die. If I fail, I die by my own hand. My entire existence was never my own. It's a cycle of predetermined fate, twisting into something I have no power over. The world I think I understand, the one I fight for, is nothing more than a carefully crafted illusion.

And Roenis... Roenis, who is suppose to be the

monster in this tale, has been mourning a woman who was sent to kill him. He had preserved her, kept her here, not as a trophy but as a solemn reminder of what had been taken from him. He isn't the villain in this story.

I am. Or at least, I was supposed to be.

A tremor wracks my bones, my vision splintering as I try to comprehend it all. My voice breaks as I speak, "Why do you do this? One moment, you're distant and unreadable. The next, you're teasing and playful. And then, suddenly, you're honest, giving me truths that shake the very foundation of what I know. It's like I'm being lured in, only to be pushed away. I can't tell what's real with you. I feel like I'm constantly set up."

He lets out a sharp breath. "You shatter all of my expectations. Everything I thought I knew is also questioned with you. Every time I think I have you figured out, you prove me wrong. I expect you to lash out, to fight me at every turn, but instead, there are moments you care and you see things others refuse to. And it terrifies me." His voice deepens, a rare vulnerability threading through it. "I don't want you blind to the truth, Syra. I don't want you caught in the chaos, or become a pawn to someone else's game. So I give you the truth, even if it hurts. Even if it drives you away, because you deserve to know."

A sob bubbles up in my throat, my hands trembling as I step backward. I can't do this. Not now. Not with him standing here, looking at me like I'm something different, something new. I need space.

I tear myself away from his grasp, chest constricting with heavy breaths. "I need air." I turn and bolt from the room, the deafening sound of my own heartbeat pounding in my ears.

He doesn't follow me as I stumble out into the streets, winding my way back to the castle. I barely registered the journey. By the time I reach my chambers, my body feels hollow.

◆

I stay in my room for three days. Three days of silence, of lying in bed staring at the ceiling, trying to reconcile everything I thought I knew with what I had learned. My stomach remains empty, the untouched trays of food piling up as the hours pass. My body aches from stillness, my mind twisting in endless loops of doubt and revelation.

Roenis leaves me alone. I appreciate it, yet I resent the emptiness it leaves behind. His presence had been a constant, an infuriating compelling force I have come to rely on. Without him, the silence feels smothering.

Datura visits sporadically. Sometimes she knocks, other times she enters without permission, her presence filling the room as she places food beside me, only to sigh when I never touch it. On the second night, she sits at the edge of my bed, tapping her fingers impatiently against her thigh.

"You're really going to waste away in here? That's not like you," her tone frustrated. "Whatever Roenis did this time, I'm sure you can stab him later. But for now, eat something."

I remain still, cringing inside at the word stab. I distract myself by just watching the shifting patterns of shadows against the ceiling.

By the third night, her patience cracks. She storms in, not bothering to knock, and flops onto the bed beside me with a dramatic huff. "Alright, I've let you brood long enough. Tomorrow, you're getting up."

I blink, finally turning my head to look at her. My voice rasped from disuse. "Tomorrow?"

She smirks. "Yes. Because tomorrow night, you have a ball to attend. And I'll be here in the morning to make sure you don't weasel your way out of it."

My stomach twists. Shit. The ball. I had nearly forgotten. A long silence diminishes the conversation. And then, for the first time in three days, I find myself exhaling, releasing some of the weight pressing against my chest.

Datura grinned. "Good. That means you're listening. Now, get some sleep. You'll need it."

That next morning, Datura returns, grinning as she throws open my wardrobe. "Thank the Gods, you're sitting up. Now, we have work to do. I'm about to make you the shiniest star at this party."

I watch her carry out two dresses, the pit in my stomach deepening.

S. C. Rafael

This day is going to be exhausting.

CHAPTER TWENTY-THREE
Roenis

The grand hall of the castle has been transformed. Lights everywhere curling around the twisting chandeliers. The walls, usually hidden with darkness, gleam with the enchanting lanterns I use within my village, casting soft pulses of silver light. Tables are draped in dark silks, their surfaces adorned with goblets and intricately carved dishes, each containing delicacies from every domain to impress the other Gods and Goddesses.

I stand in the center of the room, surveying the final touches with arms crossed. The scent of roasted meats, spiced wines, and sweet pastries fill the air, mingling with the natural cold air that lingers in my kingdom.

My mind though, is completely occupied with Syra. I haven't seen her in days. Not since the moment in the village. I haven't gone to visit her, I was giving her the space she needed. I shouldn't have pushed so much information on her. I felt like she needed to know everything. A part of me wanted her to know the whole truth and maybe that would finally break the cycle.

"Everything is in place," Datura's voice comes from my left, breaking my thoughts. She is dressed in an elegant deep-red gown embroidered with black thorns. Her brown curls pinned up and filled with red gems to match. "The musicians are ready, Asani's staff have been briefed, and the invitations were confirmed. Every divine ruler of significance will arrive, except for the Kingdom of Dreams. They're sending Orson in their stead."

Of course. They already have Syra here.

"And the food?" I ask, my gaze finding Asani in the crowd. "Perfectly prepared," she confirms, hands on her hips. "No complaints will be had tonight."

I nod, satisfied. "And… Syra?"

Datura smiles. "She's better, and she will be the star of tonight. I did my best work on her."

I nod again. Nervous to see her, but also filled with anticipation. These past three days have felt like hell without her. My gaze shifts toward Dolion, standing just beyond the entrance, quiet as always. He barley moves, his expression unreadable, watching the setup and waiting for something to go wrong.

Datura gives a knowing hum, but her attention goes toward the grand doors. "It's time. Should I open the portal?"

I start to take my place at the doors, "Yes, please."

Moments pass and then the great bells from the top of my castle toll outside, signaling the official beginning of the ball. The main doors creak open, and as if on command, the portals magic flares and the first wave of attendees enter. Gowns of all colors and styles sweep across the polished marble floors. Some guests greet one another with warm embraces, while others nod in silent acknowledgment of long-standing rivalries.

My ballroom, despite the darkness, comes alive.

I make my way near the head of the hall, greeting each guest with a nod. The Gods and Goddesses of Balance, Time, Peace, and Wrath all make their presence known. Sage approaches first, clapping a hand on my shoulder in a familiar gesture. "A fine evening, Roenis. You outdid yourself."

I merely smirk. "I always do."

As the mingling begins, I keep my senses sharp, waiting. Searching. Still no Syra.

Instead, a hush ripples through the ballroom as Sesha steps into the hall, her aura a slow, inescapable force. The Goddess of time, and yet she seems untouched by it. She is sculpted with molten brown skin, shimmering with a life of its own. Her black and gold hair cascades in waves down her back, catching the lantern light as though the strands themselves contain shifting sands.

The golden tattoos that swim over her skin aren't merely decoration. They move, change and form intricate patterns of power, like time itself obeys her flesh. Her accessories all shaped from sand and gold. A masterful display of control. Of dominance.

And of course, it isn't just the magic that makes her dangerous. It's the way she holds herself in high regard, the way her lips curve—not in amusement, but in knowing. Sesha always knows.

Beside her stands a younger version of the Goddess, a girl barely stepping into her own power, but already carrying the weight of time in her gaze. Avia. The same molten skin, the same hair kissed by gold and darkness, but the uncertainty in her stance betrays her youth. A single mole marks her left cheek, an imperfection, but still striking, as if the universe paused for a moment when crafting her, leaving a trace of hesitation.

Sage stands motionless beside me, his gaze lingering on Avia, revealing his emotions he likely wishes to conceal. I know that longing.

Leaning in, I whisper, "Go ahead. Don't let me stop you."

His head snaps in my direction, his expression disciplined, yet not quick enough to erase the flicker of hesitation. "I'd better go assist. I *am* mentoring her daughter. Nothing more."

I smirk, swirling the drink in my glass. "Of

course, Sage. We wouldn't want to tip the delicate scales of balance, now would we?"

His glare is the only response before he strides away.

I take a slow sip from my glass, trying to disguise my interest, though I know better than to underestimate either of them. Sesha's presence alone is enough to alter the course of this evening. And now, with her daughter at her side, she has something new to wield. Legacy. And legacy, in the wrong hands, is a weapon far sharper than any blade.

The room swells with movement and excitement, as more guests cascade in, and at last, the final two realms make their entrance.

Ira arrives like a wildfire consuming dry earth. Fiery, untamed, and demanding attention with nothing more than a step over the threshold. The scent of burning embers lick the air, the room itself bracing for impact. Her bright orange hair tumbles in fierce streaks, framing a face sculpted by war, her skin kissed with the hue of red, like smoldering coals. But it's her right hand that truly speaks of what she is, a warrior, a weapon, a warning. Fully red, from her wrist to the wicked, elongated talons that could rip through flesh and bone easily. She doesn't wear gloves. She never hides what she is.

Ira revels in it.

Her gaze sweeps the ballroom, landing on me for a brief moment. Her stare searing. The corner of her mouth twitches, as if she could already taste the violence beneath my skin. A dance of destruction, waiting for its cue.

She moves, and the world moves around her. And then, the universe itself sought balance, Callum enters.

Where Ira is fire, Callum is a quiet snowfall. His presence a cooling balm, a steady breeze that softens the embers she leaves in her wake. Milky white skin, untouched by turmoil, and curls the color of a calm sea, framing a face so serene it looks unnatural.

Then there are his eyes, bright blue crystal, cutting through the crowd, like he can see beyond skin and bone, beyond masks and whispered plots. He walks with a kind of measured grace, a peace that isn't fragile, but a force, gentle and unshakable.

Wrath and Peace, arriving separately, yet never truly apart.

Now, the ball has finally became interesting.

But one piece is still missing.

Syra.

I already spot Orson, her combat trainer, according to Datura's research. And on cue as usual, Datura reappears at my side, giddy with anticipation.

"She's coming."

Two simple words, yet they send a slow current through my veins. I have known she would come, yet nothing could have prepared me for the sight of her.

She wears the fabric I had acquired for her. That beautiful sheer material that seems to trap moonlight within its threads. The shades of blue and violet wrapping around her skin like mist, delicate and impossibly alluring. The way it glows with every movement, making her appear dreamlike. Such a perfect fit for a Goddess like her.

Her white hair has been styled in soft waves, half-pinned with golden strands fanning out like splintered sun rays. But it's her eyes, violet pools of power that grip me as she surveys the room, searching.

Is it me she looks for?

She lifts her gown slightly as she moves through the crowd, her grace effortless, unbothered by the weight of the attention she commands.

I exhale slowly, steadying myself as the room seems to still. The air thickens around me as my gaze devours every detail of her.

Radiant. Dangerous. Utterly mesmerizing.

"Careful," Datura murmurs near my ear, amusement in her tone. "Stare too long, and she might gain the upper hand."

I force a slow smirk. "She already has the upper hand."

Then, Syra smiles. A smile I had never seen before. And it isn't for me. I follow her gaze to Orson.

A sharp pang of the unexpected curls in my gut.

Jealousy.

She places her hand on his arm, whispering something. His eyes look toward me, his expression harsh. But Syra wastes no time, she turns and walks toward me.

The mingling has begun. Conversations trickle across the ballroom, laughter flowing through the towering banners of deep black. I watch her navigate the crowd with precision, offering only the faintest nods in acknowledgment, her true focus set on one thing.

Me.

And before I can stop myself, I move.

The crowd parts effortlessly in my wake, my stride singular in its purpose.

When we meet, a different emotion shines in her violet gaze. "Roenis."

Gods, my name from her lips. A sound I want to hear again. And again.

"Syra," I purr, savoring the syllables like they belong only to me. I extend my hand to her. "Dance with me."

A beat of silence.

The world shrinking to the space between us.

Syra studies me, her lips curving into the barest hint of a smile as she places her hand in mine.

I lead her toward the center of the ballroom, where the first notes of an enchanting melody rises through the air. As our fingers entwine, I pull her in closer, her warmth seeping into me. We move. And the others follow.

CHAPTER TWENTY-FOUR
Roenis

She is elegant. She is beautiful. And she smells of my favorite flowers.

Spinning and dancing with her feels like something I shouldn't enjoy, but here I am, holding her close, reveling in the way her body fits with mine. Her pale blue skin seems to glow by the cascading lights above. The embroidery of her gown twinkles like stars with each step. She looks weightless, unburdened. But I still see the lines in her face.

The tension from the past three days still clinging to her, hiding underneath. Yet, as we dance, her face starts to soften and relax. Whatever conclusion she reached in these past three days, I need to know.

I pull her in slightly closer, so that my lips brush against her ear. "You look radiant," I whisper, "How are you feeling?"

I feel her shiver, and the warmth forming on her neck does not go unnoticed.

"I've had time to process," she admits, her voice hushed, "I should thank you for the information, but it feels wrong to."

I spin her out, the fabric of her gown swirling around before pulling her back into my arms. "Nonsense," I counter, "I told you, you deserved to know."

She hesitates, then nods. "Well then, thank you."

We sway, lost in the slow rhythm of the music, our bodies aligning in a far more intimate embrace than intended. Her eyes searches mine, she looks utterly exposed, almost vulnerable in a way she never allows herself to be with me. It's a dangerous kind of vulnerability. One that beckons me closer, draws me deeper. Everything feels different, I shouldn't be falling for her.

I lift my hand, brushing my fingers beneath her

chin, tilting her gaze upward. Her lips part, her breath catching with anticipation and restraint. For someone so adept at masking her emotions, she let this moment breathe. Let me see her. As if she wants this too.

My pulse thunders in my ears. My thumb swiping over her bottom lip, resisting the urge to close the distance. I start to lean in, but the music changed right at the opportunity. The moment now broken.

She blinks, and clears her throat. She takes a step back. "Sorry, I need something to drink." Her voice is rough, but not unkind. More like she needs to regain control.

She maneuvers around me and disappears into the sea of bodies, her dress trailing behind her like liquid light. I exhaled, dragging a hand through my hair as I watch her retreat.

Sesha stands near the refreshments, her dark eyes locking onto me. A knowing sneer plays on her lips, and when I meet her gaze, she lifts a single brow.

I scoff under my breath and follow after Syra.

I weave through the crowd, each step pulling me to her. My hands itching to grab her, to pull her back into that fleeting moment, but I know she needs space.

By the time I reach the refreshment table, she has already claimed a goblet of golden wine, her fingers gripping the stem. She takes a slow sip, her posture straight, but the tension in her shoulders is obvious.

I grab my own drink and linger beside her. "There's no pressure tonight," I say, my voice gentle. "You don't have to force yourself to enjoy this."

She lets out a quiet, humorless laugh. "Oh, but that's the problem, isn't it?" She scans the now dancing crowd. "Everyone here knows the Dream Kingdom doesn't attend these balls. And yet, here I am. Expected to act as if nothing is out of place, while every God and Goddess in this room watches my every move."

She looks away, her fingers tightening around the goblet. "It feels like I've been lied to for so long. And now I'm just supposed to pretend? To have this feeling bubble up inside until it burst?"

My jaw clenches. I hate that she feels like a spectacle. "Then let me introduce you around," I suggest. "Let them see you as you are, not as what they think they know."

She waits, considering. Then, with a small nod, she brings her goblet to her lips again. Taking a generous sip. "Fine. But if anyone makes a comment I don't like, I'm throwing this drink in their face."

I laugh. "I wouldn't expect anything less."

I guide her through the ballroom, the silk of her gown brushing against my side as we weave through the dance floor. Whispers follow us, but I ignore them, keeping my focus on her.

The first God we approach is Sage. He stands near a column, dressed in flowing robes of muted gray and brown, the image very fitting. His soft, orange eyes glide over Syra before he dips his head in greeting.

"We meet again Goddess," he muses. "No glamour this time I see."

Syra lifts her chin. "Figured there was no point in pretending anymore."

His lips twitch. "Indeed. It suits you better. It's a nice surprise to see you at the ball, I do enjoy a good mystery."

"I do as I like, as you're aware." she admits.

Sage chuckles. "That, I believe." He studies her for a moment longer before nodding approvingly. "You are more than just whispers in the dark, Goddess Syra. It is a pleasure to *officially* meet you."

As we move on, I glance at her. "He's probably the most trustworthy of the realm."

She rolls her eyes. "He's your friend it seems, so that's biased"

Callum is next. He greets her with warmth and an easy smile. He asks about the Dream Kingdom, his tone genuine, his interest sincere. The conversation not lasting long, due to his people-pleasing antics.

Then there is Ira. She assesses Syra with narrowed eyes before smirking. "Pretty bold of you to finally attend a ball. I like your confidence, but is there fire to match?"

"I think you'll find I'm not lacking in that department," Syra replies coolly.

Ira laughs, a sharp, delighted sound. "Good. You might just survive here after all, I would like to see that fire someday."

Their conversation seems to carry a tad but longer

than I want it to. Clearly she's made a friend within Ira. Figures, since they are both fiery women.

Finally, we reach Sesha. The last Goddess I want to be around. Her eyes gleams with curiosity as she regards Syra. "This is certainly unexpected," she faintly states, swirling her drink. "The Goddess of Dreams, or *almost* I should say, finally among us."

I feel Syra slightly stiffen. "It seems I've been kept in the dark for far too long."

Sesha tilts her head. "Yes. And I imagine you have many questions."

"I do."

"Then perhaps you should start asking."

The air around them shakes with intensity, and I watch as Syra squares her shoulders, preparing for the answers. I pinch the bridge of my nose, already annoyed with Sesha, but I keep my distance, letting Syra take the lead.

She takes her in for a beat before speaking. "You've lived through many centuries, haven't you?"

Sesha smirks, intrigued but not yet cautious. "A few."

"And in those centuries, I imagine you've seen much. Heard even more." She hints. "Have you ever crossed paths with my mother?"

Sesha's expression doesn't shift. Too clever for that. "Maya?" she drawls, dragging out the name as if it's just floating in her mind carelessly. "Of course. We're not strangers."

"Not strangers." Syra repeats the words lightly, as if turning them over. "So, you've spoken?"

Sesha exhales something between a chuckle and a sigh. "A handful of times. But you know how Maya is. She moves where she's needed, and isn't always forthcoming, even with her own kind."

It's an elegant way to say nothing.

Syra doesn't buy it. I can see it in the slight shift of her stance, the way her fingers curls around the sides of her dress. She isn't asking out of curiosity. No, this is about something else. Something she'd recently learned.

"And in all those times you spoke," Syra continues, "did she ever mention what she was working toward?"

Sesha hums. "You make it sound as if she has

some grand scheme."

Syra holds her gaze. "Doesn't she?"

For a fraction of a second, something shadows across Sesha's face. Not surprise, no, she's too composed for that. But I know how to spot someone weighing their words.

"She has always been... a visionary," Sesha states carefully. "But you would know more about her ambitions than I would."

A clever redirection.

"And yet, you don't seem surprised by the idea that she had ambitions at all."

Sesha smiles, but there is an edge to it now. "Mothers often do, don't they?"

A dangerous answer. One that says everything and nothing.

Syra's shoulders squares. "Have you ever met the others?"

The shift is subtle, but I catch it. The slight part of Sesha's lips before she covers it with a sip of her drink.

"The others?" she echoes.

"My sisters," Syra clarifies. "The ones who came

before me."

A beat passed before Sesha gave her an indulgent smile. "You're quite inquisitive."

"You deflected."

Another soft hum leaves Sesha's throat, the sound playful. She lowers her glass, considering. "I suppose I did. But in truth, I haven't had the pleasure of meeting them. I'm afraid your mother kept them quite hidden."

Another carefully chosen phrase.

Syra's voice dips. "But you knew about them."

Sesha's smile deepens, a sinister knowing in her expression. "I know many things, Syra. But I'm afraid I don't keep a running list of all the gods and goddesses your mother may, or may not, have created."

Liar. She keeps track of everyones time.

Syra doesn't flinch, but her throat does bob as she swallows her frustration. Sesha is slipping through her fingers like sand, giving her just enough to stay engaged but never enough to grip.

And then, Sesha pivots.

"But I must admit," she murmurs, eyes gliding

over me with an almost lazy amusement, "it is fascinating, watching the way you look at him."

Shit.

Syra blinks, thrown off balance. "What?"

Sesha takes her time with her next sip of wine before elaborating. "Roenis." She lets my name settle like a casual afterthought. "You carry yourself like someone who knows exactly what she's doing. And yet..." She trails off, studying Syra with something akin to amusement.

Syra stiffens, her grip tightening on her glass. "And yet what?"

"And yet, I wonder if you realize how obvious it is."

Syra's brows pulls together. "Obvious?"

"The way your magic bends toward him. The way your gaze lingers a second longer than necessary." Sesha's voice is light, but there is a weight of precision that makes it clear she is not speaking idly. "Curious, isn't it?"

I watch Syra's throat bob again, this time for an entirely different reason.

"I think you're mistaken," Syra says, a touch too

quickly.

"Oh, perhaps," Sesha muses, unconvinced. "But I do so enjoy being right."

Syra's lips part as if to refute her again, but she hesitates. Her uncertainty clear, and the briefest pause where her mind is working faster than she can speak.

Interesting.

Sesha lets the silence stretch before she leans back with an effortless air. "I wouldn't worry too much, though. A bit of chemistry never hurt anyone. Well... most of the time." She winks.

Syra shakes her head as if dismissing the notion entirely, but the damage is done.

Sesha has planted the thought. She knows exactly what she is doing.

I set my glass down with a quiet clink, watching Syra regain her composure. I should have intervened. Should have stepped in to steer the conversation elsewhere. But she wouldn't have liked that.

"Enjoy the ball, Roenis." Sesha states as she walks away, her soft chuckle making it clear she knew enough.

I reach for Syra's arm, but she shrugs me off.

"I need to speak with Orson. Excuse me."

And just like that, she's gone again, moving with the kind of purpose that leaves no room for hesitation. A determination burning beneath her skin that can overtake anything, or anyone, that stands in her way.

CHAPTER TWENTY-FIVE
Syra

My body shakes with rage.

Sesha. I recognized her instantly. I've seen her roaming in my kingdom with my mother before, she stood hidden but her golden tattoos give her away. She assumed she was unnoticed then, but seeing her tonight confirms those previous suspicions. Something is wrong. Something is forming, and she knows it. A small, nagging voice in my head speaks, what if she's working with my mother? My mother did say she had people in place. How many? How deep does this web stretch?

It makes me wonder if she set up fail-safes. If Sesha is one of them.

I'll give her credit. Every question I asked, Sesha wove around them like a snake in the sand, twisting her words so they gave the illusion of an answer.

I wonder if Roenis feels the same about her. She may or may not be part of the plan. I'm not even sure if *I* want to be part of it anymore.

The certainty I once held in this mission is slipping through my fingers. This plan suddenly feels fragile—like brittle glass that will shatter under scrutiny. Every contradiction, every misunderstanding, every mistake gnaws at me.

And Roenis, I can no longer see him as the villain. I don't think he ever was.

Across the room, Orson watches me, his posture deceptively casual, but his gaze—his eyes always betrays his thoughts. He saw my conversation with Sesha. He saw me dance with Roenis. If she suspects my feelings, then I have no doubt Orson does as well.

I move toward him, my steps delicate as I approach him. The moment I reach him, he pulls me into a hug. He felt warm, familiar, but the embrace did carry an unspoken warning.

"I see you've made yourself at home," he remarks, his tone light, but the meaning behind it unmistakable.

"Well, isn't that what I'm supposed to do?" I challenge, testing him.

His hesitation clear in his stance. A tell. There's something he isn't telling me.

"With the way things look," he says carefully, "I think you've made your position here pretty clear. I just hope you know what you're doing and that you're sticking to the plan. Your mother has eyes everywhere."

A cold chill creeps down my spine.

"Speaking of eyes, would Sesha be among those under my mother's thumb?"

Orson's expression hardens for just a moment before a spec of approval crosses his features. "I don't know. Your mother keeps her true allegiances well guarded. But I do like that you're questioning things. You've handled Roenis differently than expected. He looks almost tame around you. But that doesn't mean you're safe."

The words should feel like a warning, but instead

they fuel my frustration. "I am being careful. And I've learned more here than I was ever allowed to know back home. You, of all people, should have told me the truth. Instead, I was raised in the dark, told half-truths and forced obedience. Now, I wonder, does my mother even have the full picture of the situation, or is this just one of her selfish pursuits?" I pause, weighing the next sentence before speaking it. "Let him do his magic, and we do ours. Maybe working together wouldn't be a bad thing."

Orson's eyes widen slightly, his lips pressing together. He looks down at his drink, swirling it absently. There's sadness there. A weariness. I wonder if he's thinking of the daughters who came before me. Of the ones who failed.

Is he afraid I'll fail too? Not because I lack the skill, but because I no longer want this?

"Syra," he says quietly, "I know you're strong. And I know you're smart. But I want you to make the right decision. I don't want you hurt. Or worse." He swallows, as if the words are bitter. "I've seen this play out too many times. I'm here to ensure your mother's plan stays on course. It's not that we haven't said the truth, but some things are better left in the dark.

My blood boils. "Tell my mother she doesn't need to worry about me." My voice is ice cold and venomous. "Not like she ever gave a fuck about me before." I take a step closer, eyes locking on his. "And you can quote me when you tell her—I know *everything*."

Orson stares at me, but I soon realize, maybe he doesn't know the full truth either.

I don't say another word. I pat his shoulder to give him some sort of reassurance, but it still feels dismissive. I turn away from the music, the laughter, the celebrations and I let it all fade as I walk to the staircase leading to my room.

Once inside, I close the door and sink to the ground, hugging my knees to my chest. I don't cry. I don't break. I just sit in the suffocating silence, lost in the weight of it all.

I let an hour go by. Maybe two. The silence feels like a nice break, but I still never get off the ground.

A soft knock makes me finally lift my head.

"Datura, I'm not in the mood," I say, my voice barely above a whisper.

A beat of silence. Then, a voice I recognize instantly. A voice that sends a slow, traitorous heat curling through my body.

"Well, it's a good thing I'm not Datura."

My heart kicks against my ribs. I rise slowly and crack the door open just enough to see him. Roenis stands there, a faint smile tugging at his lips.

"I'm not going back down there," I say, defiantly.

His smile softens. "No need. The ball's over. The guests are gone." He tilts his head. "Put something comfortable on. I want to show you something."

I narrow my eyes as I crack the door a little more open. He already changed into simple black clothing. Damn, I must've been sulking longer than I thought. "You always have something to show me. Pretty sure I've seen it all by now."

His grin was all teeth and sharp canines. "Everything?"

Gods he's beautiful. "What are you suggesting?"

His silver eyes trace over me and the stress of the night dissolves, leaving something warmer in its wake. Something dangerous.

"Get dressed," he murmurs. "Meet me out here when you're done and find out."

I slam the door shut so fast I nearly catch my own fingers. My heart is a traitor, pounding like a war drum. I run over and practically tear through my wardrobe, slipping into black leggings and a simple blouse. When I step outside, he's waiting with his arm crossed. He gives a small laugh at my eagerness and motions to follow.

As we walk through the corridors, his body language changes, more fidgety. It's not uncomfortable, but I can feel that he's nervous.

That, more than anything, catches me off guard.

Roenis. The God of Nightmares. Nervous.

I glance at him out of the corner of my eye. "If you're taking me somewhere to make a move on me, you could at least look less anxious about it."

He exhales a laugh. "I'm pretty sure if that were the case, I would've kept you in that delicious dress you wore."

"Oh, well, that's comforting." I blush.

Fuck. I suck at flirting.

His lips twitch. He hesitates for just a second before speaking, "I don't show this place to anyone. I figure after that night in the village, and how you were tonight, I can trust you enough to explore it."

That stops me in my tracks. He turns slightly, watching me as the realization dawns.

His library.

He's taking me to his library.

A place sacred to him. A place no one else has been allowed to step foot in. Besides his council I assume.

The tension changes. My pulse stirs with something new. Anticipation. Curiosity.

CHAPTER TWENTY-SIX
Syra

Roenis stops just before the grand golden doors of the library. His hand hovering over the ornate handle, fingers twitching as though hesitating to cross some invisible threshold. His shoulders tighten, and for a brief moment, his silver eyes meet mine, swirling with an unspoken conflict. Then, he closes them and draws in a deep, measured breath.

"Just please understand this room means a lot to me. This isn't a game, Syra. I'm trusting you with something I've never shared before." His voice is vulnerable, a stark contrast to the playful tone he was just giving me.

Without waiting for my response, he pushes the

heavy doors open. The groan of the hinges reverberates through the hallway, and those whispers I heard before flood back, as if the library itself is waking from slumber. The magic doesn't even *try* to keep him out.

The sight that greets me silences any words trying to surface. Rows upon rows of towering shelves stretches endlessly, each meticulously looks like they were designed by the most divine gods. The designs are luminescent and radiant like moonlight. Not a single shelf bears an empty space; every inch is crammed with books of all sizes, shapes, and colors, each one pulsing faintly with its own inner magic. The one attribute I notice the most, is that they glow.

The light in the room has a bold golden gleam emanating from unseen sources, but it's enough to illuminate the entire library. The shelves themselves seem alive, their surfaces smooth yet textured, and the playful curiosity in the air alone, tempts me to read them. They feel like whispers, taunting me with secrets they want to share.

I step past Roenis, whose imposing figure lingers

in the doorway, his hesitation stark against the vibrancy of the room. Behind him, the scarlet walls frame the golden doors in bold, dramatic contrast, amplifying his shadowed presence. The rich, blood-red hues intensifying his dark energy, making him appear both out of place and perfectly at home.

I take a long glance down the rows, and no matter how far down I can see, the end isn't in site. "It's… endless," I mumble, my voice almost drowning by the gravity of the space.

I wander deeper, my fingers brushing the carved edges of a nearby shelf. The faint hum vibrates on my fingers, the power coursing through the very wood. My eyes drift over the books, each cover unique. Some adorned with swirling patterns, others embedded with crystals or etched with runes. Suddenly the room shifts, switching of shelves and turning over books. I thought something went wrong, or I touched the wrong shelf, because everything starts changing.

Roenis' voice breaks through my reverie. "It's magic. Portal magic, to be precise. The room's designed to hold more than it appears." He crosses the space to a nearby table, where he picks up a violet book with black, vein-like patterns stretching across its surface. Its glow is a soft lavender, and I feel a magnetic pull toward it. Whispers brush the edges of my mind, delicate and enticing.

Open me.

Read me.

Explore. Escape. Discover.

"This one is yours," Roenis says, his voice pulling me from the trance. His silver eyes gleaming with slight reluctance. It's like he didn't want to show me it in the first place.

I blink, trying to focus. "What do you mean, mine?" My voice a pitch higher, lighter, as though the room is engulfed with enchantment, making me submit.

He holds the book just out of my reach. "These books hold a person's nightmares and fears. But they're more than that. They contain their desires, their memories, their entire being. Nightmares can guide people, shape their fate. I give them their most deepest, darkest wants and desires. Fantasies they never knew they needed." He skims his finger down the spine of my book and I shiver. It's like I feel it myself. My veins are hot, pumping scorching blood throughout my body. All I want to do is look inside.

I take an unsteady step, my hand reaching instinctively toward the book. The whispers grow louder, more insistent, but before I can touch it, he pulls it back. I suddenly feel vapors holding me down and pulling me right into a chair. My actions definitely give me away, and Roenis no doubt, can read my desires. I've experienced that first hand.

"No." His tone was firm. "You can't read your own book, Syra. It's fickle and dangerous. The magic is… unpredictable. Reading it can alter the contents—your memories, your destiny. It can trap you in a trance so deep you'd never find your way out."

I swallow hard, the weight of his words sinking in. "Then why keep them? Why have an entire library of books if they're so dangerous? Can't you just conjure nightmares as needed?"

Roenis places my book back on the shelf, and as soon as he does, it vanishes, swallowed by the shifting rows. A pang of loss ripples through me, as though I've been severed from something vital.

"Because they matter," he says quietly. "You might not fully believe me, but I care for them. Each book is a life, a story. They're fragile, and in the wrong hands, they can wreak unimaginable havoc. I keep them safe, not because I enjoy what they contain, but because I understand their importance." His voice softens, and I see the weight he carries. I see the burden of a power he never asked for. "I've learned that life shouldn't always be cursed or filled with suffering. Sometimes I envy your power to give joy in dreams. It's why I want to work together." He explains with a sigh. The raw vulnerability in his expression pierces through every lie I'd been told about him. He isn't the monster my family had painted him to be. He is something else entirely. Something more.

My chest tightens, my heart hammering in a rhythm I've gotten used to. I don't believe he thrives on the pain of others. Everything I've learned in the time so far I've spent here, is that he is caring, passionate and he just wants peace for his people and for the souls out in the world. The bastard even found a loophole of giving them desires instead of just nightmares.

When did my pretending turn real? When did the lines blur between my mission and desire? I want him. Not as a mission, not as a means to an end. I want him—all of him. I just desire to...

"Please stop." His voice is a strained groan. "*Gods*, I can feel it from here."

Heat floods my cheeks. I forgot again he can sense my desires. "I... I'm sorry. It's just the room. It's... messing with me." My words tumble out in a stammer, and I turn quickly, my steps faltering as I move to a different shelf.

Gods, Syra get your shit together.

"Can I read others?" I ask, desperate to change the subject. "Is that dangerous too?"

Roenis appears behind me in an instant, his body a shadow that wraps around me like a shroud. He reaches for a book above my head, the motion bringing him impossibly close. The veins on his forearm pulse, magic thrumming in his blood. His scent envelopes me, and I fight to steady my breathing.

"You can," he says, his voice low. "As long as you don't try to alter or destroy them."

I duck beneath his arm, desperate to escape the tension climbing between us, but the moment is already slipping out of my control. The weight of his gaze, the unspoken intensity in the air, is pulling us closer to something inevitable.

He walks towards the table and takes a seat, signaling me to do the same. Once I do, I reach for the book he's holding, and as our fingers brush, the magic surges. A pulse of energy sends shivers down my spine. The room flips, the shelves shift, and the air feels like it's fleeting. Everything blurs in my vision.

When the world comes back into focus, I'm lying in a field of swaying purple hyacinths, their petals glowing under a dark, starless sky. Roenis is beside me, his hand firm on my arm. It *feels* like a dream, but slightly darker. He isn't suppose to have this power, yet again, I feel that darker itch in its edges.

"Don't speak. Don't touch anything. Just observe." His voice booms his demand that brooks no argument.

In the distance, a black log cabin looms, its windows flooding with light. As we approach, the sounds begin. Soft moans grow louder, blending with harsher noises like slaps, cracks, and guttural cries. The atmosphere thickens with each step, and grows electric.

When we reach the cabin, I hesitate, but Roenis nudges me forward, guiding me to the window. Inside, a scene unfolds that is both raw and hypnotic. A dark-haired woman with skin as dark and luscious as night itself, lays on a bed. Her skin is flushed and glistens with sweat. She writhes against a bed frame, her body taut with pleasure and pain. She bears deep red marks across her breasts. A man hovering over her, his movements swift, his touch both tender and punishing. The intimacy of it is slightly overwhelming, a visceral display that ignites something within me.

Roenis leans to where his mouth is inches from my ear. "You're blushing." His voice is a dark, teasing caress, and I buckle under its weight.

With my silence, I feel his smirk, but I can't tear

my gaze away from the scene unfolding before us. The man slides a piece of ice into his mouth, letting it melt a little before lowering his head between the woman's thighs. I can't see everything, but her reaction tells me what I need to know. Her body arches violently off the bed, a moan spilling from her lips so sensual, it feels like a prayer to the Gods themselves. The room grows heavy with the echoes of pleasure, and the heat of my own desires blacken the edges of my vision. I feel untethered, unmoored, and then…

We are thrown back. The shift so abrupt, I'm gasping for air. One moment, I was watching; the next, I'm standing with my back pressed against a bookcase, Roenis' body caging me in. His arms rest on either side of my head, his molten silver eyes burning into mine.

Our breaths come heavy, matching the charged silence between us. My face flushed, my skin prickling with the remnants of the heat we'd just witnessed. My magic swirls beneath my skin, scratching to rip out and touch him, to tether us even closer. The tension is unbearable at this point.

"How did we end up here? Weren't we sitting?" My voice was shaky, the question spilling out.

Roenis' eyes, smoldering with unspoken truths, drift lower, taking me in as though seeing me for the first time. "Sometimes you can wander when in the trance," he murmurs, his voice dark and unrestrained. "Bodies tend to follow desire in some cases." He chuckles lightly, though the sound is strained, like he is barely holding himself together. "Somehow, our bodies wandered closer. You felt something when you watched, and guilty enough, so did I when I saw your reaction." He pauses, his gaze lowers to my lips. "I had to pull us back before we… changed anything."

The way he says it, the weight of his words sends a shiver through me. My mind brings me back to the pantry. His gaze lingers so long on my mouth, and I can't stop myself. My tongue darts out to wet my lips, a reflex, but the way his eyes track the movement makes my pulse race. He feels it too. I can see his want in his eyes.

"What is it you desire? My surrender? My kingdom? My head on a platter for your family?"

The shift in his tone is subtle but still on edge, his body tensing as if bracing for a blow. He is looking for an out. His words cut deeper than I'd expected, and I tense up in response while looking down. The burden of his assumptions wedge into me, but they aren't true. Not anymore. I know he's in a state of weakness, but I no longer crave his death, or for his kingdom to fall. Everything he is, I strive to do the same with *my* kingdom, *my* people, and *my* dreams that I give. The truth of it settles heavily in my chest. I know what he needs to see. Slowly, I let my mask fall. I look back up, showing my vulnerability. I place my hand on his face. Letting the warmth of him caress my skin.

For a moment, there is nothing. And then, his gaze erupts, melding from a molten silver to a smoldering blaze of steel. He looks at me as if I am the most exquisite thing he has ever seen. If looks can devour, then he is starving.

He is right there, a mere inch away from my face. His beautiful piercing eyes. A sultry stare with heavy lids that blaze with infatuation. I try to keep my emotions in check, but his stare makes me squirm. Does he find me beautiful too? Does he prefer my real form?

He finally speaks. "Yes." I look up at him, wondering if it's my desire he responded to, but he continues. "My mind is invaded by you." He lifts his hand to my mouth and gently traces his finger over my bottom lip. Gods I love that. I feel my magic wanting to touch him. To curl its power around him, and never let him leave. His voice rumbles and interrupts my thoughts again.

"Every touch, ever whisper, every caress and surge of pleasure that stems from your mind, that you have of me and of us…I *feel* it. Even in your absence, you consume my every thought. All I can think of is seeing you ruined, breathless, and beneath me. But it's more than that, Syra. You've seeped into the cracks of my mind and claimed parts of me I didn't know existed. You've unraveled me in ways I can't explain, and no matter how much I try to fight it, I keep wanting you. Not just your body, but you—your fire, your defiance, even your sharp tongue. Every part of you is a torment I can't escape, and I'm not sure I want to anymore."

My heart flutters, and heat blooms in my chest, spreading down to where I press my thighs together in search of relief. The ache is almost painful now, my body craving something only he can give. My gaze drifts over him, slowly, hungrily—the sharp cut of his jaw, the silver in his eyes, the way his chest rises and falls as though he's holding himself back too.

"So what the fuck are you waiting for, Roenis?" My voice a challenge, tinging with need. "Let your desire take over and stop talking alre—"

I don't get to finish before his lips crash into mine.

CHAPTER TWENTY-SEVEN
Syra

The kiss is rough and unrestrained, a clash of heat and desperation. He holds nothing back this time, his tongue demanding entry, claiming me with every stroke. A moan escapes me as he deepens the kiss, the heat of it melting away every thought. He's no longer pretending to be the composed God. This is Roenis unleashed. He is power, primal, and utterly intoxicating.

His hand tangles in my hair, tugging just enough to make me gasp. The sound pulls a low groan from him, his eyes darkening as he pulls back to look at me. His gaze is so heated, so full of hunger, that it makes me even wetter. The realization that I'm the one who does this to him, that *I* make him lose control, and I give him desire, sends a wicked thrill through me.

He grips my thighs, lifting me effortlessly, and I instinctively wrap my legs around his waist. His approving growl vibrates against my chest as he presses me harder against the shelves. The tension between us coils tighter with every touch, every kiss. His hands roam, sliding up my back, gripping, claiming. My nails rake across his shoulders, desperate to hold on to something as he sets me on fire with his touch.

But I want more. I *need* more. I want control.

With a low grunt, he pulls us away from the shelves and strides to the table in the center of the room. He sets me down on the edge with a gentleness that contradicts the ferocity in his movements. He stands between my legs as they dangle, his hands bracing on either side of me, in that second, he just looks at me, his eyes tracing every inch of my face as though he's committing me to memory.

I place a hand on his chest, feeling the heat of his

skin through the fabric of his shirt. "Take this off," I whisper, my voice husky. I trail my finger down and I can feel his delicious fucking abs.

He doesn't argue. His hands move to the buttons of his black shirt, and with a quick movement, the garment is gone, discarded on the floor. I'm taken back at the sight before me. His chiseled chest is a masterpiece of muscle and skin, his gray tone smooth and gleaming like polished stone. Silver veins crossing his torso, uneven and wild, with a slight pulsing glow. They are alive with magic, and I can't resist reaching out to trace them.

"Gods, Roenis." I breathe. He's devastatingly beautiful, and the sheer power he exudes is enough to make anyone fall to their knees.

A wicked smile curves his lips. "Like what you see, pet?"

"Breathtaking." I purr. I push against his chest, guiding him down until he's on his knees before me. He doesn't resist; in fact, his smile widens, his sharp canines peaking out. His hands slide up my thighs, spreading them wider as he leans in close. I prop one leg over his shoulder, my smugness growing at the sight of him kneeling for me.

"Are you wanting another taste?"

His eyes darken, the silver swirling like liquid metal. "Careful what you ask for, Syra."

Before I can respond, his hands grip the waistband of my leggings and, with one swift motion, a few talons grow from his fingertips and he tears them apart. The sound of fabric ripping sends a jolt of excitement within me, and I barely have time to react before he lifts me again, spreading me out on the table.

His strength and speed is fucking exhilarating.

He looks up at me, his expression mixed with mischief and hunger. Vaporous tendrils of his magic swirl around his hands as he lifts a finger, directing the energy toward the apex of my thighs. Holding me open.

"Roenis!" I gasp, but it's too late. His mouth is on me, hot and insistent, his tongue flicking against my most sensitive spot with devastating precision. My head falls back, a moan tearing from my throat as the sensation overwhelms me. It's nothing like before. This isn't a tease; it's a feast, and I am the only thing he craves. It's almost animalistic the way he glides between my folds.

His low moan vibrates against me, the sound sending shockwaves through my body. His magic joins in, amplifying every touch, every stroke of his tongue. It's maddening, and I arch against him, my hands clutching at his hair, desperate to ground myself.

He slides a finger inside me, and that familiar zap of his power is instant. Heat rushes through me, and I whimper at the sensation.

"Too much?" he murmurs against my skin, his voice dripping with dark amusement.

"Never." I manage to gasp. But when another zap surges, I slap his hand away, needing a moment to catch my breath.

His head snaps up, his silver eyes blazing with something feral.

He.

Did not.

Like that.

"You shouldn't have done that." he growls, making my stomach do flips.

In a blur of motion, he's standing again, lifting me with purpose. My back slams against the shelves, and his lips find mine once more. The kiss is bruising, demanding, and I taste myself on him, the realization only stoking the fire within me.

"My pants are ruined, yours is still on, and somehow my shirt remains pristine," I say, breaking the kiss.

He chuckles, his grin flashing all of his sharp teeth. "Let's fix that."

With intentional slowness, he tugs at the strings of my blouse, peeling it from my body to reveal bare skin beneath. His gaze darkens further, and he leans in, his lips brushing my ear as he whispers, "Perfect."

Then he smiles. And I mean a full smile. Beautiful. He wraps my legs around his waist again to keep me steady, his strength a heady reminder of how completely he has me at his mercy. The way his hooded eyes rake over me, makes me forget any shred of modesty I have and my arousal floods through me.

His touch is unbearably tender, his fingers

brushing my skin with care that feels worshipping. The contrast of his earlier savagery and this gentleness made my breath hitch. He is a storm contained, dangerous and unpredictable, and yet his restraint feels even more torturous.

I try to shift the energy, wanting to spark the fire again. I try using a stronger sense of my magic, but the restricting bracelet on my wrist holds me back. Frustrated, I flex my hand, and his eyes drops to the shackle. Without hesitation, his fingers grip the clasp, and with a sharp snap, he breaks it apart. The sudden release of my magic energizing, my veins glowing faintly with power as purple vines weave around us. I stare at him, stunned, but don't give him time to rethink it. My vines shoot out and shred the rest of his clothing with complete accuracy.

"You're free now. Leaving me at your mercy Goddess." he utters, the truth in the statement written all over his face.

His hands slide along my thighs again, lifting me a fraction higher, as he presses me harder against the bookcase. One hand cupping my outer thigh, the other trailing up my side until it finds its place over my breast. He brushes his thumb across the peak, sending sparks shooting straight down. When, he lowers his head, his tongue traces a teasing path along the curve of my breast, circling my nipple until it pebbles beneath his attention. He finally takes it into his mouth, forcing a quiet squeal out of me, which then leads to my back arching into him.

He chuckles, the vibration making me tremble. "Such soft sounds from such a loud pet," he mutters against my nipple.

"Such tiny actions from such a big God," I shoot back.

He pulls back just enough to glare at me, his eyes flashing dangerously. "Tiny actions, hmm?" He purrs. And then I feel it—the hard length of him pressing against my thighs. He is anything but tiny. My bravado falters, a whimper slipping from my lips as my body responds to the sheer length of him.

"That's what I thought." he states smugly, his lips brushing my neck as he speaks. My hand reaches down instinctively, wrapping around him, and his response is immediate. His forehead falls to my shoulder, a guttural moan ripping from his throat as

I stroke him slowly. The sound alone, Gods, drives me insane. I don't even know if it's possible to get wetter. But this need is becoming unbearable.

"Such soft sounds from a loud God," I whisper, throwing his words back at him.

He laughs breathlessly, his voice tinging with both amusement and desperation. "You... drive me insane." His lips find mine again, his kiss searing and consuming. When I pull back, it's only to see the way his brows furrow, his lips parting slightly, and his chest heaving as I continue to work him with my hand. I stroke all the way to the base, and then back up swirling my thumb over his tip.

"Fuck, Syra." He groans. His hips move with my rhythm, chasing the friction, but it isn't enough for either of us. Watching him crumble is fucking stunning. His expressions, the heat of his breath on my collar, and his sounds of approval with my movements. This hold on his control gives me immense pleasure.

His hands grip my hips, shifting me until I have no choice but to wrap my legs tighter around him again. The movement is sudden that my arms fly to his shoulders for balance. He aligns himself with me, and for a moment, he doesn't move. His gaze locks onto mine, as if searching for any sign of doubt.

There is none.

I want this.

I want *him*.

As if seeing my approval, he pushes inside me, inch by inch. I realize just how much I crave him.

The stretch is exquisite, the mix of pleasure and pain making my legs shake. My fingers dig into his shoulders as I adjust to the fullness of him, every nerve in my body coming alive. He lets out a staggered breath, his self-control barely holding.

"Gods." He mutters, his voice straining. "If I don't start moving, I'll die of bliss just being inside you."

I manage a shaky laugh. "That would be unfortunate, seeing as I'm not done with you yet."

His lips twitch, but the humor in his expression doesn't last long. Slowly, agonizingly, he begins to move. Each thrust slow, his restraint irritating as he sets a pace that teases and torments us both.

"Tell me something, pet," he grumbles, his voice

distracted. "Something true. Something not rehearsed."

The question catches me off guard. I'm speechless, but the vulnerability in his voice, the way he looks at me as if my answer means everything, make the words spill out.

"I… I don't want to kill you. I just want you. All of you. I want something real."

His movements still, a second too long for my liking, but then he's kissing me again, harder this time. It's as if my confession has broken something in him. When he pulls back this time, his eyes burn with a want deeper than lust.

"Then take it," he growls. And with that, he begins to move with harder thrusts, his control shattering as he gives in to the wildness.

I cling to him, my fingers threading through his hair, my nails grazing his scalp. My moans turning into cries as he drives into me harder, faster, his pace relentless. My magic responds instinctively, curling around us both, amplifying every sensation until I'm drowning in him. I curl my fingers around his horns, the action rewarding me with Roenis' deep moan.

I feel my release building, but Gods, it feels too good to stop. I'm not ready to fall yet. I want this to be on my terms, for him to fall apart beneath me, not the other way around. So I let my magic wrap around his wrists, pinning them as I slow the pace.

His disapproving grunt reverberates in my ear, low and beast-like, as I stop him with one last punishing thrust.

"Why are you stopping me?" His voice a growl, his eyes glinting with frustration and need.

"Because if you keep going," I whisper against his lips, "this will be over far too fast and I'm not ready yet.

I unleash another wave of magic, pushing myself off the shelf and shoving him backward. He stumbles, his arms instinctively wrapping around me to cushion my fall as we hit the floor together. A few glowing books scattering around us, their faint hum of power framing the moment. I land atop his chest, his breath stuttering beneath me, and I waste no time.

Propping myself up, I reach down and wrap my

hand around him again, reveling in the sharp intake of breath that escapes him. A low groan tears from his throat as I position him perfectly. Without hesitation, I slam down onto him, the force of it eliciting a roar from him so raw it echoes through the library.

"Fuck!" he yells. "You feel so good like this. *Too fucking good.*"

I drag a teasing finger down his taut stomach, savoring the way he shudders beneath me.

"Are you going to move?" His tone is dark, "Or do I need to punish this greedy little cunt of yours until you do?"

My gaze snaps to his, my lips curving into a mischievous grin. "Filthy words Roenis." I tease, "I'll move when you beg me. I told you once before that at some point you will."

His jaw tightens, his eyes dropping to where we are joined, the sight of my magic holding him immobile making him grind out my name roughly, "Syra."

I tilt my head, enjoying his torment far too much. "Yes, my God?"

"Please…" His voice is strained, "Move. I need to feel you."

I raise a brow, feigning disappointment. "Is that begging? Doesn't sound like it to me." I lift myself slightly, letting him feel the excruciating drag, then sink back down again.

He throws his head back, groaning, his teeth clenching so tightly it's a wonder they don't shatter. His body trembles beneath mine, his restraint slipping. And then, finally, he breaks.

"Fuck! Okay! Gods, *please*! Please fucking move. You feel too damn good," he moans, his voice filled with desperation.

The sound is music to my ears, igniting that wicked power in me. I let go of my hold on him, rolling my hips and setting a hard, punishing rhythm that has us both unraveling. His hands shoot to my waist, gripping me tightly as he pulls me higher, only to slam me back down, matching my pace with a force that leaves me wanting more.

Every thrust, every moan, every gasp, feeds the fire until nothing else matters—just this moment, just us.

The feeling is starting to climb, reaching that blissful peak. "Roenis," I gasp, my voice breaking. He seems to sense how close I am, his thumb finding the sensitive bundle of nerves. The added pressure sends me spiraling, my release crashing over me in waves as I tremble in his arms.

"Fuck," he groans, his movements growing erratic as he chases his own end. With one final thrust, he buries himself deep, his release spilling into me as a roar tears from his throat.

For a moment, we stay like that, our bodies tangled, our breathing ragged. Slowly, he eases us both to a comfortable laying position, his arms wrapping around me. I lay against his chest, his heartbeat pounding beneath my cheek.

"You're incredible," he murmurs, his voice soft and worn out.

I smile, exhaustion tugging at me. "Didn't pin you as a one-orgasm type of God."

He chuckles, making my head on his chest bounce up a little. "We're far from done, pet. But you need to rest first. I'll give you all the time in the world, and then I'll make you beg for more."

His words sends a ravenous shiver through me, but he's right, I can't even muster up a response. He shifts and lays me halfway stretched across his body. Our high slowly coming back down. I listen to his heart slow its pace, and his breathing even out.

I don't know how much time passes, but he rubs circles onto my back until sleep pulls me under. His warmth is the last thing I feel.

When I wake up, The bed is cold. He must've brought me in here when I dozed off.

I stretch my sore limbs beneath the silken sheets, my fingers grazing over the empty space where Roenis should have been. His scent still lingering, woven into the fabric and clinging to my skin like an imprint of his presence. But he's gone.

I blink away the haze of sleep and notice the set of glass doors I have been drawn to since the first time I entered his room, is cracked open. Curiosity pulls me from the warmth of the bed, my bare feet pressing against the cool floor. The room is quiet, save for the distant trickle of water beyond the doors. As I approach, I push them open further, my breath seizing at the sight.

It's a grotto. His grotto.

Shimmering crystals jutting from the cavern walls, refracting the dim glow that filter down from unseen crevices above. The space is carved by magic, bathing in an ambient shine that makes the air feel light and sacred. Water trickles from a small waterfall nestled into the rock, its steady rhythm filling the grotto with a calming hum. The pool it feeds into ripples gently. It looks dark and inviting, the reflections of the crystals dancing across its surface like shooting stars.

And there, in all it's divinity, is Roenis.

He is submerged in the pool up to his waist, his head tilting back against the smooth stone at the edge, eyes closed, and expression completely at ease. The water laps lazily at his skin, the droplets from the waterfall tracing down the sculpted ridges of his chest, his abdomen, and every defined line and dip. His horns are slick with moisture, and strands of his crimson hair cling to his forehead from the grotto's mist. He is utterly relaxed, the tension in his frame unraveling in the embrace of the water.

I swallow, watching as his fingers lazily skim the surface, sending small ripples outward. He looks different like this, unburdened, untouched by the shadows that so often leech on him. This is a piece of him I have never seen before.

And for the first time since stepping into his world, I wonder, can I be untainted by expectation too?

CHAPTER TWENTY-EIGHT

Roenis

The water cascades over me, rivulets streaming down my chest, soaking into my skin. Steam fills the air, thick and hazy, wrapping the grotto in a humid embrace. But even through the mist, I feel her stare. Her presence feeling like the static before a strike.

I don't turn right away. I want her to look. I want her to admire. The warmth of the water is nothing compared to the burn of her eyes raking over me.

A hum of pleasure rumbles in my throat as I tilt my head further back, letting the water run over my face, down my throat. My muscles relaxing beneath the stream. When I finally let my gaze drift back toward her, I catch the hunger in her expression. I see the way her lips part just slightly, the way her breath falters when I shift.

"It's rude to stare," I murmur lazily, smirking as I keep my voice low.

Syra doesn't stop though, her arms cross over her chest, but there's no hint of annoyance in her stance. If anything, she seems impatient. "It's rude to show off all of *that* and expect me *not* to stare," she quips, her voice heavy, and her tongue darting out to wet her bottom lip.

Gods, she's glorious. Even seeing her there, standing impatiently. I'm at her complete mercy more than ever. Her hair still disheveled from our time in the library and from me tossing her around, skin flushed and her body relaxed. My cock twitches at the memory of having her against the shelves, her body molding so perfectly against mine. A reckless indulgence that I should regret.

But fuck, I don't. If anything, I'd do it again in a heartbeat.

I dip down, submerging deeper into the water until it laps at my collarbones, the heat of it barely easing the ache of wanting her again. "Join me," I coax, my voice dripping with temptation.

Her brow arches, her lips curling in amusement. "If I do, I can't say I'll behave."

The things I want to do to her.

"Who said I want you to behave?"

She doesn't hesitate long. The loose shirt I'd draped over her after our last bout of pleasure, falls to the ground, leaving her bare before me once again.

And Gods, I'll never tire of this sight.

My eyes roam, drinking her in. The way her breasts slightly rise with each breath, the way her skin glows in the grotto. She stands with a confidence that makes my chest tighten, her hands finding her hips as she watches me with hooded, knowing eyes.

She told me last night she didn't want to kill me.

She told me she wanted me.

But tonight still hangs in balance. If she changes her mind, she can end me with a single strike of her dagger once night arrives. I'll be vulnerable to her in every possible way.

And still, I'd let her have me.

She steps into the water, breaking my inner spiral of thoughts. Her movements slow, the tension in her body fades the moment the water touches her skin. A hum of content slips past her lips.

"Gods, this water is magical." Her pleasure is a symphony, and I want to hear more.

She tilts her head back, floating, her body moving in slow ripples away from me.

Oh no. That won't do.

I reach for her, gripping one of her legs and pull her towards me. A soft squeal bursts from her, and I grin. "Hey! I was enjoying that," she protests.

"Too bad," I grumble, tugging her close until she's practically wrapped around me. "I'd rather enjoy you."

Her legs settle around my waist, her hands splaying across my chest, the warmth of her skin against mine ignites that fire.

Mmmm. I quite enjoy her closeness. I adjust, letting her feel me, hard and needy, pressing against her. Her eyes widen, a delicious blush painting her cheeks. The color contrasting and mixing with her skin, giving a rich violet hue on her cheekbones.

"What's wrong, Syra?" I purr.

She doesn't answer with words. Instead, her fingers brush over my bottom lip, tracing it slowly, delicately.

"You're so beautiful," she whispers, her voice raw.

Fuck.

Those simple words make my heart stutter, my breath sharpen, and before I can stop myself, I grasp her chin and tilt her face at the perfect angle.

I kiss her, softly at first, savoring the way she melts into me, the way she sighs against my lips like she's been waiting for this. I want to take my time, but soon, the softness isn't enough. My tongue slides past her lips, deepening the kiss, claiming her. Her small moan of relief sends a jolt straight to my cock, and she shifts against me, pressing closer, desperate to feel me.

I'm already lost, already aching to be inside her again, when she suddenly pulls back. "Wait," she pleads. "I want to do something first."

I watch her, intrigued. "Is there an area in the pool where you can sit comfortably?" She asks.

I frown slightly, wondering where her mind is

going, though my body already burns in anticipation. "There's a small ledge by the waterfall. Why?"

She only smiles, genuine, sweet, and dangerous.

She can kill me with that look.

She grabs my arm, guiding me to the ledge. When we reach it, she pats the stone surface. "Sit."

I lift myself onto it with ease, the water streaming off my body. My cock stands thick, and when she pushes herself between my legs, I finally understand.

Oh, fuck me.

Syra runs her hands up my thighs, her fingers a torturous glide. Her gaze is ravenous, burning, and hungry.

"It's only fair I get a taste of you now," she purrs.

Her words are a spell, a brand against my skin. My power hums, feeding off her desires. Her hand wraps around me, earnestly, but the effect it has is lethal. A hiss escapes my lips as she strokes me, her thumb teasing the tip, spreading the bead of arousal already leaking from me.

Then her mouth is on me.

I tilt my head back, my eyes closing. A ragged moan tears from my throat as her lips part and she takes more of me in, inch by agonizing inch. Her tongue swirls around the head, her moans of content vibrating against my skin, sending sparks of pleasure rocketing up my spine.

Gods, she's going to ruin me.

My fingers tangle in her hair, gripping, guiding, as she takes me deeper, hollowing her cheeks. The heat and the wetness of her mouth, it's enough to send me over the edge already, but I hold on.

Barely.

Her pace is slow at first, savoring. Her hand moves in tandem with her mouth, squeezing just right, and I can feel myself falling. I curse, groaning her name, but she doesn't stop. She watches me, pride flashing in her violet gaze as she picks up speed, swallowing me whole.

"Fuck, Syra." My voice is hoarse, strained. "That feels so Gods-damned good."

She hums, the vibration again is enough to send me over that daring edge. My grip tightens, my hips jerking, and Gods her *fucking* tongue.

She keeps winding it around the base of my shaft, then working it around until it flicks on the bottom, swirling it under the base of my tip.

Fucking scandalous, the feeling spiking the buildup of my orgasm.

I break. I spill inside her mouth, my muffled roar still echoing through the grotto as she takes every last drop. She swallows, milking me for every bit of pleasure, and I swear I see stars.

When I finally regain myself, I don't give her time to breathe. I drag her onto my lap, kissing her fiercely, positioning her above me. Her thighs falling on the outsides of mine. My cock is perfectly aligned with her entrance and already hard again. I let her feel every inch as I slowly push her down onto me.

I keep my thrusts into her slow, teasing and deep. She gasps, her nails biting into my shoulders.

"Gods, Roenis," she moans.

I grip her hips, now setting a brutal pace.

"Yes," I growl. "I am your God, Syra."

I want her sore. I want her drained. I want her knowing exactly who she belongs to.

The beast in me stirs, clawing at the edges of my control. My muscles tense, my form wanting to shift, to rear its head and claim her in ways no man could.

Syra's face is sheer bliss, her lips part, her moans rising, but then—

Her eyes meet mine. And she notices my struggle.

She places her hand on my face, a grounding touch. "Let go."

I snap.

My talons rip free, my frame growing, and muscles thickening. My horns pulse as the beast takes control. The hunger in me strong.

She gasps, but it isn't fear—it's excitement. Her giggle silences into low moans as I thrust deeper. They quickly switch to cries of pleasure. Her hands fly up, gripping my horns, and I growl, the sensation dragging me deeper into my frenzy.

Water splashes, the grotto turning into a tempest of our movements. The serene oasis now a battlefield of pleasure, a volcano ready to erupt.

I know she's close. I can feel it, her tightening, her shaking, her gasping breaths.

I retract part of my talons, finding that perfect spot, the one that makes her shatter. A single brush, a swirl of sensation, and she breaks. Her cries echo, her body trembling violently as she clenches around me.

That sweet, unbearable tightness pulls me under with her. I roar as I cum, my release barley spilling anything the second time. I'm deep inside her, my grip powerful as I hold her through the chaos.

For a moment, neither of us move. Just our breaths, hammering hearts, and bodies stirring in the water.

Then, a laugh rumbles from me unexpectedly.

Syra lifts her head, blinking at me. "What?"

"This place is supposed to be my solitude. My peace." I grin.

She smirks, miming a zipper over her lips. "I can be quiet. Didn't mean to ruin your quiet space."

I chuckle. "Gods, you didn't ruin it at all, but now every time I come here or step into my library, I'll think of you. Filled with need every time."

She wiggles playfully. "Good." She scoots off and starts swimming to the middle, stretching her limbs like a satisfied feline basking in the sun. The water glides over her skin.

"Maybe we can both escape here often."

The idea of it, of her here like this, again and again—stirs something possessive in me.

"Mmmm." I hum, leaning back against the rock, watching her float. "Then we would never leave I'm afraid. And that's not very God or Goddess-like of us, is it? Ignoring our duties to the Human Realm?" I tease, though the thought of forsaking everything for this temptation is all too easy.

She rolls her eyes but smiles, that mischievous glint returning to her gaze. "Okay, fine." She pauses, treading water as if considering something. "Speaking of duties, I do have a few questions for you. If you're willing to indulge me."

Her tone shifts just slightly, and it sparks my curiosity.

I lift a brow. "Oh? Now I'm really curious."

CHAPTER TWENTY-NINE

Syra

The nerves rack my body. I'm trying to concentrate on the questions I want to ask, but all I can think about is his body. Watching him break, watching him lose himself, even slightly, is mesmerizing. I saw his true form that night with the child. This time it's partial, but I love seeing all these different sides to him. Our dynamic has definitely changed, but I have no regrets.

I already made up my mind. I know what I want, but I would still like some answers on a few things. As I swim around, the warm water doing little to calm the nerves, I ask my first question. "You broke my bracelet last night. Am I safe to assume I'm no longer your pet?"

He smiles, showing those damn canines again. "Tired of me already? Yes, you are no longer a restricted guest, but I would still like you as my… *pet.*" He emphasizes the word, his voice dropping deeper.

I can't help my blush. Damn him.

"I couldn't be tired even if I tried, but moving on, the night you made me stab you…" I trail off, watching closely as a hint of guilt crosses his silver eyes. "…I know you can feel desire from me, but that night, you told me my mother didn't love me. You knew the right thing to say to set my anger to its boiling point." I keep my stare locked on him. "That wasn't a desire. You somehow knew that information." I had some time to think and maul over in those days before the ball.

His eyes shift down, staring at the water as if the reflections hold the answer. The silence is loud, broken only by the faint sound of the waterfall. When he speaks, he sounds defeated.

"Your book."

My eyebrows shoots up. "You read my book?

When?"

"After I kissed you that first time in the pantry."

"Why?" The question slips out before I can think about it.

His lips part, but he hesitates before exhaling a breath. "Because that moment replayed in my head a thousand times. I started to feel something for you, and I didn't want to be lied to or fooled again. When I read your book, I was more focused on whether you still wanted to kill me—which you did—but you also had desire for me. I didn't predict that your book would shift and show me your mother and your other desires. Your decisions were still changing, nothing was set in stone yet."

His head hangs low, his hands brushing through his beautiful wet red hair. Without thinking, I swim closer, lifting his chin up with my fingers. His eyes shine with guilt and sadness.

"I'm not mad," I whisper. "I would've done the same."

His hand slides over mine, warm even in the water. Then, gently, he turns it over and presses a kiss to my palm. His simple act, so soft yet so powerful, sends my heart on a rampage that pounds through my chest. I swallow against the sudden tightness in my throat.

"What other questions do you have?" he asks, "I'll answer them all."

I study him, searching for deception, but there's none. Only honesty. He means it.

For once, I find I don't want to interrogate him, at this point I think I know he does everything he can for the people he cares about.

Instead, I allow myself to bask in the warmth of this moment, of the way his presence wraps around me like night itself. But as the weight of our conversation settles, I know I need time. Time to process the last twenty-four hours, to have it sink in without distraction.

I take a deep breath and pull away slightly. "I need to wash up," I say, my voice softer now. "I'll see you later?"

Roenis studies me, then nods. "Come find me whenever you want."

◆

***

Back in my chambers, I dry myself and slip into something light. The room feels heavy with all of the things I've felt and done since arriving in this kingdom. But tonight, there's one last thing I need to do.

I move toward my vanity, pressing my palm against the silver rimmed cool glass. My magic hums beneath my skin as I whisper my full magic out. A shimmer of purple light weaves through my fingertips, crawling over the surface until the mirror's reflection ripples like water. And then, my mother's face appears.

Her expression is unreadable at first, but her sharp eyes bear into me with that same scrutinizing look she always wears. "Syra," she says, her voice clipped. "What is with this interruption? I've already spoken with Orson with his report from the ball."

I inhale deeply, steadying myself. "I'm calling off the mission."

Silence. Then, her expression shifts, something dark crosses over her face. "Excuse me?"

I'm assuming Orson didn't report anything about my activities.

"I'm not doing it," I say, firmer now. "I won't kill him."

Her lips press into a thin line. "You seem to think this is your decision to make."

"It is," I bite back. "And I've made it."

She leans forward, her voice dropping into something more insidious. "If you don't complete it, someone else will. The mission will get done, Syra. Whether by your hand or another's."

A chill scrapes in me. "Is that a threat?"

"It's a fact," she replies. "You were chosen for a reason. Do you think I would leave everything to chance? You are bound by your duty as the next Goddess, by blood. That has not changed."

My hands tighten into fists at my sides. "Did you get Orson's message from me?" I ask, voice like steel. "I know everything."

Her uncertainty flashes in her gaze. Just for a second. But, her expression returns to a cold smile curling at the edges of her lips. "And yet, here you are. Still making the mistake of going against my orders, which I see with the fact your glamour is gone."

"I won't do it."

Her eyes narrow. "We'll see." She looks confident. It was something in her eyes, like she has a trick up her sleeve.

I don't give her a chance to say anything else. Removing my fingers from the mirror, I cut the connection. The mirror goes dark, my own reflection staring back at me.

It's done. Now, I need to find Roenis and tell him. He will know what to do next.

I check his chambers first, but they're empty. My heart beats faster as I make my way to the library. I work my way through the corridors, each step echoing unnaturally. When I finally reach the grand golden doors, I hesitate. Something feels… off.

His library is always closed. He wouldn't leave it open right?

No one else is allowed in Roenis' library. It is sacred, a sanctuary of knowledge bound by his magic. The fact that the doors are slightly ajar sends a warning scream in my head.

Pushing them more open, I step inside, my eyes scanning the towering bookshelves. The scent of aged parchment fills my lungs, grounding me for only a moment before the tension in the room wraps around my chest like a vice.

Roenis isn't here.

Instead, I find Dolion.

And Sesha.

They stand near the center, their postures rigid, their conversation silences the moment I enter. Their eyes lock onto me like *I'm* the intruder, an inconvenience. My pulse spikes, my stomach tightening. A foreign presence stains this sacred place, and Roenis will kill them for it.

Sesha smiles, almost snake-like. "Syra. Fancy meeting you here."

Dolion doesn't smile. He simply watches, dark eyes raking me over. My skin prickles. This isn't a coincidence.

I hear whispers, the same ones from before when Roenis showed me my book. My eyes are drawn immediately.

There in Sesha's hands, is my book.

I freeze, my breath catching in my throat. Roenis told me no one could access the books without his will—without his magic. Yet there it is, my story, clasped within Sesha's slender fingers. A chill freezing my blood.

Something in my mind clicks. Pieces of information rearranging themselves into a picture I should have seen long before now. Dolion. Sesha. Their odd behavior, the hushed conversations, the way Dolion always seemed to hover near Roenis but never with true loyalty in his eyes.

And then, another memory hits me like a bolt of lightning.

That night in Roenis' village. The tavern. Dolion was speaking to a hooded figure, their conversation urgent. I had brushed it off then, distracted by the night's chaos, by Roenis and everything he was unveiling to me. But now, now I see it clearly.

Sesha tilts her head slightly, as if she can hear the gears turning in my mind. "Something wrong, Syra?"

My throat tightens. "Yes, you being here is wrong."

Dolion steps forward. "You seem unsettled."

"I wonder why that is," I say, my voice steadier than I feel. I keep my stance firm, unwilling to let them see how deep my suspicion is running. "What exactly are you two doing here?"

Sesha chuckles, brushing a strand of dark hair behind her ear. "Oh, we could ask you the same thing. But I imagine Roenis has let you in his library, hasn't he?"

I don't answer. Giving them confirmation of anything feels like a mistake.

Dolion sighs. "He's not here, if you're looking for him."

"I can see that. Now stop changing the subject. No one—" my voice flattens, "and I mean no one, should be in here."

"Interesting," Sesha murmurs as she tilts her head. "And yet, here you are."

My magic claws beneath my skin, a warning from an instinct. Something isn't right. They're toying with me, seeing how much I know.

But I've learned to play this game, too.

I arch a brow. "Because as of today, Roenis and I

will be working together. Now, for my question."

Sesha's lips curl, her amusement fading. "That depends on whether I feel like answering."

Dolion clings next her, tension radiating from his frame. A tell. He's anxious.

Recognition clicks. She was the hooded figure that night. The way he spoke in hushed urgency, as if conspiring—it was her.

I step forward. "Tell me, Dolion," I say, "who was it you were speaking to outside the tavern that night?"

His expression hardens. A muscle jumps in his jaw.

Sesha's eyes gleam with satisfaction as she answers for him. "I think you already know that answer, Goddess."

I lift a hand. "I wasn't speaking to you."

My gaze locks onto Dolion, fury crackling beneath my skin. Vines lash out in an instant, snaking around their legs, rooting them to the ground. The magic vibrates, angry.

"I'll ask again. Why the fuck are you both in here? Why is she holding my book? And why were you sneaking around the village the other night?"

I feel Sesha's magic before I hear my answer. Her voice reverberating around me, close yet impossibly distant.

"So many questions from such an incompetent Goddess," she spits, mockery laced in every syllable. "Your mother truly believed you'd be the one. Such a shame you turned out to be yet another failure. But this time—" her smile is a razor's edge —"we have a backup plan."

I whip around, magic surging, but she's gone.

It's too late.

She's in front of me now, closer than she should be.

"Goodnight, Syra."

My book snaps open.

The whispers rise again, almost deafening this time.

Darkness crashes in. And then, I'm swallowed whole.

CHAPTER THIRTY

Syra

I'm choking on air. My vision is completely fuzzy, and my mind can't place where the hell I am. Nothing feels real. My senses are dark, and it feels like I'm floating in nothingness. I linger for a few moments, and then I feel a pull—a force dragging me toward an unknown. A flash of light streams, though I'm not sure if it's within my mind or if I see the light from behind my eyelids. Either way, I slowly start to feel like I'm being pieced back together.

I open my eyes, and I'm in a dark field. It's nothing like the beautiful meadow Roenis took me to when we first traveled into a book.

Shit! I'm in my book.

No. No. No. NO NO NO!

This isn't good. I'm not supposed to be here. Am I stuck? Fuck, where's Roenis? I need to find a way out. If I don't, my mind will become a prisoner in here.

The air around me feels suffocating, like something is pressing against my skin, digging through my thoughts. The world shifts, and the ground beneath my feet trembles as a mist rolls in, consuming the field. Shapes begin to emerge within the fog, twisting like living shadows. The images are flickering between reality and illusion. I turn sharply, my pulse thundering in my ears, but the moment I move, everything is tilting again.

Roenis is there.

His body sprawls out before me, crimson blooming across his chest like petals of wilted roses. His silver eyes are dull, lifeless, staring at the sky that does not exist. My breathing stops, my stomach wrenches, and my knees threaten to give away beneath me.

"No," I whisper, stumbling toward him, my hands trembling as I reach for him. "No, this isn't real.

You're not—this isn't—"

A dagger gleams in my hand.

My dagger.

It's slick with his blood.

I drop it like it burns, my chest constricting as my vision tunnels. My heartbeat pounds, drowning out every other sound, until her voice slices through the silence.

"You have failed, Syra."

My mother.

Her voice booms around me, echoing in the void, in the sky, in my very bones. The mist thickens, turning a deep shade of violet, swirling like a vortex of my power. The field warps, widens, and suddenly I am surrounded by mirrors. Each one reflecting the same scene, just a different failure. Roenis dying again and again, each death worse than the last. My dagger plunging into his chest. His body turning to ash in my arms. His voice whispering my name, begging me to stop.

"No, no, no! This isn't real!" I claw at my arms, at my face, trying to ground myself. My mind is twisting between what I know is false and what I cannot escape.

"This is your doing," my mother hisses, her voice present through every reflection. "You were never strong enough. Never capable. You let yourself fall for him. You let yourself be weak. So I gave you a little push."

"Shut up!" I scream, slamming my fist into the nearest mirror, shattering it into a thousand shards. But the reflection doesn't fade, it only multiplies. More images of Roenis dying, more versions of my hands stained with his blood. My scream is weak, my throat already raw. I try to run, but the ground keeps crumbling beneath me, leeching into an endless void.

Hands grab at me from the darkness. Cold, skeletal fingers, pulling me down and dragging me deeper into the nightmare. I thrash, but my body feels heavier with every passing second. The air is chanting my failures over and over, a chorus of torment that refuses to let me go.

Then, suddenly a touch, fleeting yet familiar. A distant voice speaks to me.

Roenis?

I reach for it, for him, but the darkness swallows the hope.

No. No, I won't let this consume me. I dig deep, reaching for my magic, for anything that can break this spellbound nightmare. My veins pulse with energy, violet vines sparking to life around my fingers. I channel it, trying to rip through the illusions, to tear apart the walls of my own mind.

Nothing.

My magic flickers and dies, like a candle suffocated by wind. I grit my teeth, forcing more power into my limbs, but the moment I do, the nightmare tightens its grip, twisting my own magic against me, feeding the horror instead of dispelling it.

I need more. I'm not enough.

I'm not enough.

I'M NOT ENOUGH!

Panic rises in my chest, but I shove it down. There needs to be another way. This book is my creation, my mind, my power. If I can't use brute force, then I need to outthink it. I close my eyes, ignoring the screams, the mirrors, and the weight of Roenis' corpse in my hands.

Focus.

This isn't real. I have to find the seams, the cracks in the illusion. Every spell has a flaw. Every prison has an exit.

And I will find mine.

CHAPTER THIRTY-ONE
Roenis

Giving Syra space is harder than I expect, but a rare sense of ease settles within me. She's choosing me. Choosing us. I feel the weight of her desire, and for once, it isn't tainted by the urge to kill me. Something in her has changed these pass two days, and finally she seems content with her choices.

I distract myself in the garden, plucking flowers, their delicate petals brushing against my fingertips. They are the ones I use to make the fragrant oils she loves. But the simple act of preparing them does little to settle the unease rising in my chest.

Suddenly, there's a rupture in the air. It feels like an opening. Someone is using the portal.

I go still, every muscle taut with suspicion. No. She wouldn't leave. She would need me to open the portal. Unless... Dolion.

The thought sends fire through my veins. I break into a sprint, moving with purpose. The path to the portal is burned into my memory—through the trees and around the castle's right wing. My boots barely touch the ground before I round the last corner, my heart dropping with the realization.

Sesha.

She stands halfway through the portal, her golden eyes gleaming with triumphant malice. She gives me a slow, taunting wave before she's gone, swallowed by the portal.

Syra.

FUCK! Where is she?

A snarl rips from my throat as I whirl around, my magic roaring to life. I make my way inside my castle. Trembling as my power explodes from me in waves, the beast inside claws against my ribs, demanding release. Fear snakes through my rage, gripping tight around my lungs. My shadows whispering where to go.

Fear. I haven't felt it like this in centuries.

The magic prickles at my senses, the remnants twisting through the air. The energy is wrong. My stomach clenches as I follow the pulsing source of power, a dark certainty dragging me forward.

The library doors are open.

How? How the fuck did this happen? The only two people capable of opening both the library and the portal are Datura and Dolion. Datura is in the village, so all my rage hones in on Dolion. The stench of his magic lingers, bitter betrayal stinging my senses.

Dolion's blood will paint the floors when I'm done with him. If anything happens to her because of him, he will wish upon the Gods that I never find him.

My eyes sweep the room, catching the faint residual magic skating across the marble. My gaze snaps to a folded paper laying upon the floor.

I snatch it up, scanning the words, and my vision blurs with fury.

It seems the threads of fate have tangled in my favor. Your little dream has slipped through your fingers—though, I suppose she was never truly yours to begin with. If you wish to see her again before her mind swallows her whole, you know where to find me.

Don't keep me waiting. I despise wasted time.

-Sesha

The paper crumples in my grip, my body stiffens as power releases in a violent burst. Vapors explode from me, violently lashing at the walls, and swirling around my body.

They took her book. That's the only explanation for this cryptic bullshit.

I close my eyes, reaching for its magic, calling for it. Silence. A void where her book should be.

My hands fist, squeezing so tight, my nails pierce skin. My list of those who will suffer and wish for mercy, is growing.

I call again, this time summoning Sesha's book. It materializes in my grasp, golden and heavy. Golden threads of time swirl the front, and sand spills from its edges, pooling at my feet in lazy patterns.

Two can play this game. The difference? This is

my fucking battlefield.

I call to my portal to open it, feeling Sesha's for a clearing. Her's is open. She's clearly expecting me as her note suggests. I shift with my magic, making it to the portal faster than before, my power hungry and desperate.

The Kingdom of Time is an abomination of logic. The sky is a never-ending veil of moving constellations, changing from day to night in unpredictable waves. Towering rounded structures built from sand and glass, stretch impossibly wide, growing and reforming with sand magic in an endless cycle.

Winds of liquid gold cut through the land, reflections flickering with glimpses of past, present, and future. Time bends here, an illusion and a weapon all at once. The place hums with an unnatural stillness, yet I feel the pull of a thousand different moments brushing against my skin.

Two figures stand at the entrance of her portal, their golden masks expressionless. "Sesha awaits, God of Nightmares."

I don't acknowledge them. I push forward, my

heart moving in a fast rhythm. My magic swims at my fingertips, ready. The walls of the building change and change again as I pass, the path reforming behind me, trapping me deeper inside her domain.

My eyes find Syra.

She kneels in the center of a dimly lit chamber, her body eerily still. Strands of white hair spills over her shoulders. Her eyes, no longer violet—are blank, fogged over with an unnatural white out glaze.

She's not here. She's trapped in her own book, mind ensnared in whatever nightmare she's fighting inside. Fucking Sesha.

My chest tightens, fuck I need to help her get out.

A climbing clap echoes through the chamber.

Sesha steps forward, golden robes flowing behind her against the floor. "You took your time," she accuses, tilting her head with mock disappointment. "But I suppose you were given short notice."

My magic pulses, shadows licking at the ground. "Release her."

Sesha sighs, shaking her head. "Oh, Roenis. You know that's not how this works. She read the book.

She has to fight her own battle."

"Why did you take her?"

Sesha laughs, the sound grating. "Because she's part of the final plan. We're doing things differently, remember?"

Just then, the shadows lurking at the edges of the chamber begin to stir, and one by one, they step out.

Maya. Dolion. Orson.

Maya's smug face gleams with triumph, her lips curling into a smirk. Dolion stands beside her, arms crossed over his chest, his stance lazy, cocky, as if he truly believes he's on the winning side. But it's Orson's face that catches my attention. Unlike the others, he doesn't exude confidence, but instead faking it. There's hesitation. Doubt. As if he's realizing what this is really about.

My anger takes over.

Shadows propel me forward, faster than thought, faster than sound. Dolion has no time to flinch before my hand clamps around his throat, lifting him off his feet. His fingers claw at my wrist, a choked gasp slipping past his lips.

A sharp snap echoes through the chamber.

Dolion's body crumples to the floor, his head twisted at an unnatural angle. His eyes stare lifelessly at nothing, the arrogant smirk wiped clean from his face.

I step over him like the insignificant stain he is.

Maya glances at the corpse. Sesha huffs, unimpressed, because he was nothing more than a pawn. A sacrifice to get what they needed. But I won't give them the luxury of using anyone else against me.

I take a step forward, my voice low, deadly. "Each one of you will be dying a cruel death."

Sesha's smirk falters.

I don't wait. Magic surges from me, filling the chamber with darkness, my vapors lunging toward her. The moment they strike, golden sand rises in a violent wave, colliding with my power in an explosion of force that shakes the very foundations of the room. The walls groan under the weight of our clash, stone cracking, dust spilling from the ceiling like the first tremors of an impending collapse.

She has no idea what I'm willing to do to get Syra

back.

Sesha moves fast, retreating behind Syra's limp form. And then, she lifts a dagger. Not just any dagger. Syra's dagger.

I freeze.

A cruel smile stretches across Sesha's face as she lifts her hand. Her golden sands swirl, pushing Syra forward like a marionette. Her limbs jerk unnaturally as she forces Syra upright, her head lolling, her silver-white hair cascading over her face.

"Syra doesn't need to be conscious for this," Sesha purrs. "She just needs to be holding the blade when it sinks into your chest."

The words scrape against my mind like rusted metal. My hands form into fists, vapors thickening around me, pulsing with fury. I can't fight her.

"You're hesitating." Maya's voice cuts through the echoed chamber. She steps forward, her violet suit catching the dim light, her expression one of sheer delight. "You should have known, Roenis. This has been the plan from the beginning."

Orson follows beside her, and I see his doubtfulness twisting through his features. His fingers twitch near his blade.

Maya to self absorbed to notice.

"I was hoping Syra would fail," she continues, "so I could be here to watch you die myself."

The realization slams into me like a punch to the stomach. This was never about Syra's success. Maya never intended for her to win. She set her up to fall—to be used as a pawn in her new twisted game. And now, she's reveling in it. Not just wanting to kill me, but also to break her. Forcing Syra to be the instrument of my death.

I grind my teeth, urging myself to breathe past the rage clawing up my throat. My eyes flick to Orson again. He isn't looking at me. He's looking at Syra. And I can see the battle lines are bleeding together.

I latch onto that sliver of hesitation.

"You were her trainer, weren't you?" I say, voice sharp, hoping my words reach him. "You taught her how to fight. How to survive. And now you're going to stand there and let them do this?"

Orson's throat bobs as he swallows, his hands still flexing at his sides.

Maya scoffs. "Don't listen to him. He's

desperate."

I take a step closer, my magic flowing out like fog now. Dark, dangerous clouds of suffocating mist. "If you go through with this," I say to Orson, an angry whisper, "you won't just be against me. You'll be betraying *her*."

Orson's hesitation finally snaps.

And then, his hand reaches for the sword at his waist, shattering it with magic I've never seen before.

The steel liquefies, morphing into powerful violent silver vines that lash through the air. The motion, the style, the form…it almost mirrors Syra's. My eyes widen.

Holy shit.

I don't have time to process the connection before the vines snap forward, ensnaring Maya with vicious intent. Maya's power booms outward in a desperate surge, trying to shake him off. The force rattles and bends the very space between them. But Orson holds his own.

Sesha stands untouched, watching it all unfold, but she's more focused on her own task. Syra lunges at me.

Her movement is fast, unnatural. It's her body, but not her will. Her dagger glints as she twists midair, striking out with alarming speed. I barely move in time, the blade catching my shirt and slicing through the fabric. A shallow sting burns across my ribs.

I can strike back. I should.

But this is Syra. I won't spill her blood, even if Sesha controls every inch with her fingers.

I duck, pivot, and narrowly avoid another strike as she aims for my throat. Her fogged eyes—cold and empty, move around from in her mind. No hesitation. No mercy. No clue whats happening on the outside.

I growl, vapors start to pool under and around me. "Sesha," I snarl, dodging Syra's next blow, "If you think I'll kill her, you're dumber than I thought."

Sesha only tilts her head, amused. "I don't care what happens to her. I just need her to kill you."

Enough of this.

A deep tremor rips through my chest. Shadows

spilling from my pores like living creatures, thicken into a monstrous form. My fingers lengthen into my black talons, my limbs stretching, and strengthening. My horns expand, their white bases shifting into obsidian as my transformation takes hold.

I let my nightmare form take over fully.

An inhuman snarl rips from my throat, my breath thick with the scent of sulfur and death. The lights that occupy the space flicker wildly, struggling to illuminate against my presence. The temperature plummets. Coldness takes over, leaving foggy breaths in its wake.

Syra attacks again. This time, I meet her blade head-on.

Her dagger clashes against my clawed hand, sparks flying from the impact. I twist, my power expanding in a whirlwind of movement, forcing her back without harming her. She stumbles, but recovers sluggishly.

She comes at me again, a blur of speed. Our battle turns into a dance of evasion and deflection, steel against nightmare. I don't retaliate with full force. I can't. Instead, I focus on maneuvering, waiting for an opening.

It comes. A split second of hesitation, her arm tensing, a moment of resistance in her face. Syra's still in there, fighting against her nightmares and Sesha's control.

I use it.

I lash out, my claws hitting the dagger instead of her hand. The weapon flies from her grip, clattering to the floor.

Sesha's expression drops.

Syra's body sways slightly, as if her own will is fighting too.

I shove forward, ignoring Syra and launching straight for Sesha.

She raises a hand, summoning a distortion of magic, but I barrel through it, grabbing her by the throat and slamming her against the ground. The force cracks the stone beneath her. Fucking satisfying.

She chokes out a gasp, but before she can react, I conjure the book into my free hand.

Her book.

The moment it opens, a pulse of energy spills outward. The pages glow, shifting with unnatural power. Sesha's scream is instant, and the sound is fucking music to my ears. Her body seizes, her golden eyes glossing over just like Syra's, paralyzed by the trance of her own nightmares.

But I don't stop there.

I let the nightmares deepen, pouring unforgiving power into the book's pages. The magic takes hold of her entire being—her flesh, her bones, her soul—dragging her down, pulling her into the very story she fears.

Her body collapses inward, dissolving into ink, into words, into *nothing*.

The book slams shut with a thunderous crack, its cover shifting around, before stilling altogether.

Silence.

A moment later, the sound of Maya's scream shatters the air.

CHAPTER THIRTY-TWO

Roenis

I try to keep my breath steady as I turn to face the noise. My eyes pinpointing the sound rattling through my bones. Maya.

The remnants of Sesha's destruction leaves a scent of scorched magic and charred stone. I had already beaten her, torn through her very existence, and yet the battle still doesn't seem over. Not until I take care of Maya too. Her power keeps surging, seeking to undo and kill anything in its way.

I make my way towards Orson. The power I shifted into, now fading away as the shadows trail off behind me. When I get closer, I notice the space around them keeps pulsing light. The unnatural colors of pink and blue come from Maya's magic. My vision in the dark cuts through the haze, and I can see Orson's steel vines still wrapped around her. She writhes against it, her body twisting with spikes protruding from her skin.

The binding holds, but Maya is never one to submit. Her hands stretch out and with a vicious burst, pointed thorns erupt from her flesh. The silver steel hisses as her magic shreds through it. Fragments of his metal scatter across the floor. Orson leaps back in time as she breaks free.

Maya's feral grin spreads as she springs her arms forward. Thorns shot toward us, each one sharpened like spears. I sweep my hand in the space, allowing my vapors to devour the projectiles before reaching us. Orson grunts beside me, his arm covered in the steel, shifting to reform back as thin whips.

"She doesn't stop," Orson shouts, irritation slipping into his tone.

"No," I agree, cocking my head to crack the tension I'm starting to feel. "I've been dealing with her shit the past five centuries."

I steal a glance toward the far end of the chamber. Syra remains where she had fallen, eyes still fogged over, locked in that damn trance. I need to hurry this up so I can help her break it. The nightmares that are consuming her, trapping her within its depths, must be draining her. She's unaware of the battle raging around her.

I glance back and notice Maya watching me.

Her eyes flick to Syra's still form, and something wicked flashes in her eyes. A weaponized thought.

Fuck.

She lunges first, a downpour of thorns shoot from her palms, slicing through the air in chaotic patterns. I counter again with a cloud of my magic, casting a type of umbrella effect. Orson takes his opening, his arm swinging around using the thin steel whip as he swings at her ribs. She turns, her magic scraping across his arm but failing to cut through completely.

She snarls, stumbling back, but rather than retreat, she summons *another* barrage of spiked thorns, launching them toward Orson's exposed side. The barbs tear through his defenses, piercing the shifting steel before he can fully create another whip. He grits his teeth, the liquid metal knitting back together as he rips the embedded thorns from his body.

I don't give her a second to recover. I let my shadows surge from beneath her, wrapping around her ankles, locking her in place.

"This is over," I state.

Maya laughs, the sound grating in my ears. "Not yet."

She snaps her fingers, her magic detonates. Pink and blue energy sends me skidding backward, my horns grazing the cold stone wall. Orson braces himself, his feet digging into the marble, but Maya has already set her sights elsewhere. Her motivation focuses towards the dagger lying on the ground, forgotten from the earlier fight.

Syra's dagger.

I lunge, but Maya is faster. She dives, her hand closing around the hilt, and in a blink, she's upon Syra, pressing the blade to her throat.

"I can always create another," she sneers, breath skimming against Syra's skin, the blade biting just enough to draw blood.

Syra doesn't react. Her breathing remains even, her glazed-over eyes unfocused. She's still lost, blind to how death hovers just above her throat.

I still, my magic faltering. If she kills her, I will follow. Nothing will make sense. I can't witness this again.

Orson moves first—in a motion so fluid it's basically undetectable. He snaps his wrist, a surge of liquid steel forming out again, and shooting towards her. The force strikes the dagger, sending it spinning from Maya's grip before she even notices what happened.

She gasps, the action catching her off guard.

Orson doesn't waste that moment. He catches the falling dagger, his metal-coated fingers tightening around the base. With a single, brutal thrust, he drives the blade straight into Maya's chest, right in the heart.

Her breath snags, and her face stunned.

I watch as the liquid spread from Orson's touch, melding the dagger into her very skin, forcing it deeper, fusing with her body. Her power flickers, sputtering out like a dying flame.

"No—" Maya chokes, hands clawing at the wound, but it's useless. The metal seeps so deep within her, it's locking her magic inside, suffocating it from the source. It won't fully kill her, but it will do enough to subdue her indefinitely.

She staggers, her knees slamming into the cold floor. Her breath coming in short, panicked bursts. Her gaze darts to Syra, then to me, then Orson, desperation creeping into her features.

I step forward, retrieving Sesha's book from the holding space I used. The cover heavy from earlier and pulsing with the same eagerness after devouring Sesha. I let the pages shift for the second time, sensing the weight of fate about to be sealed. I look down at Maya.

"You should have stopped, now look who's desperate." I mock.

Maya trembles, her body betraying her. Even with the dagger lodged deep in her chest, even as the steel poisons her from within, she refuses to yield.

I can admire that, but no where in this realm will there be a moment I save her. I will *never* give her that mercy.

I give a slow exhale, and open the book. Magic spilling from its spine, and again a vortex of swirling energy forms. The pages searching, making the pull become unbearable.

Maya lets out a strangled scream as the force grasps her, dragging her toward the book's open pages. I've watched this twice now, both giving me the satisfaction of ridding this realm of filth and hatred.

Her hands claws at the air, as if trying to resist, but it's too late. The book's power consumes her just as it did with Sesha. Her power muted, with no way to escape.

I snap the book shut.

I will be locking this book away in a special place once I reach my library. I let the weight of the moment settle into my bones. Then, slowly, I turn and make my way to Syra.

I reach out, brushing my fingers against her cheek, watching for any sign of recognition.

Nothing, but I will get her back. I *have* to.

Beside me, Orson wipes his hands on his pants,

shaking his head. "What now?"

"Now, I need to get her out. Keep me stable, my mind is going in. I'm sure she also just received a surge of power now that Maya is no longer a part of the realm. It officially makes Syra the Goddess of Dreams."

"Shit." Orson spits out. "I forgot about that. What a worse time for that to happen."

I nod. "Yeah. And not only do I need to dig my way out *with* her, but she's going to be outpouring all this power with no place to release the first initial pulse."

I settle myself, inhaling deeply, feeling the weight of the moment press against my skull. Entering someone's mind is not like stepping through a door. It's slipping between the cracks of reality, pushing through the fragile lines of consciousness. I close my eyes, extending myself and seeking the path that will lead me to her. It's instinctual, an ability buried deep within my magic, but it still takes precision and a hell of a lot of concentration. One wrong move and I can fracture her already unstable mind or worse, lose myself in the endless web of her nightmares.

The moment I breach a wall, a jolt of static, shocks my body. Her power slams against me like a tidal wave. I grit my teeth, anchoring myself so that I can press forward against the resistance. Her mind is complex, switching between clarity and chaos, and I can feel the struggle to contain the eruption of her new divinity. Colors start to pulse, images flashing in and out with half-formed landscapes, desires, and nightmares. I weave through them, following a path toward her core where I know she's trapped. I'm finally in, no more walls, but the closer I get, the more the weight of her power presses down on me. It feels like gravity testing me. If I don't get her out soon, we might drown in her new awaken power.

CHAPTER THIRTY-THREE
Roenis

Syra's mind is suffocating. It feels fucking heavy, almost like the weight of the memory is something beyond a nightmare. It charges my body the moment I sink into her consciousness. I keep getting pulled in by her untamed new power. It's chaotic, unstable, and far more complicated than the last time I had ventured into her desires and nightmares. With Maya gone, her power has grown, and I don't think she realizes how untapped and limitless it can be. I take a step forward figuratively, pushing deeper. The space around me begans to shift, weaving sparks of ember in the area. Some parts look like they are folding in on itself, but then finally, I'm thrown into it.

I'm standing in a battlefield of mist and shadows. Ahead of me, Syra stands, her frustration painted on her face. Her vine magic is writhing like overused ropes. And before her, is...*me*. A fractured version, a nightmare copy. He stands still, the crimson of his hair darkening with the illusion of blood. His silver eyes, void of light, reflecting the death she's about to deliver.

I try to move toward her, to call her name, but my voice is swallowed by the space.

Syra is panting. Her face set with determination, but there is so much pain in her eyes. Even as she lifts her hand, even as her magic dagger flings forward, the grief is there. She strikes me. As she does, her vines wrap around my throat—his throat —tightening, constricting until the nightmare version of myself gasps soundlessly, his knees buckling beneath him.

Then, it begins again.

I'm watching the same battlefield. The same version of myself stand before her. The same pain flashes across Syra's face, hesitating, and then she kills me again.

And again.

And again.

Each time, her expression fractures a little more. She wipes at her face, smearing something I know isn't just sweat. But she can't stop. She's trapped, bound by something that's out of my control. Out of her own control too. Her nightmare is consuming her into this endless loop.

I push again, this time I can move slightly forward. Gritting my teeth against the force, feeling like If I get too close, it will shove me back, but slowly I inch closer. If I let the nightmare take me too deeply or rush, I'll be lost here with her. But I'm not going to lose her. Not like this.

I try reaching. My hand passing through the cold, shifting space of the loop. "Syra!"

She doesn't turn. She can't hear me.

I clench my jaw. This is worse than I thought. Her mind isn't just trapping her in the past; it's making her live her greatest torment over and over again. Her power now going wild. Becoming self-destructive. If she doesn't control it soon, it will devour her completely.

I close my eyes, feeling the thrum of the power around me. It's not mine, but it's familiar. I have to get her to take hold of it, to bend it to her will instead of letting it break her.

"Syra, listen to me! This isn't real! You need to control it!"

She strikes again, her magic lashing through the air, tearing through his body. As he crumbles, so did the battlefield again. Her shoulders tremble, her hands burning from the constant use of the magic. She knows something is wrong, she just can't see the way out.

"Syra," I growl, stepping into the moment just before she delivers the next strike. This time, I catch her wrist.

Her body stiffens, as if the touch is something foreign to her. Her gaze snaps up to me, wide and filled with confusion. "You… you're not supposed to be here, is the loop changing?"

"Neither are you, and so you *are* aware it's a loop."

She shakes her head, trying to pull away, but I

hold firm. "I have to keep at it. I need to find a way out. If I don't—"

"You will break yourself before you break free." I lean in, forcing her to meet my gaze. "This is *your* mind. *Your* nightmare. But it doesn't have to be. Take control of it. Stop letting it control you."

Her lips part, her breathing uneven. The floor of the illusion starts pulsing like it's on the verge of transformation.

She swallows hard. "How?"

"You tell me." I release her, stepping back, giving her space to decide. "This is your mind, Syra. What do you want it to be? Use your power. I know you can feel it. It's stronger now, so use it."

For a moment, she's still. She quivers, the space becoming unsteady, like waiting for a command. She inhales deeply and closes her eyes.

The change is immediate.

The darkness softens, the mist dissipating. The battlefield melts away, replaced by a warmer image —a garden. I feel the wind flow pass me, see the way Syra's body relaxes, and how easy it is for the power to flow from her.

Golden light bleeds through the clouds that are blocking her freedom.

We are no longer in a nightmare. It's like she rewrote everything. Weaved a dream within my magic.

The scene changes again. Now, we stand within my library, lined with towering shelves of books. There are windows stretching infinitely, showing a sky light with stars, endlessly shooting across the sky.

Maybe I'll add windows with that type of magic, just for her when we get back.

I watch as she turns slowly, taking in the scene. The glow of her magic like a ring of aura latching onto her. She blinks, almost in disbelief, before exhaling something close to relief.

"I… I did this?" she whispers.

"Yes," I said, my voice quieter now.

She looks up at me then, something new in her gaze. "It feels different. Powerful."

"You're weaving dreams." I state calmly.

The dream drifts again, and now, we are standing in a human village. The air filling with the scent of rain and thunderous waves rumbling in the background, but the people aren't afraid. They're laughing, running about in the puddles and living without the weight of fear clinging to them. I see myself there beside her, not as a shadow, not as a God, but as a partner.

A warmth spreads through my chest, "Syra…"

She turns, and in her eyes, I see the full force of her power, her dreams and her nightmares interlacing into a fresh power. But as she looks at me, the world around us shatters.

A pulse of magic bursts from her, violet and gold colliding, tearing through with such force that I'm thrown backwards. The threads unraveling, and I'm ripped from her mind. When I open my eyes, I'm back in the chamber, gasping, my limbs heavy with exhaustion. But I don't care. Orson holds me in place after being thrown and my gaze snaps to Syra.

She's awake.

She stands up, her chest gasping in rapid breaths. And when her gaze finds me, I nearly forget how to breathe.

Her eyes—

They're a luminous swirl of violet and gold now.

She is far beyond just power. She is a full Goddess.

I have never seen anything more magnificent.

A hand releases me. Realizing Orson was still holding me in place. The moment he lets go, he rushes past me, throwing his arms around Syra and pulling her against him. "You're awake," he breathes, his voice exhaling relief, his arms wrapping around her as if he can keep her there from now on. "Don't do that again kid."

Syra clings to him, her fingers digging into his back as if anchoring herself. She buries her face against his shoulder, and in that long moment, neither of them speak. Then, she takes in her surroundings, and she pulls back just enough to look at him. "Orson, what happened?" Her voice is hoarse, like she was screaming herself raw in that dream.

Orson swallows, his gaze flicking to me briefly before he answers. "Sesha is dead, along with Maya. She's gone…they both are. Roenis trapped and concealed both of them in Sesha's book. We did what had to be done."

Syra stills, her hands gripping his forearms, her eyes searching his. "Dead?" she questions, as if she needs the word to settle. "Gone?"

Orson nods. "In a way, yes. They are no longer in this realm. She is severed from her magic, Maya's hold on you, her hold on *everything* is no more." He exhales, running a hand down his face. "They would never have stopped. It left us no choice."

Syra's face gives away to the sadness she feels, but she doesn't cry. She nods slowly, the weight of it sinking into her bones. "I knew somehow it would come to this, I played a lot of scenarios in my head on how to stop the mission, and her," she admits. "I just didn't expect it to feel like this." Her fingers flex against Orson's arms, her body still shaking from the aftermath. "Like the world has flipped, and my insides cracked open."

She lifts a hand to her chest, pressing her palm over her heart. "I can feel it. Power. So much power, coursing through me, humming beneath my skin, like it's trying to escape. I don't know how to contain it."

"You don't have to contain it, Syra. You don't have to fear it. You just have to learn to wield it. Orson will teach you."

Orson glances my way. His secret is his burden to share, but at least now, she'll have someone who understands the intricacies of dream weaving. Someone who won't let her fail.

Then she turns to me—those beautiful eyes locking onto mine, affection swimming in their depths. My chest tightens. Before I can make the first move, she wrenches free from Orson's grasp and runs straight to me.

My heart splits wide open, as if it had only ever been waiting for this moment. For her. Always for her.

And when she crashes into me, her lips—warm, and fucking soft—steals every last air I have left.

CHAPTER THIRTY-FOUR
Syra

The moment my lips crash into his, the world melts. I'm falling, drowning and burning, but Roenis is right there catching me, saving me, and putting out the fire all at once. His arms wrap around me, and he lifts me.

A startled gasp leaves me, swallowed instantly by the deepening kiss. My legs wrap around his waist where they belong, and my fingers tangle in his hair, threading through the silken strands. A low growl rumbles against my lips, sending that delicious feeling down my spine. Gods, he tastes like something dark and dangerous, like honeyed wine, and I can't get enough. He just feels right.

Mine.

A pulse deep in my core, unfurls like a flower letting the power spark alive. A want that my vines are responding to. They sprout from my arms before I can stop them, slipping from my body and winding around his. They start over his shoulders, then down his back, and finally curling around his horns. They crave him. *I* crave him.

Roenis jolts slightly, breaking the kiss with a breathless chuckle. "Syra—" His voice is husky, and when he tries to shift, his arms barely move. A playful grin tugs at his lips. "I'd very much like to keep breathing, little Goddess."

I blink, finally registering the way my vines have thoroughly ensnared him. They aren't just wrapped around him, they're holding him hostage, gripping every part of him like he's mine to keep.

Which he is.

I can't help it, I burst into laughter, forehead dropping against his. "Oops." But I don't let go. If anything, I tighten just a little more, making him groan dramatically.

"Syra," he strains, but it's full of fondness. "You're

squeezing the life out of me."

I grin. "You can handle it."

His eyes darken, "We don't have time right now to test that theory."

And then he kisses me again, stealing every ounce of control I thought I had.

Before I can completely lose myself in him again, a very loud, very pointed cough cuts through the haze.

"I would hate to interrupt," Orson states, voice edged with urgency, "but if you two are quite finished suffocating each other with magic and hormones, *I'd* very much like to get the fuck out of the Time Kingdom before everything inevitably goes to shit."

Roenis exhales against my lips, I feel the subtle tension creeping into his hold, the way his fingers grip tighter against my waist. His silver eyes turn towards Orson, as if he's debating whether we should keep making out just to annoy him further. After a few moments I see the defeat on his face.

My vines reluctantly retreat, slithering back beneath my skin like a sulking child. I glance over at

Orson, who stands with arms crossed, wearing the distinct look of a man who has zero patience for lovers tangled within each other.

"He's right," Roenis states, pulling my attention back to him. "With Sesha gone, Avia will take her place. The surge of power will hit her hard, and just like you, she won't be able to control it, not right away." His arms loosen, easing me back onto solid ground, but his touch lingers, as if reluctant to let go. His jaw tightens as his gaze sweeps over the rubble-strewn chamber. From the structure alone, I suspect we're beneath the main castle, buried in the lower levels.

"I'll need to contact Sage," he continues, concerned. "He'll have to intervene. Avia's transition won't be easy, ascending to Godhood never is. And her new role as Goddess of Time…" He exhales sharply. "That's a burden in itself."

Avia. She is about to inherit an entire kingdom and an ocean of divine magic, all with little to no preparation. Maybe I can help her. But how will she feel, knowing that we are the reason everything had changed?

A pulse of urgency stabs through me, my heart rate speeding up. "We have to go. Now."

Both men snap their attention to me, confusion spilling across their faces.

"I feel someone coming," I press, the sensation gnawing at my senses. "We need to leave immediately. Did Sesha take a portal here?"

The gaps in my memory noticeable now, fractured by the time I spent unconscious.

Roenis nods. "She opened it for me and held it until I arrived. I don't know if she closed it. A lot happened in those few moments, I didn't see her leave to shut it."

Orson is already in motion, muttering a string of curses as he strides ahead. Roenis takes my hand, his grip tight, like he's afraid he might lose me again. When I steal a look at him, a silent war between what he wants to do and what he must do swims in his eyes.

"We'll face this together," I whisper, squeezing his hand.

His lips twitch—just barely—but then he pulls me forward, and we run.

The cold wind howls through the broken chamber as we navigate it. The urgency hasn't faded, if anything it's only grown. Every step echoes and the weight of the situation is pressing down on me. We have to find it. This portal is make or break.

Roenis keeps a firm grip on my hand, leading the way with purposeful strides. Orson ahead is scanning every corner as we navigate the wreckage. We're still in shock that we haven't ran into anyone in this kingdom.

"There." Orson points towards an archway that leads to the outside. The portal is still shimmering like the surface of undisturbed water. My stomach tightens. We might just make it, no obstacles. But if it doesn't let us through.

I shove the thought away. There's no room for doubt.

Roenis doesn't hesitate, he pulls me closer before stepping toward the portal. Relief floods my chest as we push through. A rush of cold magic licking my skin, and the familiar weightlessness of transportation pulls us fully forward until we are flung out onto solid ground.

The Nightmare Kingdom's gardens.

We came through the back entrance and the moment my feet hit the blackened floors, relief vanishes as I register the three figures waiting for us at the base of the stairwell.

Datura. Kenji. Grifton. No Asani though, he might still be in the village.

Their expressions range from unreadable to outright furious. Datura steps forward in a dark night robe that's ruffled, and her eyes narrow to sharp slits. "What the hell happened?"

Kenji crosses his arms, leaning against the column, but there's nothing casual about his stance. "We were given no information."

Grifton exhales, his expression tight with concern rather than accusation. "What happened? We need to understand everything. We felt an extreme shift, and people are freaking out. Asani went to keep the people calm and distracted."

Roenis lets out a sigh, his grip on my hand tightening briefly before he releases it. His voice, when he finally speaks, is heavy with exhaustion. "Sesha and Dolion kidnapped Syra. They took her with the intent to use her against us. Against me. I tracked them down and intervened before things could escalate beyond control."

Kenji's brows furrow, his arms unfolding slightly. "Kidnapped?"

"Yes," Roenis affirms. "They used her book on her. I didn't go after Sesha to start a war—I went to get Syra back. And in the end Sesha, Maya and Dolion are...gone."

A heavy silence follows.

Datura looks confused. "Gone?"

Roenis nods. "Maya and Sesha are now concealed away—no longer viable in the realm. As for Dolion, I snapped his neck for betraying our Kingdom, and me. Besides that, we have a much larger situation at hand. Two Goddesses are gone, and in their place, their successors will take the role as Goddesses. Syra and Avia."

The realization settles over them. Grifton rubs his jaw, glancing between us. "That's a dangerous shift of power."

Roenis looks toward Datura. "Contact Sage. He needs to be here now."

Datura studies him for a moment, recognizing the gravity of the situation before giving a nod. She steps away, murmuring an incantation under her breath, and the magic pulses through the air. The summons is sent.

A long silence stretches as Grifton and Kenji watch me, as if relieved to see me back safe. I give them a small smile. I missed them too.

After a few minutes, Sage steps through the back entrance like we did. Communication was fast, but it seems like he was already prepared to be summoned. Orange eyes like melted amber, scan the room. But he's not alone.

Avia emerges beside him.

The room freezes.

Avia looks smaller than I remember, but there's a calmness in her expression, something completely opposite of her mother. She steps forward with a poise that isn't quite practiced but isn't hesitant either.

Roenis stiffens, his silver eyes flashing dangerously. "I believe I summoned only you here, Sage."

Sage remains composed. "She's here because she should be. Because *clearly*, this was always meant to happen."

Roenis takes a threatening step forward. "You knew?" His voice comes out rough like gravel. "You knew about Sesha's plans, and you let it get this far?"

Sage meets his fury with unshakeable calm. "I knew what had to be done, and I knew I couldn't interfere beyond the preparations I made. If I had acted too soon, it would have risked more than just the balance of power—it would have thrown everything into greater chaos."

Roenis's hands curl into fists. "You left us blind!"

"I ensured no one was left liable in that castle while the events took place," Sage counters. "I put protections in place to minimize collateral damage that Maya planned. And now, because of that, we can move forward without war breaking out."

That's why her Kingdom seemed empty.

Roenis looks like he wants to rip something apart. His horns glow faintly, his rage tipping out. But before he can retaliate, Avia steps forward.

"I didn't agree with my mother's ways." Her voice cuts through the tension, soft like butter but a form of authority is rooted there. "I never have." She looks at Roenis, then at me, understanding flashing in her expression. "I don't want war. I don't want any more manipulation. I don't blame either of you for what happened."

The weight of her words feel true.

"I will take my place as Goddess of Time," Avia continues, "but I won't follow the path my mother did. I'll learn to control my power, and I'll do it under Sage's guidance."

The room remains tense, but a sliver of understanding sweeps over us as we slowly accept the outcome.

Roenis studies her for a long moment before extending his hand. She goes to shake it, but he retreats just a little before stating, "If you even hint at betraying us, or plan any schemes—"

"I won't." Avia meets his eyes, grabbing his hand firmly. "I want to live in peace among all Kingdoms."

Her words firm like a quiet decree. No ill will. No

vengeance. Just the possibility of something better.

I feel the weight of uncertainty start to lift.

This isn't over. But maybe—just maybe—we're finally stepping towards something new.

My smile breaks out. "You'll be an amazing Goddess."

Avia looks towards me again and smiles back. "You will be too, Syra."

Epilogue Syra

The room is heavy with heat. Our bodies tangled in shadows, with the exception of the light from the doors hiding his grotto. They cast tinted blue streaks over Roenis' bare skin as he hovers over me, his silver eyes dark with hunger. The scent of him, Gods, is addictive.

His fingers trace slow lines over my body. He worships every part of me. An exploration that leaves a burning sensation every where he trails that damn finger. He is patient tonight, teasing me, drawing out every moan and every shudder until my body trembles beneath his touch. I arch into him, my hands mapping the ridges of muscle along his back before tangling in his unruly red hair.

"You're making me impatient," I murmur against his lips, gasping as his mouth trails along my throat, teeth scraping over sensitive skin before soothing the spot with his tongue.

He chuckles, the sound reverberating through my body as he presses closer. "And yet, you love it."

I do. I love the way he kisses me like I'm the very air he breathes, the way he moves against me, the way he makes me feel whole and adored. His hands tighten on my hips as he sinks into me, keeping the pace tenderly slow.

"Roenis," I moan, clutching at him, feeling his vapors wrap around my vines. The feeling of our magic combined is peaceful. I let myself surrender, lost in him, in us, in the moment that consumes everything but the feel of him inside me, the weight of his body, and the devastating pleasure of it all.

We fall together, a symphony of gasps and whispered names, of tangled limbs and clawing hands. And when we finally collapse, chests heaving, skin slick with sweat, I have never felt more at home.

We lay in the aftermath in silk sheets, my head resting on his chest, listening to the steady beat of his heart. His fingers draw lazy patterns along my spine, grounding me in the softness of the moment.

"My power feels different now," I state, stretching my fingers, watching as faint violet threads dance between them, more controlled, more effortless. "Like it's truly mine."

Roenis presses a kiss to the top of my head. "It was always yours. You were just limited by expectations that weren't meant for you."

I exhale, smiling at the truth in his words. "It's easier now. I can weave dreams without it giving out on me. And when I touch the nightmares, they don't pull away anymore." I hesitate, tilting my head to meet his gaze. "I think I can weave with them, not just alongside them."

His brow arches. "You want to merge our powers?"

I nod, excitement stirring in my chest. "Not completely, but in a way that enhances them. Instead of separating it, we can create something balanced."

He hums thoughtfully, his fingers threading through my hair. "It's ambitious. But if anyone can do it, it's you."

I smile, pressing a lingering kiss to his collarbone before rolling onto my back. "I talked to Orson today."

Roenis' fingers still against my skin. "And?"

I sigh, staring at the ceiling. "He told me about how he was used to fuse his power with my mother's. To make me stronger when she created me."

Roenis doesn't speak immediately, and I glance at him, expecting tension. Instead, he's waiting for me to continue.

"I was surprised," I admit. "I never knew he had that kind of magic." A small smile tugs at my lips. "But I wasn't angry. If anything, it made me feel closer to him. He's always been there for me, and it doesn't change anything.

Roenis exhales slowly, his hand settling over my stomach. "I'm glad he told you."

I turn to him tracing the sharp lines of his jaw, the curve of his lips. "I don't want secrets anymore. Not from the people I care about."

His silver eyes soften. "No more secrets, then."

I lean in, brushing my lips over his, lingering in

the warmth of his breath before whispering, "Good."

But before I can settle back into his arms, Roenis rolls us over in a swift, effortless motion, pinning me beneath him. A slow, wicked smirk curves his lips as his fingers swipes down my body with intent.

"Now, pet," he purrs, his voice dark with promise. "We're not done. Since I'm not a one-orgasm type of God, as you so boldly accused me of before."

Heat coils in my stomach, a delicious shiver running down my spine as I meet his gaze, daring and eager. "Prove it."

And he does. Again and again.

Tilted Scales Preview

Sage

The grains of sand flow through the air, golden against the darkening sky. It moves like an unseen current of magic. We stand in the Hourglass Forest outside of the Time Kingdom. Avia stands at the heart of the opening, her hands outstretched and fingers splayed as if conducting an orchestra. Every sway of her hands make the shifting time-imbued dust form patterns of mesmerizing elegance.

I watch her from the shade of the trees, my hands clasped behind my back, every muscle in my body wound taut with restraint. I have seen her practice before, seen the determination in her brow, the way she bites the inside of her cheek when focusing, and the way her lips part ever so slightly when she concentrates too hard. But tonight. Divine gods, *tonight*, she's amazing.

A true Goddess.

The role does not fit her yet, not fully. She is still molding herself to it, the magic still finding its rhythm within her, but Gods help me, she makes it look effortless. The sand comes alive as she guides it, escorting strands of life into something tangible. I had spent over a century mastering the art of Balance, and yet watching her, I feel lacking.

She falters, just for a moment, the grains stuttering midair before collapsing in a circle of golden dust around her feet. A frustrated sigh leaves her lips and I force myself to step forward rather than remain frozen in place, swallowed by my own thoughts.

"You're trying too hard." I murmur, my voice betraying nothing of the turmoil inside me.

Avia turns, her gold eyes meeting mine in the moonlight. There's challenge in them. The beauty mark on her left cheek only makes her more striking, an accent to the determination in her expression.

"I have to try," she counters, brushing errant grains from her fingertips. "Time won't simply obey me out of courtesy."

A corner of my mouth twitches, amused despite myself. "No, it won't. But it also won't yield to force alone. You have to feel it, Avia. You have to let it move through you, not just around you."

She exhales, rolling her shoulders before casting a glance at the scattered remnants of her failed attempt. I step closer, feeling the pull between us like an inevitability. "Again." I say softly, reaching past her to guide her hands. "This time, don't command it. Invite it."

The moment my fingers brush against hers, our spark ignites again. I have to stop touching her. She is like torture, yet I keep doing it.

She stills. A fragile silence stretching between us, thick with everything I have tried desperately to suppress. Her skin is warm, her pulse a steady beat beneath my fingertips, and my own heart hammering in my chest. I'm starved.

I have spent years toeing the line between being her mentor and becoming someone more. I have buried desire beneath logic, reason, and duty. But Avia is a force of nature, and no matter how hard I try to balance myself against her, she tilts my scales every time.

She doesn't pull away.

Instead, she turns her hands, letting her fingers rest against mine. "Sage." she says, my name a plea.

I will tilt all the scales just to hear it again.

I swallow hard, my throat dry. "Again." I repeat, my voice steady. "Feel it."

Her eyes search mine, seeing the cracks beneath my composure, as if recognizing that all she has to do is push and I would fall.

But she doesn't. Not yet.

She exhales again, her gaze shifting back to the sand and this time when she moves, the air itself seems to hum in response. Time bends to her will, and I, a God of Balance, find myself bending as well.

Acknowledgments

Writing *Tainted Dreams* has been a journey of late-night writing sessions (even a few sleepless nights), and a balancing act of work, motherhood, and creative blockage. This book wouldn't exist without the support of those who believed in me, even when I doubted myself.

My coworkers, family and friends cheering me on, has really pushed me to finish. I feel so proud that my idea finally came to life.

To my readers: Whether you've followed me from the beginning or are just stepping into this realm—thank you for trusting me to lead you through Syra's and Roenis' journey. I hope you loved these characters as much as I do.

To my family and friends, who have endured my ramblings about magic, forbidden love, and shadowy book daddies—your patience, encouragement, and smut reactions, kept me going.

To all my favorite authors who came before me, you are the ones who remind me why I write and why I love reading: to explore, to challenge, to *feel*.

And finally, to the dreamers, the ones who embrace the impossible and chase the magic—this book is for you.

With all my heart,

Sabrina

About the Author

Sabrina Rafael is a dedicated author specializing in fantasy romance, creating captivating stories that blend with enchanting new worlds. She grew up all over and finds home within her writing. With an associate degree in Film Production Technology, Sabrina brings a cinematic perspective to storytelling, crafting vivid scenes and charming narratives. Writing has been a lifelong passion, beginning in childhood and evolving into a creative journey where reading inspires imagination and wonder. Sabrina continues to explore possibilities and hopes to inspire readers with her stories.

www.ingramcontent.com/pod-product-compliance
Lightning Source LLC
LaVergne TN
LVHW011942060526
838201LV00061B/4184